I0664793

MY GIRLFRIEND'S UFO

By

James Fairchild

This book is dedicated to all veterans
of the military and intelligence services
of America and the Allied Coalition
who with their sacrifice
have made my freedom possible

FIRST DOWNFALL PRESS EDITION

Copyright 2009 by James Fairchild

All rights reserved. No part of this publication may be reproduced, stored in a retrieval system, or transmitted, in any form or by any other means, electronic, mechanical, photocopying, recording, or otherwise, without the prior written permission of the publisher. Printed in the United States of America.

Cataloging-in-Publication data for this book is available from the Library of Congress.

This is a work of fiction. Any resemblance to actual persons, living or dead, events or locales is entirely coincidental.

Downfall Press is a registered trademark.

ISBN: 978-0615145839
Published by Downfall Press
www.downfallpress.com

Of all of the things I was expecting to find when I arrived at the abandoned ranch after Uncle Sven died, at the top of the list was not the wreckage of a UFO.

That's not what it is properly called, I suppose, but it's certainly what I called it when I first saw it, I said "My God, it's a UFO."

I was standing in the barn that night, beside the backhoe, which I had used to dig up the barn floor, when I first saw it, after I had first screened the video Uncle Sven had left for me. It was late in December and a backhoe was needed to excavate the frozen Montana earth, and it certainly did the job all right.

I don't know what I was really expecting to find; Uncle Sven's note was somewhat cryptic, and I really had not given it much thought, thinking it would be nothing more than some family heirlooms he had wanted to protect from thieves after he died, but here I was, confronted with the sure and certain fact that good old Uncle Sven was a much more complicated man than I had given him credit for.

I suppose I should start at the beginning; the story would make a lot more sense, but I was fairly new at keeping a journal at the time, so I pretty much wrote the story as it happened.

Sven Larson died in the peace and comfort of his Montana ranch in December of that year at the age of eighty five. He was my uncle, and for some reason unknown to me, had named me the executor of his estate. This did not make much sense, as his two brothers were still alive, but I was a good forty years younger than either of them, and had a business degree, which made me as good a candidate as any for the job, since he had no children of his own.

I had gotten the call from his doctor. Apparently, Sven had known his number was up for some time, having been diagnosed with pancreatic cancer, and with the efficiency and thoroughness that was his trademark, had organized the end of his life completely. He had prepaid his funeral expenses, picked out a plot and paid for that too, updated his will and closed all of his accounts.

According to the doctor, Sven had realized the day of his death that Today Was The Day, and he had, that evening, cooked up a very large steak, smothered it with onions and mushrooms—after wrapping it in bacon—added side dishes of mashed potatoes and corn, ate the entire meal while washing it down with no less than an entire bottle of Aquavit [that's Swedish booze, or jet fuel if needed] and then polished it all off with three chocolate éclairs. He then took his usual dose of painkillers and retired to his bedroom, where his placed one last phone call to the doctor asking him to stop by in the morning, after which he laid down to sleep and died quietly about four o'clock in the morning.

Dr. Wilde found him there the next day, hands folded across his chest, and found that Sven had left a note directing the doctor to call me.

I received the call about 6:00 AM, Western time, at my home in California. I was surprised to get the call, I guess I had thought Uncle Sven would live forever. He was in perfect physical condition, like most farm boys, and still fit into his World War II uniform.

I caught a Frontier Airlines flight to Billings that day, rented a truck from Hertz [making sure to get unlimited mileage] and drove across half the state to Sven's ranch.

When I got there, Sven's body had already been taken to the funeral home. Dr. Wilde had left a note on the kitchen table inside the ranch house. This was the country, and no one locked their doors out here. Particularly when Sven had brought home half of World War II with him after the war.

On the table was a sealed manila envelope with my name on it. I'm Jim Larson, and after I opened that envelope, my life changed forever.

I sat down first, and stretched my legs out, then picked up the envelope. Funny how you remember the little details when you get the shock of your life.

His will was inside. It was one page; he had left the ranch and all of his estate to me, for some reason. That was pretty much it; he had the ranch, some old farm trucks, his personal Ford, and a single bank account with his accumulated savings, for which he had granted me authority to access. There was a note from the funeral home showing that his funeral expenses were all prepaid, and a number to call with questions.

Finally, there was the videotape. This was my first surprise, and it should have warned me.

Sven didn't even watch television. He read a lot, and his friends joked that he had read all the books in the state of Montana.

I had no idea that Sven even knew how to operate a video camera, but he clearly did. This one was a VHS tape, so he wasn't entirely up to date, but it was a remarkable achievement.

I looked around for a video player. The ranch house had been built in the 1930s, and was a four bedroom place, with an enormous kitchen and living room, and a porch running around the house. Later a garage had been added, and the cellar had an actual coal chute and coal bin. When the price of oil got ridiculous, Sven had simply resumed burning coal for his simple needs.

The video player was in the living room. There were further clues here that something unusual was going on. The video player was sitting on top of a portable television, and the boxes they had come in were still sitting on the living room floor. Sven had clearly bought these two items specifically for this purpose.

At any rate, unwitting of the direction my life was about to change, I sat down in front of the TV, turned it on, put in the videotape, and hit the play button. There was a moment of static, and then the image of Uncle Sven filled the screen.

Looking at him then, I remember thinking that he didn't look like a man about to die. He had a ruddy complexion, and a thick shock of white hair, and was six foot four inches tall, and over two hundred pounds. The cancer which killed him had clearly not yet successfully slowed him down when this video was made.

Then, he sat back in his old leather chair, and began to speak.

"Hello, Jim," he said, "by the time you see this, I'll be dead, and I sure appreciate your coming out to take care of my business."

Right, like I would turn down a request from my uncle.

"I've left some notes," he continued, "and I'd be appreciative if you'd tend to King's grave after I'm gone."

With that, the video ended.

Well, that was certainly a surprise. Sven never did talk much, so the thirty second video was his style, but what was this about King?

King was his dog. King had died, like, twelve years ago. He had spent a zillion bucks keeping him alive as the old hunting dog battled leukemia. When he died, Sven had buried him in the barn. Since the barn was no longer used for cattle or horses, we used to kid Sven that his dog had the biggest mausoleum in Montana.

He had never mentioned King since, and had never gotten another dog. So I was quite surprised to hear that Sven's number one priority after his death was the grave of his dog.

That's when I started thinking that there might be something more going on that just the grave of old King. Surely, I thought to myself, Sven had something he didn't want anyone to know about, and he had buried it in the barn. I should get the backhoe out and check out King's grave. I decided to do exactly that later on that night. At the time, I thought it might be family heirlooms.

In the meantime, I went upstairs to the guest bedroom, where I had spent many summers. I used to come out here in the summers from my home in Connecticut, and Sven had taught me how to ride, the art of the roundup, the annual planting and harvesting, how to shoot and how to repair everything from oil wells to tractor engines.

I had only an overnight bag, with some shirts and three pairs of jeans and socks, and a shaving kit. I had a suit for the funeral, so I hung that up.

I changed into a pair of jeans and a sweatshirt to guard against the Montana winter, and looked around the house. It seemed not to have changed since I was a teenager, and Sven sure hadn't wasted any money on paint. But it was neat and clean and comfortable.

In the kitchen I turned on the old gas range, which had an actual griddle on it, and checked the fridge. It was full of steaks, no surprise, and I found that I was very hungry, and in short order had two of them ready.

Sven had an excellent collection of Aquavit in the house, but I had a healthy respect for that stuff, so it was water for me.

As I ate, I realized that it was the first time in my life that I was eating alone in this house. Sven had married a Norwegian girl after the war, and she had kept house for him until some idiot in an oil tanker killed her on the highway when I was sixteen. Suddenly it seemed very quiet.

But the steak smelled good, and my appetite returned, and I finished the steaks.

Afterward there wasn't much to do. The ranch itself was located in the middle of a remote part of Montana. The nearest neighbor was five miles away. The road to the ranch was just gravel. As the night came on, no other lights were visible as far as the eye could see.

So I put a fire on, and watched the flames for a bit; but then curiosity got the better of me, and I pulled on a fleece overcoat and work gloves, and headed out to the barn.

Since Sven had given up cattle and horses some years ago, he kept farm equipment there mostly. I noticed that the tractors were up on blocks, and the harvester was covered with a tarp. Only the backhoe was uncovered, and it was plugged into the wall circuit so the engine block wouldn't freeze. This should have been a further clue, but I still wasn't thinking I would find anything unusual, so into the cab of the backhoe I went, and started it up.

It started easily, and I unplugged the engine block from the wall. While the engine warmed up, I got out and looked for King's grave.

We had put him in a metal ammunition box, of which there was no shortage around Sven's place. At the time, I thought everyone had an uncle with a surplus of metal ammunition boxes on his ranch. I learned later about Sven's habit of collecting weapons.

King, once his body was in the metal box, had been buried in the corner stall about five feet deep. I recognized the site, and brought the backhoe over.

My plan, at the time, had been to move King from his present resting space to a permanent site.

I thought I would have the grave excavated in half an hour, and would be asleep in my bed within the hour, and would re-bury him tomorrow. The backhoe responded to the controls, and in a few minutes I had excavated the earth. I was operating the controls very gently when I heard the scrape of metal, so I turned the backhoe off and got out to inspect the hole.

Whatever it was, it wasn't King.

First of all, King's grave was not there. I had been present when he was buried, and had helped lower him into the ground. The metal box in which he had been buried was simply not there.

Instead, there was a black metal surface at the bottom of the hole. I climbed down into the hole and inspected it with a flashlight.

It was cool to the touch, not surprising as it was buried in Montana earth in the middle of the winter, but usually metal in that sort of cold will give you frostbite. This metal was no more than slightly cool. It had not scratched, either, when the backhoe scraped it.

Finally, the black surface of the metal seemed to absorb the light.

Well, this was not what I had been expecting. I wasn't sure what to do now, but I certainly wasn't tired or sleepy, and the backhoe was right there, so I climbed back in and continued digging.

It took a little over an hour. Whatever it was, it was nearly the size of the entire barn. It was quite long, and in a triangular shape, much like a delta wing fighter. At first, I thought it was simply a metal sub floor, but it had the smooth contours of an aircraft, so I dug around the bottom and sides till I could get in and look around. It was about the shape of an F-106 Interceptor.

It took a very long time to realize what it was that I was looking at. At first I thought it was an ordinary airplane. Sven, after all, had been a pilot, and had owned several aircraft in his life; he had flown fighters in the war. I knew that often surplus aircraft after the war were simply buried where they stood as it was too expensive to haul them away, and I thought that Sven, a frugal man, had simply done this with one of his airplanes.

But as I got into the pit and did a close examination, I found that the thing had no markings. There were no doors or hatches. There were no windows. And there were no engines or landing gear. It was just a long triangular flying machine.

So after about forty minutes of trying to identify the aircraft type, I finally realized what it was, why Sven had asked me to be the executor of his estate, and why he had left a cryptic message to me about the grave of his dog.

It was about one thirty in the morning. There was only one thing to do. I got back into the backhoe and covered the thing back up again.

I don't know why I did this. I remember thinking at the time, that the neighbors would come in the morning to express their condolences, and that I didn't want them to see a UFO sitting in the barn.

It took far less time to cover it up than it did to uncover it. I put a cover on the backhoe and plugged it back into the wall. I then swung the barn doors open at both ends, and the gently falling snow began to blow inside. By morning, I reckoned, the floor of the barn would be frozen solid and covered in snow. If Sven had never told anyone that he had one of these in his barn, I wasn't going to be the one to break the news.

I fell into bed and fell instantly asleep. Thus came to an end the day which had changed my life forever.

CHAPTER TWO

I awoke the next morning with a moment of brief disorientation, not remembering at first where I was or why I was there.

Then I remembered that Sven had died, and felt sorrow; and immediately after that, I remembered the machine in the barn, and suddenly felt worried.

I was on Western time, so I awoke very early in the morning, and the sun was not up yet.

The floor was cold on my feet. As a matter of fact the entire house was cold, there being the little matter of the Montana winter. I raised the temperature on the thermostat, and the heater kicked in.

I was far too wired to go back to bed, and did not have much else to do today except attend the funeral. I had some time, which came in handy, since I had some very heavy thinking to do, and having quiet time in an empty house was going to be useful.

So while I cracked open some eggs and prepared the highest cholesterol breakfast I had eaten in twenty years, I went through my options.

This was a small town, and Sven knew everyone in it. By now the news that I was here would have been communicated to everyone locally, which meant that they would stop by today to express their condolences.

I, on the other hand, did not look forward to meeting with Sven's friends and neighbors; it would take more energy than I had. I was having enough trouble myself dealing with the loss of my uncle without having to help other people deal with their issues.

Then, there was the issue of the Thing In The Barn. On this issue, I had actually already dealt with it and knew what I was going to do.

I had served in the military, and knew that for years there was a rumor going around that the Air Force had gotten their hands on some sort of flying machine which, so went the story, had crashed in a place called Roswell, New Mexico, in the late 1940s. This flying machine was supposed to have a very unusual power supply, and was said to be of non-terrestrial origin.

The story was made doubly interesting by the fact of the location of the crash, which was in direct proximity to the base housing the 509th Bombardment Group, at the time the only long range bomber command capable of carrying and delivering the atomic bomb. They had, in fact, been the group which had carried out the missions to Hiroshima and Nagasaki.

Whether or not the Air Force had succeeded in getting ahold of the wreckage was of little interest to me. The part of the story which I was now remembering with some concern is what had happened to the civilians involved.

Years after the crash, a number of civilians came forward with a very disturbing story. A number of women who had seen the crash or whose husbands had been involved in the recovery stated, under oath, that uniformed members of the American military had come to their homes and threatened them and their children with murder if they ever went public with the story. At the time they gave their statements forty years later, these women were now grandmothers, and said they were going public in order to protect the futures of their families, the idea being that suspicion would fall on the military if they or their children ever came to harm.

I realized my eggs were burning, and used the spatula to put them on a plate. I sat down and began eating while I sorted things out.

If there was any truth at all to this story, I wanted to have as little to do as possible with Uncle Sven's mystery aircraft. As far as I was concerned, it was now buried under five feet of Montana earth and another foot of snow, and it could stay there for all eternity. I had no intentions of ever digging it up again, and I had no intention of ever mentioning it to anyone, and the secret was going to die with me.

The title to the ranch now passed to me, and there was enough money in Sven's accounts to pay the property taxes for a hundred years, so I was just going to let it sit forever. If I never sold the ranch, no one would ever dig a new foundation, and whatever it was that was buried under the barn would never be found.

At the time, this seemed like a pretty good plan. The funeral was in a few hours, and I had a return flight booked tomorrow afternoon. In less than forty eight hours I would be home, and all of this would be a memory.

Feeling better about the whole situation, I finished some really excellent eggs and far too much bacon, and hit the shower. Half an hour later I was dressed, shaved and ready to face the day. The sun was still not up yet, so I lit a lantern and went out and closed the barn doors which I had left opened last night.

I really should have known better, that this was all not going to wrap up as easily as I had hoped. Life is never that easy. When I got back from the barn, Kirsten Vorra was in the living room.

If you do have to run in to one of your old girlfriends unexpectedly, it's best to be reasonably cleaned up. I remember thinking that when I first saw her again – I thought "I'm sure glad I took a shower!"

Actually, it was a pretty silly first thought. But when you're dealing with a death in the family and discovering a UFO in your backyard in the same day, you can be excused for having not entirely logical thought processes. Especially where Kirsten was involved.

The Vorra family were our neighbors, that is to say, they had the next ranch over, several miles away. We were separated by a patch of government land, which her father leased to run cattle for pasture. The Vorra and Svenson families had come over on the same boat from Scandanavia just before the Civil War and had homesteaded together. Like our family, the Vorra children had largely scattered across the country after they grew up, and now the ranch was being leased out for grazing land.

Kirsten and I had a history. When I was fourteen, my father wanted some personal time with Mom, so he sent us all of to Sven's ranch over the summer. That's when I made Kirsten's acquaintance. I was out riding one morning and spotted this skinny blonde riding a pinto, and rode over to say hello. She was my age, and the two of us were bored with farm life and had a lot of energy and spare time, and one thing led to another, and before long we were an item.

Over the following summers we renewed our romance, and when we turned eighteen we both stopped coming to Montana. I remember that Kirsten had married a military guy, and that he had gotten killed in the first Gulf War, making her a widow after only a very brief marriage.

And now here she was, in my living room. I could not have been more surprised.

I entered the front door, stomping the snow off my feet, and got a clear look at her.

Now, as then, Kirsten was undeniably one of the most beautiful women ever put on God's green earth, and remember that I live in California, where there are a zillion of them, and she put them all to shame.

She was still skinny, with that mop of blonde hair cascading over her shoulders, and the piercing blue eyes looking out at me, a tall woman as most Swedish girls are, with her 36-24-36 figure tucked into a weathered pair of blue jeans and an old flannel shirt.

She had to have known that I'd be at the ranch, but she still stared at me for a moment when I entered the room, as if to reassure her who it was.

I remembered my manners, and took off my hat and smiled.

"Well, hello there, you," I said. No one ever accused me of being a diplomat.

And then she smiled, and the whole room lit up.

"Hello yourself," she replied, standing up, "I thought you might be up at this hour, saw the light on, thought I'd stop in."

"Of course. No problem." I took off my fleece jacket and hung it on the wall.

"Do you have any family with you? I don't want to wake anyone."

"No, Kirsti...it's just me." That was her nickname, it's what everyone called her.

This was interesting. Our ranch was literally in the middle of nowhere, and to get here at this hour of the morning, she had to have been on the road for forty minutes. In the snow. On a gravel road.

I went to get coffee. "Do you want some breakfast?"

She shook her head. "No, I've got to lose some of this fat."

I sneaked a look at her. If there was any fat anywhere on that body, you'd need a microscope to find it. More likely, she was familiar with my cooking and didn't want to die of food poisoning.

She pulled a cup out of the cupboard. "I will have some coffee, though."

So she put her cup over, and I tiled the coffeepot and poured her a healthy dose of Sven's favorite coffee. We both put sugar in our coffee and sized each other up.

She spoke first. "I'm sorry about your uncle."

I nodded. There was nothing to say.

"He was a great guy," she continued. "I'll miss him. He always made me chocolate brownies on Sundays."

This was news to me. I had not known she was up here regularly.

She saw my expression. "I came over on Sundays and cleaned the place up. He was having problems with the arthritis in his hip."

Score one for Sven. Dr. Wilde had told me Sven had no other medical problems. He must not have told her that he was dying.

But I wanted to know about her. "Are you staying at your folk's place?"

She nodded. "I've been getting my life back together, and my parents are getting on, so I'm looking after them while I finish my degree online."

A blonde with a degree, this was a day for surprises. "What are you studying?"

She looked at me with those big blue eyes, and said "Aeronautical engineering."

It would not have been more of a shock to learn she was studying nuclear physics. Kirsten was a really smart girl, but high school had bored her to death, and other than skiing and cheerleading, she had never expressed any interest in continuing her education. Still, she was in fact a top student, so it did not surprise me she had been accepted to any program she chose to apply to. But designing aircraft?

"Really? Aeronautical engineering? I didn't know you were interested in aviation. What got your interest going along those lines?"

She sipped her coffee. "Well, my husband, Warren, he was a pilot."

I had not known this. "Kirsti, I'm so sorry, I heard that he had been killed in the Gulf War."

She was silent for a moment. "He was a good man."

There was this really long awkward silence.

I had no intention of pressing her on this matter, but she continued, "He flew the A-10. He really loved that airplane."

Him and everyone else in the entire Allied Coalition. The A-10 was a close combat support aircraft. It could fly low and slow and you could hang an entire arsenal under the wings. During the war it knocked out dozens of enemy positions and supplied vital intel to the ground troops. It was the infantryman's favorite aircraft, and troops frequently cheered when it flew over.

"So that's what got you interested in aircraft design?" I stirred my coffee and leaned against the counter.

"Oh, no. I've wanted to work in aviation since before I met Warren, but I was going to wait until he got out of the service to get my degree. Now that he's gone, I have a chance to get it finished."

She paused and looked over at me from behind her coffee. "It was your uncle Sven that got me started."

That made sense. Sven had been a pilot. He could talk airplanes for hours without stopping. It had been his one passion.

I smiled. Sven always loved blondes. It occurred to me, then, that Sven's wife had been one of the Vorra girls, which made her Kirsten's great aunt. Like most folks in little towns, we were technically related by marriage.

"So," I said, little realizing what would come next, "Sven got you interested in aircraft?"

"In a way. Some time back he showed me that wrecked spacecraft you've got buried in the barn, and I've been studying it ever since. Did you want to have sex now, and talk about this later?"

CHAPTER THREE

Well, I don't remember what I thought next, but I do remember it involved a choice between talking and sex, and I picked sex, as I usually did with Kirsti Vorra, and the next two hours passed in a very exhilarating reunion.

Only after we were finished did she bring up the topic again. "Let's get out of here before the neighbors get here. We can go over to my house."

She bounced out of bed, and for a minute I just let my eyes take in the sight of her, and then I followed her into the shower, where after a while we were able to get clean and dressed.

When a woman is as beautiful as Kirsten is, she doesn't need makeup, which means she needs very little time to get ready, so in less than twenty minutes we were in her truck headed over to her place.

I had put a sign on the door giving the details of Sven's funeral, so that those neighbors who came by would be able to know when and where the ceremony was to take place.

There was a lot to talk about, but bouncing over the frozen ground in her Ford pickup made conversation impossible, so we didn't talk much until we got to her place.

The Vorra ranch was a great spread. The key element in their land is that they had running water 365 days a year – not even the Montana winter could freeze over their creek. This meant that their cattle had access to water, although I had no idea as to what the Vorras were doing in terms of animals or crops this year.

Their barn had a connecting covered walk, so we pulled the truck in, plugged in the engine block, and walked to the ranch house protected from the elements. It was going to be a very clear, but very cold, day.

We sat on their couch, which faced a bay window [insulated] which overlooked the entire valley below them. It was a spectacular view. Then again, if you wanted a view, all you had to do was look at Kirsten.

Sitting there next to her, I pulled my thoughts together. There was a great deal to be settled here today, and the long flight here, the unexpected events in the barn, and the sexual encounter were all leaving me pretty wiped out. So I drank my entire cup of coffee—to Kirsten's astonishment—and settled down to business.

"So....how long have you known about....that Thing In The Barn?" I wanted to know.

She had gone into her kitchen, gotten the coffeepot, and refilled my mug, before she sat down next to me.

"Six months." She looked at me over the rim of her cup.

A day of surprises. Little Kirsti Vorra had been sitting on top of a huge secret for half a year. "How did you find out?"

"My father contracted Alzheimer's disease. I came here partly to take care of him before he died. He would ramble on about almost any topic, but his mind cleared just before he died, and he told me that your uncle Sven had a secret buried in his barn, and that I should go and talk to him about it. That was in June, so I went to see your uncle Sven, and he filled me in."

Like being hit with a sledgehammer. So her father had known, too. Furthermore, good old uncle

Sven had chosen to disclose the secret of the century solely to a blonde with a high school education, instead of, like, the Air Force, who I assume would be glad to hear about it.

"Kirsten...exactly how many people know about this? And how did your father find out?"

Now it was her turn to be surprised. Clearly, my question was not what she had been expecting.

"You mean," she said, putting her coffee down, "that you don't know?"

"No, I don't know," I said, somewhat impatient, "but I'd sure like to find out."

A long sigh followed. Then she took a deep breath, and for the first time, I heard the story of what really happened, all those years ago in the sky over Montana, and why I had been chosen to carry the secret.

Sven, as Kirsti told the story, was a pilot. I had known this. He furthermore owned a single engine Piper, since apparently he knew the Piper family from his days in the service and preferred this aircraft. I knew this too.

What I did not know was the next chapter. Sven was flying back from Billings to his ranch at some point—Kirsten did not remember the year, exactly, but it was during the Korean War—in the early evening. This was not a problem, as the visibility was unlimited, and the sky was clear.

The problem first arose when Sven realized he was being followed. The story as he told it to Kirsten was that he became aware of a light behind him, which he assumed were the lights of another aircraft. He was quickly overtaken, and the other aircraft drew up parallel with him. When he looked over, he realized that it was not like any other aircraft he had ever seen.

Still, this did not bother him. This was when jets were just becoming standard in the National Guard, and Sven, who had flown in the Korean War, assumed it was a military aircraft. The other aircraft had the vague outlines of a jet, and that's what Sven thought it was.

Still, what happened next concerned him. The other craft directed a very powerful light into his cockpit, almost blinding him, and he wrenched the wheel away, turning in a circle away from the other aircraft.

The other ship immediately zoomed off into the distance. Sven leveled out his Piper Cub, and continued his flight. But the mystery ship returned, and flew past him so close and so fast that the turbulence from its passing rocked the propeller plane. Furthermore, it circled around to make another pass at him.

Now, Sven, like a lot of Swedes, was a pretty patient man, but get him riled up, and he could turn into a rattlesnake.

Unfortunately for the other ship, as it turns out, Sven had flown Skyraiders in Korea.

The Skyraider was a slow, lumbering, piston powered aircraft, but it was absolutely perfect in certain roles, and one of those was ground attack. As a result, the enemy did not like the Skyraiders, and would always call in air support when they showed up. The enemy air support would consist of MiG-17 fighters.

The MiG-17, alas, is a jet fighter, which means that it was a whole lot faster, move maneuverable, and more lethal than an old propeller plane.

But faster, as the MiG pilots would learn in the last few minutes of their lives, is not always better, and no one was better at teaching this lesson than Sven Larson, at the time an experienced pilot with an attitude.

As it turns out, the MiG pilots, as they approached the slow moving Skyraiders, would race up behind them with the idea of attacking them from behind.

The Skyraider pilots, of whom Sven was one, knew that all you had to do was to suddenly decrease your airspeed to a near-stall, and the MiG, which could not slow down as fast, would overshoot you, and then the Skyraider would be behind the MiG, and since the Skyraiders were armed with rockets and cannon, the whole story would be over about two seconds later, with the Skyraider filling the MiG with holes.

This is exactly what happened that night in Montana. Sven thought he was being buzzed by some joyriding Air National Guard pilot, so he suddenly slowed the Piper Cub down and descended rapidly.

The other ship, coming from behind and above him, had no chance to decrease speed or regain altitude, so it shot right past him. Sven's plane was not armed, and it didn't need to be. He had dropped so much altitude, the other ship was not able to recover and pull up in time, and it proceeded directly into contact with the Montana countryside, crashing in a truly impressive manner and tearing up the field as it did so.

This Sven had not been expecting, and when he realized the other pilot had gone down he immediately landed…which was convenient, since he was now over his own ranch, less than a mile from his actual residence.

The radio in the aircraft was picking up nothing but static that night and Sven was not able to call for help. He thought he could use the telephone to call for help when he landed, and that had been the original plan. He put his Piper down as close as he could to the wreck, grabbed his first aid kit, and went over to render assistance.

That was when Sven got the surprise of his life. The mystery ship had pulled its nose up at the last minute, and done a fair belly landing. As he ran toward where he assumed the cockpit would be, Sven was surprised to see very little damage to the craft.

There was, however, no cockpit, or engines, or lights, or landing gear, or markings, or much of anything else. According to Kirsti, Sven reached pretty much the same conclusions I had in about the same amount of time: this was no Air Force plane; it was not from anybody's Air Force in this solar system; and that whoever or whatever was inside had gotten pretty banged up on landing.

Olaf Vorra, his neighbor, had been out late that night, chasing one of his animals that had gotten sick, and had seen the entire aerial duel, complete with crash, and had ridden his horse at a full gallop over to Sven's place.

The horse had refused to go within a mile of the mystery ship, almost bucking Olaf from his saddle, so he dismounted and finished the journey on foot, the horse being the only one of the three of them with the sense to get as far away as it could.

That's how Olaf found uncle Sven...standing about a hundred feet from the front of the landing site, smoking a cigar with one hand and holding a pistol in the other, about eleven o'clock at night.

When banging on the hull with the pistol produced no response, the two men retreated to the barn, where, with a tractor and cables, they returned to the site and proceeded to drag the wreck into the barn, under cover. The barn doors were then closed, and locked, and for the next forty years, apparently, Olaf Vorra and Sven Larson sat on the biggest secret in the history of aviation.

The reason for silence was the same as mine. Sven and Olaf had heard the rumors, too, of pilots who saw and reported unusual activity or aircraft types, who then disappeared from the squadron and were never seen again. They had a pretty good idea of what would happen to them if they reported it.

Then Olaf Vorra had died and passed the secret to the only daughter who had returned to care for him in his last days; and then within six months, Sven Larson, my uncle, followed him into eternity, leaving only his cryptic message on the videotape.

Things were looking up here. If we were the only two who knew about this, all I had to do was convince Kirsten that keeping quiet about this was a real good idea, and I was home free.

I was pretty sure she didn't like the idea of the inside of a prison cell, or as I have also heard, an insane asylum, which is where the government was currently locking up people with direct knowledge of this sort of business, so I thought I still had a chance to get out of here today and leave all of this behind me.

I smiled.

This got her attention. "You seem pretty cheerful, for a man with this problem," she said.

Problem? Who, me? My problem was safely buried under five feet of Montana tundra, and would spend the balance of eternity there. I didn't have a problem, and I said so.

"Kirsten, the reason I'm smiling is that I've just realized that the only two people who know about this are you and I. That is correct, isn't it? Have you told anyone?"

She shook her head.

I went on. "If we so much as breathe a word of this to anyone, the government will be all over us...and we'll never have a moment's peace again, for as long as we live. My plan is to leave that thing exactly where it is: buried under five feet of earth."

Now it was her turn to smile. "I was hoping you'd see it that way."

I took her hand. "Not to worry. I have no desire for this kind of fame and fortune. I want to live a quiet, inconspicuous life, a long ways away from here."

"Me, too," she said, and curled up next to me.

For a long time we just looked out the bay window. I thought I was doing pretty well. I'd discovered a huge potential life-wrecking problem, and had managed to deal with it in a matter of hours, and had still gotten to hold Kirsten next to me again. This was all going to work out.

"What time is the funeral?" she asked.

"Two o'clock, at the chapel in town." Sven had been a Lutheran, so there was only one of those locally, and the whole town would be there.

To my knowledge, I was the only member of his extended family attending.

The town was about fourteen miles away over a gravel road, but the Ford would have no problem with it.

"Let's get some sleep," she said, pulling a huge comforter over us, "it's going to be a long day."

And so we drifted off to sleep, the last few peaceful hours that either of us would have for a very long time.

CHAPTER FOUR

Sven's funeral was quite an event for the little town he lived in. Almost everyone in town had been born after him, and had been the recipient of his hospitality at one point or another, and Sven had always been a good neighbor and helped everyone who needed help for any reason. As a result, his funeral was standing room only.

The minister said some very kind words about uncle Sven, which was really nice of him, since Sven had never gone to church. Apparently, that had not stopped him from contributing to the various charities the church sponsored.

The Air Force sent an honor guard, and at the cemetery they fired the traditional salute. I was presented with the flag, which I accepted from a young man who looked to be far too young to be in uniform.

Then, overhead, a thrilling sight...the Air National Guard had sent a missing man formation. The fighter jets screamed overhead, filling the valley with the thunder of their engines, a final salute to one of their own. I was later to learn that one of the highest ranking current members of the Montana Air Guard had been a young lieutenant who had served under Sven in Korea, and had ordered this formation in his honor.

I was to learn a great deal about Sven and his relationship with the Air Force in the months to come, but at the time I thought it was just a really nice gesture.

Kirsten protected me from the long line of neighbors and well wishers, thanking each of them personally for coming, and accepting flowers, cards and notes from everyone.

When it was all over, we got back into the Ford and headed back. This was pretty awkward. We both realized that we had to decide if we wanted to spend the night together again, or alone in our respective homes.

When we got to the turnoff for Sven's ranch, Kirsten pulled over and looked at me.

She looked at me. "Do you want some company tonight? Or would you like to be alone for a while?"

Normally I would have asked her about her family, but I knew that she was all alone in that ranch, too.

"I have to feed the cat," I responded, "but you'd sure be welcome, Kirsten, if you'd like to stay the night." Then, because somewhere I found a shred of decency, I continued. "There's a guest room...if you'd like your own space."

Which was a nice a way as I could find to say "if you don't want to sleep with me," but that turned out not to be necessary.

She put the Ford in gear and turned toward Sven's place. "Thanks, but I think I'll just curl up with you tonight."

We smiled at each other. This was sure different, talking about sex with your teenage lover when she was all grown up. We used to make time for each other in the meadow by the river; now we had two entire ranches to run around in, and we could have sex as often as we wanted.

We got to the ranch in short order and while she found the kitchen, it being agreed that my cooking would kill both of us, I went out scouting for the cat.

There was this scruffy tomcat who hung around Sven's place. He wasn't really Sven's cat, really, he just kind of lived in the barn and kept the mice in line. Sven put out food for him and put a cat door in the barn for extra cold nights.

I found the cat chow, put it on a paper plate, and went back inside the house and watched out the window. Sure enough, the tomcat came bounding out of his hiding place, devoured the food, and disappeared again.

Well, that took care of the cat. That left Kirsten. What to do about Kirsten?

So I asked her. "What am I going to do about you?" I went into the kitchen and wrapped my arms around her and kissed her neck, which I knew drove her crazy. I have very few principles.

"Well," she said as the broiled yet another one of Sven's seemingly endless supply of steaks, "if the past is any guide, you'll use me for sex repeatedly, and then fly away and forget about me for a few decades."

I kissed her again, more slowly this time.

"Make a decision," she said sweetly, obviously having gone down this road before, "which would you like, the steak or the girl?"

At this time, actually, the steak seemed pretty good. It was ready now, and I could always have the girl later. She was right, we did use each other for sex a lot.

"The steak," I proclaimed, "and the sooner the better."

"Figured as much," she replied, and my steak was delivered neatly onto one of the monster platters Sven kept around for feeding harvesting crews.

She followed the steak with a delivery of mushrooms. It seemed a little odd to be eating's Sven's steaks. It didn't seem natural at all.

I looked around. After we left, this property would be leased for grazing cattle. Likely, no one would live in this house; it would be turned over to a property manager. Sven had disposed of his personal effects before he died, so the house was virtually empty. I had a flight from Billings to California later today. Within hours, this house would be closed forever. I suddenly realized that this would be the last meal served in this house; that we would be its last inhabitants.

Sixty years of history would end here by nightfall.

I looked over at my companion. Kirsten always wore underwear and an apron when she was cooking, and ditched the apron when eating. I could never figure out how such a skinny kid could eat steak the way she did and never put on a pound. Probably, I reflected, due to the cross country skiing she did on a regular basis. Wouldn't hurt me to get some cross country time in one of these days. Today she was wearing a combination from Victoria's Secret.

That got me back to thinking about tomorrow, and Kirsten. She had gotten a bottle of red wine out and poured us each a glass.

"To us," she said, and we clinked glasses and drank.

I started work on my steak. "I have a flight later on tonight, back home."

"And where is home?" she asked, blue eyes curious.

"Home, is a town by the sea in California."

"And what do you do there?"

"As little as possible." This was true. I was known far and wide as a lazy person. "And what of you, my blonde friend, what have you been up to?"

"I model winter wear for ski manufacturers." Well, that did not surprise me, she had that girl next door All-American look. She could sell metal brackets if she was in a hardware catalog.

I laughed. "And where do you live?"

"Well, right now, I live here. But I have a condo in New York, mid town."

"Will you be returning to New York?"

Clearly she already had a plan. "I have a flight in the morning. I just had to make sure you were willing to keep the secret."

I needed no urging on this issue. "You may rely on my discretion. I have no desire to pursue this matter further."

Well, that was progress. We were no longer calling it "the crashed UFO in the barn," we were calling it "this matter".

"So what about your degree in aeronautical engineering?" This I was curious about.

"I have my private pilot's license."

Watching a girl in Victoria's Secret underwear talk about learning to fly while she is eating a steak is somewhat erotic for some reason.

"I'm sure you are a fine pilot," I said, as I finished my steak, "and I hope you will occasionally fly out to see me."

"Why I would be delighted," she said, mock-formally, "as you know I always have enjoyed flying with you."

And we both laughed, and left the dishes for later, and as we had done when we were younger, we put a blanket in front of the fireplace, loaded it with wood, and then made long, slow, passionate love in front of the fire while the sun set over the wide Montana sky.

Afterwards we both took a shower. I had a flight to catch tonight, and Billings was a very long trip away.

I had my overnight bags packed in minutes. By the time I was ready to go, Kirsten had already left.

She was like a cat that way. She never liked to say good bye; she would just be gone when you got out of the shower.

I looked out the front window, but her truck was gone too.

Kirsten Vorra was a remarkable woman. For a moment I wondered what my life would have been like if we had continued our relationship from high school into college, and after.

Probably, we'd be already married and divorced. I could never sustain a long term relationship anyway. My relationships usually lasted about two hours. A long term relationship was eight hours, but only if she slept over afterwards.

No point in dwelling on what might have been. I set about closing up Sven's house.

I shut off the gas, but kept the electricity on as there was a circuit to keep the pipes from freezing. I locked all the doors, hardly a necessity in this part of Montana. It really took very little time to close up Sven's entire life.

In less than half an hour my rental car was packed and I was out front. It seemed so jarring, to actually be closing a chapter of the Larson family history, but here it was. If anyone in the family wanted to run a ranch, it would still be here, but I knew none of my nieces and nephews were planning on becoming a rancher. Too much work involved.

I did not look behind me as I left.

CHAPTER FIVE

The road to the highway is gravel, so it's pretty slow going. I had to keep it at forty miles an hour, and even then, the rental car was having real trouble not losing traction on the gravel. I was grateful the road was mostly frozen. In three more months this road would be a muddy trench.

I suppose that's how I spotted Kirsten's truck. It was about half a mile in, and at first I thought she had car trouble and had pulled over. But the truck was parked too far off the road for that.

So I drove off the road toward her truck to see if there was anything wrong, and that's when I realized she was in the cemetery.

The little cemetery in our county contains the remains of almost everyone who has ever lived there. It isn't much; it's very out of the way, with a small picket fence to mark the boundaries. Every Memorial Day the kids come out here and put American flags on the veteran's graves. We had been out here earlier today to bury Sven.

But she wasn't at Sven's grave. She was a bit further down, among the earlier burials. She saw me drive up, but then resumed looking at the grave, where she was seated with a single flower.

I sat next to her. The grave she was keeping company was marked with a simple stone, the kind the VA gives to veterans when they die. It said "Warren Fairchild, Major, United States Air Force," and the dates of his birth and death. He had been taken at an early age.

I suddenly realized that this was the burial site for Kirsten's husband, killed in the first Gulf War. Maybe pulling over was not such a good idea after all.

Kirsten had she shoes off and she had brought a flower, a single rose.

"Do you need to be alone?" You can be brutally short with your close friends.

She looked over at me, took my hand, looked back at the headstone. "It was the radar, you see."

Probably she'd been drinking. One does not usually discuss radar in a cemetery. But she sure looked sober.

And then she continued on, and I realized what was troubling her. "James was flying a mission over Iraq. The Republican Guard had a limited number of Chinese radar guided missiles. In the A-10, he was an easy target."

My God, he must have been. With an enemy antiaircraft battery and a radar lock, it must have been over in seconds. The A-10 could not even hope to try to evade a missile. It did have countermeasures, but they did not always work.

"I was in New York at the time. The Air Force sent two of his friends over to tell me."

There was nothing to say, so I did not say anything. She became a war widow on short notice.

"We had only been married for a year."

She stretched out on the grave and looked up at the endless Montana sky above her. I gingerly lay down next to her, feeling extremely awkward, with my lover near her dead husband's grave.

"So the question becomes," she said, "if I could prevent this from happening from some other woman, would I? I think yes, I would."

I had absolutely no idea what she was talking about, so I said "I have absolutely no idea of what you're talking about."

She looked at me as if I were an idiot. "The radar. What if you had a technology that could defeat radar?"

It seemed to me that we had a pretty good handle on that. The F-117 fighter and the B-2 bomber were quite radar invisible. I mentioned this.

"But the F-117 and the B-2," continued my blonde girlfriend with the high school education, "owe their radar silhouettes to their design and a special paint. What is you had a technology that would make any airplane invisible to radar?"

Well if you did, you'd be pretty popular at a certain aerospace company I knew about.

"So," she said, making up her mind about something, "if the Air Force had this technology, and they could evade radar, then women like me would not have to lose their husbands and live their lives alone."

I had a really bad feeling about this. "You're thinking about, the, ah, Item In The Barn."

She nodded. "It's invisible to radar."

That got my curiosity going. "How do you know?"

She got to her feet and began to walk to her truck. "I've flown it."

I got up too, but I stopped dead in my tracks. If this was true, it meant that this little blonde whose entire relationship to aviation was that her husband had been a fighter pilot, had been flying an artifact from another world around the Montana horizon.

She looked at me. "Your uncle Sven taught me how."

Of course. Sven was a pilot. It only stands to reason. He had five decades to research the crashed lander; he had been retired from the Forest Service for the last thirty years, so he had the time to do the work. And somehow, this girl had gotten him to give her flying lessons.

Kirsten had grown up a lot. Married, widowed, and given access to the story of the century. I knew what was coming next.

"I want to give the Lander to the Air Force," she said. Then, because she saw the look on my face, she continued, "I can do it alone. I'll tell them you knew nothing about it."

She looked back at the grave of her husband, killed by a missile with a radar lock. "If I can help it, no other woman will ever have to go through what I've been through."

Time to pick my words very carefully. "Kirsten, you're not thinking clearly."

She nodded. "Yes, my doctor says I'm suffering from pathological grief."

Well, she must have loved her fighter pilot, because it had affected her deeply.

"You're not well, Kirsten. Why don't you come out to the coast for a week, you can use the guest cottage, relax a little, think things over."

She was not easily misled. That was the problem with these Swedish types, once they got an idea into their heads, it kind of stayed there.

"No," she continued, heading toward her truck, "I don't care what happens to me. I don't want this to happen to anyone else. I'm going to tell the Air Force."

Well, I certainly cared what happened to her, and I had met some of these security types, and I wouldn't trust them with my family. I had no intention of being on a government watch list for the rest of my life.

On the other hand, we were, in fact, at war. Every day, men were flying into danger. It looked like it was going to get a whole lot worse before it got any better. There was no question that this technology could be of use.

But what if the Air Force already had this technology? The rumor was that they had been working on this since the Roswell incident, decades ago. It seemed to me that they should have the problem solved by now.

This was getting to be a tricky question. Just as suddenly, I realized I knew the answer.

How could a private citizen deliver to his government, in this case ourselves and the good old USA, a discovery of monumental importance, without being hounded by security for the rest of his life?

The answer was, by a single telephone call. And I knew just who to call.

"Kirsten," I said as I helped her into her truck, "have you ever heard of the OSS?"

CHAPTER SIX

We drove to the airport, after I promised I would explain to her my proposed solution to our situation. I returned my Hertz, and then, in the cab of her truck in the rental car parking lot, I laid out what I thought, at the time, would be a good plan.

I should point out at this point that I was overly optimistic about our chances.

"All right," she said, parking her truck and killing the ignition, "you have my attention. Who or what is the OSS? And how can they help us?"

I drew a deep breath, and then began the story of how the modern American intelligence community was born.

"Once upon a time," I started, "there was a man named William Donovan. He was a lawyer, and during the Second World War he created and ran the US intelligence service. It was called the OSS, or Office of Strategic Services. After the war was over, the OSS was dissolved and some years later, the CIA, or Central Intelligence Agency, was created to take its place."

Kirsten thought this over. "So this OSS, it ran during World War Two. So how can they help us now?"

Firmly committing myself to a course of action, I responded, "because my maternal uncle, William, worked in both the OSS and the CIA for forty years after the war was over. He's retired, lives in Connecticut now, but he keeps in touch with the Agency. If anyone can help us, he can."

That is, if the old boy wasn't too old to help out, but he did send me a Christmas card every year, with greetings written in his elegant penmanship, and I was his favorite nephew.

Kirsten looked at me. "Can you call him? Do you think he will help us?"

That was really a good question. I had no idea what his security clearance level was, or who he knew in the intelligence business, but I did know what William could keep his mouth shut. And I knew a way to test the waters.

I looked at her. "Are you going back to New York?"

She nodded. "I've got a condo in Manhattan."

This was working out pretty well. If I could pull it all together.

"I'll go with you," I decided. "Let me call him and we'll meet in New York."

That settled, we headed into the airport terminal where I changed my reservations and got a flight to New York City. Another telephone call went to the service looking after my house in California, and then to the bar for a stiff drink before calling uncle William on the telephone.

William lived in Connecticut. The word Connecticut is an ancient Indian term which means "cold freezing place with much snow most of the year" or at least I think it does, or should. I had been born there, and departed for the much warmer climes of California about thirty seconds after I received my high school diploma. Getting ahold of William meant reopening a lot of family connections and that was not going to be easy.

My father's family had been Swedish immigrants. Mother's family, on the other hand, were some of the original Pilgrims, and had settled Massachusetts and Connecticut in the 1600s. Their Puritan work ethic had made them successful early on, and they had been able to hold on to a lot of their success over the years.

As a result, William, who was an attorney, currently handled the family affairs from his law office. We had once owned a very large manufacturing business in Connecticut, but in this century we were mostly into real estate. All of this was locked up in a trust which had been set up before Theodore Roosevelt got into office, which meant it was still in force.

I left the blonde in the bar and found a private place in the air terminal. I rang William, not expecting to reach him personally, but the old boy actually answered his phone.

"Hello young James," he said, probably recognizing my telephone number from Caller ID, "good to hear from you. How have you been?"

I wondered if he would call me "young James" until I was fifty.

"Hello, William. Good to hear your voice. I have a legal question I would like your help on. Is now a good time?"

When I turned 18, uncle William insisted I call him by his first name, which made me feel a little weird, since he was older than I was, but he had told me that we were both adults. Such informality from him meant something, I knew, so I had always followed his wishes.

The phrase, "a legal question", however, had another meaning entirely. Like most families, ours had a few skeletons in the closet, and ours was a doozy, and William and I were in charge of keeping one particular secret buried. We had a code phrase, "I have a legal question" meant that it was time to address this issue.

Understanding instantly, William followed protocols and arranged to get off of the telephone.

"Not now, young James, but perhaps we could meet at some point. Is there a priority to this?"

"Can you meet me in New York at the usual place?" Since we had not met there in, like, a decade, I was hoping he would remember.

"Of course." As if he did this every day. "When would you like to meet?"

"Tomorrow morning. Eight o'clock. Breakfast is on me. I appreciate your help, William."

"Very well, then, eight o'clock AM in the city in the morning. Have a good evening, young James." And he hung up the phone.

So, uncle William was still in the game. Excellent.

The truth was, I was about to take advantage of him on a grand scale. But I would do so knowing that if I had not gone through him first, he would be insulted.

I leaned against the wall, and thought about The Diamond Room, and William, and the Oh So Socials.

After World War Two, the existence of the OSS became public knowledge. It did not take long for people to notice that the roster of OSS agents read like a Who's Who of the American upper classes. This was largely due to the fact that the agency had recruited at some of the better schools, usually the Ivy League, which was pretty well stocked with smart people who spoke a number of languages, which is what you need in a war.

At any rate, the OSS had been successful beyond the wildest dreams of its progenitors, and afterwards they held reunions like any veteran's movement, where the press dubbed them "The Oh So Socials" in reference to their blue blood roots and tendency to party in places like Newport and Palm Beach.

When the CIA was formed, it took a very long time for US intelligence to recover the abilities it had once possessed during World War Two, and a number of the OSS veterans had assisted in birthing the agency to accelerate the process.

They had always served in silence, and on their resumes they never listed what they had done or where they had served, with their law firms providing deep cover for them.

Of course, any successful organization always had a need for new blood, and I had once been of assistance to the government of the United States in something other than a military capacity, and I had done so through a former member of the OSS, namely, my uncle, William. Accordingly, I had a permanent contact within the intelligence community, with a reputation for being a Useful Person, and I intended to make good use of it now.

My one contribution to the world of intrigue and diplomacy revolved around a U-boat, a room full of diamonds, a Princess, a Grand Duke, and something called Operation Deadlight.

It sounds more exciting that it was, but it is an interesting story, and since William and I played a part in it, it's important to know.

A long time ago, in a country which I will not name, there was a Princess who was fourteen years old. She was set up in an arranged marriage with a Grand Duke from another country for political purposes. At the time, you could be married to someone, but it was not a romantic marriage, so you could see whoever you wanted to on the side, and that was the original idea.

What actually happened, is that the Princess and the Grand Duke apparently fell for each other, in a very big way, and the Grand Duke, who as I recall was at the time all of sixteen years old, decided to give his beloved a present befitting her station in life.

He created something called The Diamond Room. It became in international sensation overnight, and became one of the top ten art treasures on the planet instantly.

The Diamond Room was a series of panels which covered the walls and ceiling of the chapel of her castle.

These panels were made up of mirrors and diamonds, so with a minimum of light, the entire room would be ablaze with the incandescent reflected light of thousands of diamonds and mirror particles.

At any rate, it was his wedding gift to her, and they were married in that room, and for the next hundred years it was the standard by which all other royal weddings were measured.

Then, her country was overrun by the Germans in the Second World War, and the Diamond Room disappeared.

After the war, the Germans said they didn't have it; the Allies said they didn't have it; and the castle had been bombed into ruin, so it was assumed by all that The Diamond Room was just one more casualty of the Second World War.

As you have probably guessed by now, this was not the case.

Our family involvement in this whole affair was just accident. Really.

During the final days of the war, Uncle Sven was serving in Europe. He had gotten leave, and so he decided to visit Scandanavia. He was in Norway the day the war ended, in a little village on the coast.

The way it was told to me, Sven was staying in a local inn. There was a knock at the door in the morning, and when he answered it, the innkeeper was there, saying the Germans were in the village and wanted to talk to him.

Alarmed, Sven looked around for a back door, but the innkeeper told him that the Germans wanted to surrender. So, Sven got into uniform and went to the town square and met with the German commander.

As it turns out, there were no Germans stationed anywhere near the village. These particular Germans were from a U-Boat that had been scheduled to rendezvous with a Luftwaffe bomber which was scheduled to touch down at the local airport. They had received the orders to surrender and had come into town and had in fact located the Luftwaffe crew. When they heard there was an American in town, they offered to surrender to him.

This is how Sven found himself accepting the surrender of an entire U-Boat and a Luftwaffe bomber crew. It took a while to translate everything, and find a radio and ask what to do with the U-Boat, but as it turned out, the U-Boats were ordered to proceed to England, where the English were taking possession of the U-Boat fleet. The code name was Deadlight.

So, after five hours of talking on the radio, Sven directed the U-Boat Kapitan to sail for England, which he did, taking the Luftwaffe crew with him, leaving Sven alone again in the village.

He did, as a matter of protocol, stop by the airfield and inspect the German bomber, and that's when things got really interesting.

The bomber was a six engine affair. This made it pretty rare, as it was apparent that it was one of the few with the range to fly intercontinental. This made it of interest to US aircraft designers.

Sven radioed his findings to SHAEF [Supreme Headquarters Allied Expeditionary Force] and offered, since he was a pilot, to fly the thing to the United States. At the time, captured enemy aircraft were being studied at a military airfield in Nevada.

This he was instructed to do, and in short order Sven had the thing running, and managed to get it aloft and pointed toward the United States.

He had to stop for fuel, and, crafty fellow that he was, he arranged one of his fuel stops in Montana.

What Sven had left out of his original reports, was that the bomber was loaded to the gills with crates, and that these crates held the original paneling material for The Diamond Room.

But when Sven arrived with the bomber in Nevada, it was empty.

He had taken the simple expedient of landing on his own ranch, unloading the crates, and then taking off again for Nevada, where he delivered the German bomber to a group of scientists studying captured enemy technology.

He then returned home, where he unpacked the crates, thinking he'd gotten a nice souvenir of the Second World War, and suddenly discovered that he was now in possession of one of the most recognizable artifacts in the history of the world.

Realizing he could never go public with this, he had buried under his farmhouse, where time would not have affected the treasure it concealed. The question now was, what to do next.

When his younger brother—my father— married a woman who had relatives who had served in the OSS, the solution become obvious.

When, as Sven explained it to me, he became "too damn old for it to matter anymore" he called me into the living room of his ranch one summer night and explained his predicament.

He then posed to me a question: would I take up this matter with my uncle William?

I knew what had to be done immediately. When I returned to Connecticut after the summer was over, I took a weekend off and went down to William's beach house when I knew he'd be in residence. He was always glad to see me, despite his using the beach house primarily as a site for assignations with debutantes, and allowed me to crash there.

Once his paramour had departed on Sunday night, I poured William a very large rum—British Navy stuff, expensive---and asked him the following question.

Suppose, I said to him that night, overlooking Long Island Sound while drinking rum and smoking illegal Cuban cigars, suppose that The Diamond Room had not been destroyed at the end of World War II. Suppose that an ordinary GI Joe had found it and had somehow managed to get it shipped home, and that it was currently safe, sound, and well concealed in the American heartland.

Furthermore suppose, I went on, that the GI was now getting on in years, and would like to transfer The Diamond Room into appropriate hands, i.e., the Federal Government of the United States, but wished to avoid prosecution for misappropriating enemy property.

Would the OSS be willing to serve as a broker to transfer The Diamond Room into the custody of the CIA, keeping the identity of the GI private?

That moment, I suppose, is when William realized I was an adult. Actually he should have realized it when he caught Valerie Moore and me in the pool house, but we were only teenagers at the time.

Now here his nephew stood, in his own beach house, asking him if he would be willing to use his intelligence community connections to acquire a priceless art treasure.

To his credit, William took it pretty calmly, as if he got these questions every day, which I later learned was pretty close to the truth. He put down his rum, took a pull at the cigar, and looked across the room at me with a new respect.

"Let me see, my boy," he said, "Let me see."

And so he did. He called his contacts within the OSS, who called the CIA, and this is what happened next.

At the time, the US government was embroiled in a controversy regarding its conduct at the end of the war. Apparently they had given safe passage and citizenship to a number of German scientists via an arrangement known as Operation Paperclip. Some of these scientists, it turned out, had committed crimes against humanity while in the employ of the Third Reich. The press had found out about this, and citizens were outraged. It was very bad publicity for the government.

When William sent a discreet inquiry to CIA via the OSS regarding The Diamond Room, the response that came back was no, not at this time, but please call back when the heat dies down…like, in about twenty years. The government had decided to distance itself as far as possible from any possible exposure to ill gotten gains from the Second World War.

William had relayed this information to me, and we had agreed that when the time was right, that I would call his office, and ask to discuss "a legal matter."

So now, my uncle thought that this mystery GI had died, and I was going to discuss the fate of The Diamond Room with him, when in actuality I had a much bigger agenda in mind, namely, The Thing In The Barn.

I was actually planning to kill two birds with one stone, and if this all worked out, I could get rid of all of my problems at once.

I returned to the airport bar, located my blonde, and took her to a quiet corner of the airport and laid out a plan.

The best solution would be to place the crashed UFO into the hands of the government, while ensuring that the US government did not lock us up for the rest of our lives, or worse.

One approach we could use is to arrange the transfer of The Diamond Room through my uncle William.

If the government behaved itself and handled that matter discreetly without making wreckage of our lives, I would then approach William again regarding the crashed UFO to make a similar transfer.

At the time, it was our best option. Kirsti listened carefully and nodded agreement.

With that settled, we headed for the departure gate, and prepared for the flight to New York.

CHAPTER SEVEN

The flight was headed for Newark Airport, which we both preferred since it has an Airtrain that runs directly into Manhattan. It was a long flight, so I had time to reflect on my uncle Sven's life.

He was the son of immigrants; he had grown up on a ranch which had been farmed for the first time by his parents, who had gotten title to the land only after the US Cavalry had fought the bitter Indian Wars. Many of these Indians still lived in the area, and Sven knew most of them.

He had then joined the US Army for WWII at the age of sixteen, and had part of the mighty US Eighth Air Force that had pounded Germany into submission. He had gone from a simple rural life to vicious mechanized combat, and then had flown jet fighters in the Korean War.

Add to that his run-in with a UFO, and all in all, Sven had lived quite an eventful life. No wonder he returned to a quiet, boring farm life afterward.

It was his young wife, I suppose, who he had been trying to protect, when he did not report his UFO encounter, nor the crates under the farmhouse holding the priceless panels of The Diamond Room, but then she had been killed on the highway, and Sven's life must have seemed quite empty.

Dr. Wilde had told me that when Sven got the news, he refused any sort of treatment, saying "it was his time." I think he was just tired of living.

And now here I was, wrapping up two very large loose ends.

I flipped up the armrest and curled Kirsten's body next to mine. For the remaining four hours of the flight, we slept.

There were no delays on landing, another benefit of using Newark Airport over Kennedy or LaGuardia, and we took the Airtrain directly into the city of Manhattan.

Since the reformers got ahold of the mayor's office, they had done a good job of cleaning up the city. Crime was way down, and the subways were clean, fast and efficient. In less than forty minutes the subway dropped us at the 42nd street station, and we had traveled from the isolated wilderness of mid Montana to the most densely packed city in North America.

Kirsten lived in this area, I learned, but we were not going to go to her condo. Instead, we were going to the Princeton Club.

The Princeton Club is a hotel right next to Times Square, and it is run for the benefit of Princeton alumni in the City, who have a place to stay, meet or dine, as their needs dictated. The building also houses the Columbia Club, and since dear old William had gone to Princeton, and since I had gone to Columbia, it was the perfect place to meet.

When we arrived, the door was opened by the same doorman who had been there when I was an undergraduate. Turns out, he had been working there since before I was born.

The Club had recently been remodeled, so everything was quite up to date. The bellman took Kirsti's bag, I checked us in, and within minutes we were in a very nice hotel suite, where we promptly stripped and got into the shower to wash off the airplane and subway grime.

William was going to meet us here at eight o'clock, but since this was going to be business, we ate breakfast first, ordering room service.

Kirsten, as usual, ordered a bigger breakfast than I did, which you can do if you cross country ski every week which she does, whereas I had to content myself with a measly cereal and toast, while I secretly hungered for a large steak with eggs and bacon.

The nice thing was, Kirsten always eats in her underwear. Today was the "What is Sexy" collection from Victoria's Secret, where she maintains an account. For a moment I forgot my breakfast, as a matter of fact I forgot why I was even in New York, just staring at that perfectly toned, perfectly tanned, blonde body of hers.

She caught me staring and smiled. I looked away.

"Jim," she said, looking earnestly at me, "it's ok to stare at me, I'm fucking you, I like to look at you too."

Hey, if you ever need a casual lover, get one of these Swedish girls.

I went to the third floor library at 7:45 AM. The place was entirely empty. The Club has a computer room, and that's where the current club members do all of their work nowadays.

But the library is spacious, comfortable and private, which is why William and I always met here.

Kirsten waited upstairs. She was not particularly concerned, probably because she had never seen how badly the government can screw up the lives of its individual citizens. Besides, she had to do her hair.

The librarian, an elderly woman from the class of '55, asked me if I needed anything, and when I said no, she told me to call I needed assistance, as she would be at the front desk picking up returned books. I thought it more likely that she would be having a quiet cup of tea somewhere, but it was very nice of her to ask if I needed help.

That left me alone in the library, and some much needed time to reflect.

What would William say about this? I thought about William for a moment, and what he had been through in his life.

Born in New England. Prep School. Princeton. World War II. The OSS. The CIA. And then retirement. There wasn't much that William had not seen in his lifetime.

So how strong was his connection to me, I wondered. I was his favorite nephew—as a matter of fact, his only nephew—but I did not know if William would be willing or able to protect me from an inquisitive government when they found out what good old Sven had been hiding in his barn all these years.

And Sven, what about him. He had a UFO buried under the barn. He had The Diamond Room buried under his house. I knew for a fact he had an arsenal of weapons from World War II and Korea hidden around the ranch, complete with ammunition. What else had Sven hidden on the ranch, I wondered.

And Kirsten. Was this just a casual encounter? Did she want our occasional sex to develop into a relationship? How badly had her widowhood damaged her emotionally? Was she going to recover?

And the UFO. Where was it from? What had happened to the crew? What was its power source?

I had a lot of questions this morning, and no answers, but I knew that within a week, I would have a definitive resolution to all of them. I just hoped it would be a positive outcome.

William strode through the library door. He was still slim, fit, and had that perfect posture still. Today he was wearing chino slacks and a blue blazer with the Princeton tiger on it [the tiger is their mascot].

"Hello, nephew," he said, shaking my hand and sinking into the chair next to me, "what news of your priceless art work? Has the time come to give the Federals custody?"

He had a vocabulary from the 1940s. No one else that I knew called the government of the United States "the Federals" as if they were a bunch of employees.

"Hello, Uncle," I replied, "good to see you," and I meant it. William was now my only relative from my mother's side who was still alive and mentally intact.

"And you too, my boy," he replied. "So don't keep an old man waiting. What's the story on The Diamond Room?"

"It's all yours," I said, watching him carefully, "just keep me out of it."

He had a mug of coffee with him, which he sipped sparingly. "And where shall I find it?"

"It's in Montana. At the ranch of my uncle Sven Larson, who died last week. The crates are buried under the house, underneath the coal bin."

Old farmhouses had a coal chute, and a bin in the basement. Coal trucks would dump a load of coal there each month for the use of the resident. Sven's was still in use when he died. Only I knew what was buried there.

"Do you know the condition of the material?" he asked.

"Buried in steel lined and closed vaults. It should be fine." The cold weather wasn't going to hurt diamonds much, and I know that the material which made up The Diamond Room had been buried in metal crates that had originally housed missiles, so deterioration and weather damage was not going to be a problem.

"And what of you, young nephew?"

Surprise question. "What about me?"

"What are you looking for out of all this?" he eyed me as if to assess my character.

I had not thought about this. I suddenly realized that I had been thinking of The Diamond Room as a problem, when it reality it was a priceless treasure. I guessed he was wondering if I wanted a reward. I set him straight.

"What I want, uncle," I began, "is for the US Government to take possession of The Diamond Room, and I don't want to know how, or when, or why, and I never want to be involved in it, and I never want to hear about it again, and I especially don't want a bunch of nosy investigators poking around my personal life."

A long speech for me. William digested this.

"Any interest in a reward?"

As a working man, the reward for the recovery of The Diamond Room would permanently change my financial picture, but it wasn't worth the loss or privacy.

"No. If there is one, you keep it."

That brought a smile to the old boy's face. "Not a problem, not a problem. You may consider this matter closed, and I will ensure that you are never troubled on this matter again."

"Thank you, uncle." I handed over a slip of paper with Sven's address on it. "This is the location of the ranch."

His eyes took on a faraway look. "The Diamond Room. This will be quite a coup even for me, you know, recovering this particular item."

He was trying to make me feel important. William had arranged defections for the highest level officials during the Cold War, and had arranged the rise and fall of governments, so this was small potatoes, but I appreciated the gesture.

"I appreciate your help on this matter, uncle." I could not do this without him, so it was my turn to make him feel good about his involvement.

He put the coffee down. "Any time you'd like a career change, my boy, it's never too late to call."

I knew what he meant. William had tried to recruit me for intelligence work when I was an undergrad at Columbia, and now he was trying again.

At the time, I spoke three languages, was ex-military, young, flexible, adaptable, and unattached, so I was a perfect candidate for recruitment.

William had been very subtle about his approach. He had used a honeypot.

A honeypot is an old intelligence term for a female agent who is sent to attract a prospect. He had done his homework, all right. At the time I had more lust than intelligence, with a known weakness for blondes that would stay with me my entire life.

At any rate, one day while in Low Library at Columbia, I had run into a beautiful young blonde by the name of Ann-Marie, who told me she was an anthropology major. I should have suspected something when she did not know where the statue of Alma Mater was on campus, which is pretty hard to miss, but like I say, I had more lust than brains.

After a few more encounters, she made her move, trying to entice me to join The Agency. I had realized immediately what was going on, and after escorting her out of my dorm room for the last time, I called William.

He denied it indignantly at first, but finally confessed, saying something about "the family business", and I made him promise never to try anything like that again, and told him if I ever changed my mind, I would call him first.

This gave him the impression that I would at least think about it, which I had no intention of ever doing, so he stopped sending beautiful young women my way.

Ann-Marie's real name was Gwendolyn St. James. I ran into her a year later at the Columbia-Harvard game. She was a student at Radcliffe. She apologized for the deception, and even bought me coffee afterward. I did not forgive her until after we had sex. Repeatedly. Nice kid. I wondered where she was now.

"No thank you, uncle," I replied, returning to the present. "But I shall always keep your offer in mind."

He nodded. We were just about done here. "Who is the young lady?"

I frowned. "How did you know I was not alone?"

"Really, nephew. I have known the doorman since before you were born."

OK, well, that was fair then.

"She's a friend." That was a gentleman's way of saying she was a lady, even if she was sleeping with me, and should be respected.

"Ah, a friend," he said, nodding his understanding. "Would you like the use of the beach house for the weekend?"

Now, that was a truly generous offer. The beach house, while very old, was extremely cozy, very private, and extremely romantic. I had not expected him to extend his hospitality, but did not want him to feel he was obligated.

"Thank you, William, but I have no wish to impose. We'll be fine in the city."

He lit a cigar, quite illegally. This was a library, after all. "Nonsense. I'll have to go to Washington to put together a team to recover The Diamond Room from your uncle's house. The beach house is yours for the weekend if you like. Why don't you spend a few days there, and I'll fly my team to Montana. When we've recovered the crates, I'll stop by on my return to Washington. What do you say?"

The thought of having Kirsten alone for three days in a beach house was enough to make any bachelor cheer up. Kirsten was a nudist, after all.

I took one of his cigars and lit up too. Well, if he meant it, I was sure going to take him up on it.

But I would have to ask Kirsten. I knew she loved the beach, so that should be an easy sell.

"Tell you what, uncle," I said, puffing away, wondering where he got these Cuban cigars, "I'll ask the lady."

He waved his cigar. "It's all yours, nephew. You know where the key is. Make yourself at home."

I nodded agreement, and we sat there in the library, puffing cigars, which we would never get away with, except that William had been a member here for over fifty years.

CHAPTER EIGHT

Uncle William left after his cigar. He took the train to Washington, where I assumed he would assemble the retrieval team. I finished my cigar and stole a breath mint from the front desk so Kirsten wouldn't know I'd been smoking a cigar.

Once in the room, I found her brushing her hair, which I have always found to be erotic, so I sat down at the desk, put my feet up, and tried not to look interested. This did not work.

She caught me looking, and began taking long, slow strokes through that luscious mane of hers.

"How did it go?" she wanted to know.

"As best as might be expected. William is going to send a team to recover the crates. We'll have an update in a few days. If all goes well, and we trust them, then we'll tell them about The Thing In The Barn."

She nodded her consent. "We're all set, then."

"We are all set." I looked around, stole another look at her perfect breasts, packed neatly into a sport bra as she got into her dress. "There is one other thing."

She looked worried, but I reassured her. "William asked if we wanted the use of his beach house over the weekend. It's down on the Connecticut coast."

That got her attention. Like most blondes, she loved the beach. I think it's their Viking heritage.

She gave me a look. "Would we be alone?"

I smiled. I knew she'd go for it. "Yes, we'll be very alone."

She thought a minute. "I don't have to be at work until Monday. I could take the weekend off."

I stood up and began packing. "Let's get started. We'll need to get out of the City before the traffic becomes impossible."

"How will we get there?"

I reached for the phone to call the concierge. "William left his car for us. We'll drive. We can be there by lunchtime."

She nodded and continued dressing, then began to pack. Unlike most women, she packed lightly.

In half an hour we were downstairs, checked out and I presented the doorman with William's car check ticket. I was not prepared for what came next.

Shortly thereafter, a very elegant looking Rolls-Royce pulled up at the curb. I admired it for a moment, until I realized the doorman had opened the door and was looking at me.

"Your car, sir" was all he said.

The Rolls was a 1946 Wraith convertible. It was the first of the great postwar Rolls-Royces, with the great sweeping fenders and the huge leather seats. I had no idea William was motoring around in this thing.

I tried not to let my surprise show, and opened the door for Kirsten, who was entirely unable to conceal her instant love for the car. I helped her in, closed the door, tipped the doorman, and got into the right side, and pulled away.

"This is your uncle's car?" she said, running her hands over the leather.

"Apparently." The last time I'd seen William, he was using a Morgan speedster. I guess he was moving up in the world.

"Very nice!" she smiled and sank back into the seats.

The car had no trouble with the traffic. It took time to get out of the city, but before long we were on the highway and headed for Connecticut.

This is where we first saw the toll bridges. In California, the roads are free. That's why they call them freeways. So we would up paying extortionate fees every few miles for the trip to the coast.

As we neared the coast, I pulled the monster over and put the top down.

Kirsten tied a scarf around her hair, and we drove the final miles to the beach cottage enjoying the cool coastal weather.

The beach cottage is a small affair, built in the 1600s to be near the port back in the days when the family was in shipping. It was remodeled about twenty years ago, and William had a Jacuzzi spa installed, put in air conditioning, and, more lately, WiFi and plasma screen TVs.

The bedroom had a king size bed, the bathroom had soft lighting, and the kitchen was always kept stocked. It was the perfect bachelor pad, which is what William was using it for.

It was remarkable to think, that this was our original ancestral home. Now it was a vacation hideaway.

Well, this weekend it was a rest and relaxation spot. I pulled the Rolls Royce into the garage, grabbed Kirsten's bag, and introduced her to the place.

"This is it," I said, holding open the door, "make yourself at home."

She headed directly for the bathroom. I put the bags in the bedroom and then headed into the kitchen. William was a fan of the Starbucks iced coffees, and he kept a selection in the fridge, so I opened one up and let the caffeine run into my system.

Kirsten had on a bandeau top and shorts on in minutes.

"So where's the beach?" she wanted to know.

The beach is actually about a quarter mile away. I changed into a pair of denim shorts and we walked the short distance.

The Atlantic Ocean is a bit different from its western counterpart. The sea is colder, the seaweed more prolific, the weather more rough. More than a few sailing ships had come to grief on this shore. Today it was fairly mild, so we pulled our sandals off and let the sand get into our toes. We strolled along for a bit, and then she sat down, resting her back against a bluff and watching the waves roll in. We had the beach entirely to ourselves.

"This is nice." She took my hand and looked out at the horizon.

"Yes." There was not much to say. It was nice today. Glad we weren't having a thunderstorm, which happened a lot this time of year.

For a long time neither of us said anything.

"It was nice of your uncle to help us."

I nodded. Actually, I had to give the old boy credit. He could easily sit around and enjoy retirement, he had certainly earned it. But he had made time to take care of his nephew, and for that I was grateful.

"I sure hope it works out," I said, and meant it. There could be all kinds of fallout from the recovery of The Diamond Room, but I was certain of one thing, if you wanted something kept secret, you called William.

I knew this because I knew something Kirsten did not know. During World War II, William had been part of something called Operation Alsos. During an overflight reconnaissance mission, William's P-51 had suffered engine failure and he had come down in hostile territory, where he was promptly captured and handed over the German SS. To his credit, William successfully destroyed the aircraft on landing.

The Germans, who by that time were within a month of losing the war, were getting pretty desperate, and had nothing to lose. William had been interrogated ruthlessly, but he had stuck to his story saying he was simply doing recon missions for the Army Air Corps, and since there was nothing to contradict his testimony, eventually the SS turned its attentions to other priorities, like getting to Switzerland before the Allies caught them. William had been liberated by Patton's men as they swept through Germany, and Operation Alsos, the recovery of the German atomic bomb project, was never compromised.

I knew that William's perfect posture was actually the result of spinal fusion performed after the war, an operation that had to be done because the SS had cracked his vertebra during his interrogation.

As a result, he became known as a person who could be trusted with secrets, and I knew he had handled all kinds of sensitive projects for the US government.

So if anyone could recover The Diamond Room and keep quiet about it, it would be William.

I thought it through. He would arrive in Washington today, assemble a no-questions-asked crew of men, commandeer an aircraft suitable for hauling cargo, and would be in Montana tomorrow, likely landing on Sven's own airstrip. They would have the crates dug out of the coal chute within a matter of hours, and would return to Washington by Sunday morning.

So, Kirsten and I had a weekend together. Could be worse.

I wrapped an arm around her and kissed her neck. She kissed me back, and she leaned her body into mine. I held her close and felt the warmth of her hair.

I suppose it seems romantic, and since the beach was abandoned we could have had sex right there, but the fact is we were both worried and tired and jet-lagged, so we were pretty much happy to just sit.

I realize she had fallen asleep on my chest. I rested my head on hers and drifted off myself. For a time, we enjoyed the peaceful sleep of the innocent.

CHAPTER NINE

When we woke up, the sun was beginning to set in the west. We didn't get up at first, merely lay curled up next to each other, too lazy to get up and do anything productive. That was all right – it was our day off.

I had not spent a weekend with Kirsten Vorra in years. This was going to be interesting. I supposed I should make her dinner or something, since she was my guest.

"Would you like something to eat?" I asked.

She looked out over the ocean. "That would be nice."

"I'll make some seafood. I think I saw scallops in the fridge." I had remembered her love of seafood.

I gently disentangled myself from her. Sleeping next to her always aroused me, which I always managed by going to the kitchen and making her something to munch on, so she wouldn't think I was just using her for sex.

But this time she sensed my discomfort and laughed.

"Hey, it's ok, it's nice to see you're still interested!" She stood up, brushed the sand off, and we headed back into the house.

The cottage was cooler and out of the sun, so it was more comfortable.

I poured her a drink, and set to getting dinner ready. I had a friend who was a graduate of the Cornell Hotel School, and in college we had always gotten this guy to find the best chef in town, so over the years I had acquired enough culinary skill to prepare an adequate meal, as long as it was only seafood and salad.

She propped her head in her hands, elbows supporting her chin, and watched me as I worked.

"Do you have a girlfriend?"

Well, that question came out of nowhere. I prepared an evasive answer.

"Not really. I don't have time."

She thought about this for a minute. "Why not?"

I suppose that shows her priorities. We had recovered a priceless art treasure and an artifact from another world, and she wanted to talk about whether or not I was involved with someone.

"Too much work. I'm tired at the end of the day. I don't have time to come home at night and be sociable."

"But you have time for sex." This was hard to argue with.

"I don't have to be sociable for sex," I said, and truer words were never spoken.

She smiled at this. "I suppose you're right."

I looked at her. She was astonishingly beautiful and smart as a whip, there was no reason for her to be alone.

"What about you?" I wanted to know. "Are you involved with someone?"

"No."

"Why not?" I had turned the tables on her.

I got those big blue eyes. "He'd have to be better than you."

We both laughed at that one. I put a plate in front of her, and a salad bowl. William had those salad-in-a-bag things in the fridge. She picked up a fork and began picking at the lettuce.

"I really don't know what I'm going to do with myself. I thought I'd be somebody's wife at this age."

I pretended to work on the scallops. Truth is, I had seen a lot of widows like this after the war. They lost all interest in life when their man died. Some of them had gone mad with the grief of being left behind. Some had killed themselves.

I wondered, as I stirred the pan, if my little blonde friend was considering ending her own life. Her parents were dead, her husband had been killed, she had no children or close friends, and her only career was modeling clothes. She was the highest possible risk. Years had passed since the end of the war, and clearly Kirsten was not healing or moving past her grief. She was probably having sex with me just to fill the void.

I suppose this is part of being an adult. You have to deal with death, and tragedy, and unfulfilled hopes, and see your friends and family suffer, and deal with the government.

If Kirsten was contemplating The End, nothing I could say was going to dissuade her.

That's when it hit me. I was probably right. Kirsten was, by her own admission, suffering from pathological grief from the loss of her husband. She was, in her own way, winding up her affairs by arranging the transfer of The Thing in The Barn to the Air Force. When that was done, she had no further commitments or ties to this world.

I was burning the scallops.

With a practiced move, I brought the pan up and slid them onto our plates. I had added some steamed vegetables. It would look fine in any restaurant. I could also cook eggs, but that was my entire culinary repertoire. My normal diet was Twinkies and Pop Tarts. I would probably be expelled from France if I ever visited.

I said with a cheerfulness I did not feel, "With your looks, you probably get five marriage proposals a week."

She gave a wan smile and tried a scallop. It took her mind off of her situation. "Hey, you haven't forgotten how to cook!"

My scallops are famous. Everyone likes them.

"Thank you, my dear, I am glad you approve." I then opened a Riesling I had found sitting in William's wine cellar, and we were set for dinner.

She tried the wine, and with the food, the wine, the beach, and my company, she slowly began to relax. In a few moments, she put down her wineglass and looked at me.

"So what would you like to do this weekend?" she asked.

I had that answer ready. "Sleep in late, have sex often, deplete the wine cellar as quickly as possible, and go to the beach at every opportunity." This was the same answer I had been giving since I was seventeen.

She laughed, which made me feel good. "You haven't changed a bit!"

"You're quite right," I replied, "except that I sleep in a lot later." Which was true.

She took another sip of the Riesling. "Me too," she said.

This was shaping up nicely. I hoped I could give her a nice quiet weekend with good food and company, and to cheer her up a bit before she returned to the city. It was the least I could do for a friend.

By this time she was actually eating the scallops, which was good, since it meant her appetite was intact. I was working on my own glass of wine and I had an idea.

I knew her better than anyone else. If I could get her talking, perhaps I could help her work through her grief. This was a good idea for two reasons – one, to help her, and the other, that she would do all the talking, since I had no intention of doing anything involving thinking this weekend.

This seemed like a pretty good idea at the time. We had a lot to talk about, and an entire weekend to do it in. I learned later that you should never ask a question to which you do not wish to know the answer.

"So where do you think it came from?" I asked her.

She understood I was talking about The Thing In The Barn. "I don't know. I was never able to figure that out."

"Did Sven have any ideas?" I wanted to know.

"We know it was a short range craft, for atmospheric flight. It had to have come from a mother ship."

Well, that was news to me, but I wasn't the expert on alien spacecraft.

She continued. "There was no food storage. There were no supplies on board for a long mission."

It was then I remembered she had been inside the craft. "How did you get in?"

She made a gesture with her hands. "You have to push on a certain part of the hull. It opens a hatch."

"What was it like?" This was pretty interesting, getting a top secret briefing from a young blonde wearing only underwear while drinking a first rate wine.

"The cockpit is very small. The pilots were very short compared to us."

That must have been interesting. Sven had gotten the hatch open. He had to have found the bodies of the pilots.

"How many were there?"

"Just two. Your uncle took pictures."

"What did they look like?"

"It was hard to tell. They apparently both died on impact. They had a kind of safety harness on, but the bodies were very disfigured."

Well, crashing into the ground in Montana would do that to a body, I thought.

We were silent for a moment. Then I thought of a fairly important question.

"Where are the pilots buried?"

"In the cemetery. Sven had headstones made up for them under the names Lars Larson and Ole Larson."

Ha. Sven had used his own family name, and had buried them in our family plot.

I would have liked to attend that autopsy, I thought. I followed that up with another question.

"How did you ever get it into flying condition?"

She shook her head. "I didn't. Sven did. He said the problem was not with the ship, it was with the pilots. The ship didn't take very much damage. It just killed the pilots."

That made sense. She had said that the craft had belly landed.

"What was the power source?" I wanted to know.

"According to your uncle, it was nuclear. But he never said whether it was fission or fusion."

Funny to hear a blonde talking about the types of nuclear reactors.

It was her turn for a question. "You don't seem too interested. It's a pretty important discovery your uncle made."

I didn't think so. "Frankly, I could care less. I know we have life on this planet, it only stands to reason there's life on others. We've launched spacecraft to the moon, I figure someone would eventually build a spacecraft and come here. As long as they don't fly down Interstate 5 causing havoc, I don't care what they do or where they came from."

She thought about this. Then she turned her big blue eyes on mine. "So what are you interested in nowadays?"

I took a slow pull at the Riesling. "You know, Kirsten, I don't care about much anymore."

She sighed. "You used to care. You used to care about a lot of things. What happened?"

"I'm too tired." This was true. I worked crazy hours. When I got home, I fell directly into bed. I didn't even have a hobby anymore. A long time ago, I used to like restoring cars. Now I bought the cheapest car with a hundred thousand mile warranty and traded it in when the warranty expired before I had to do any work on it.

She shook her head regretfully. "You were a lot of fun back in high school."

"I didn't have to work a hundred hours a week in high school," I pointed out, quite reasonably. "My fun quotient has dropped a lot."

"What about your girlfriends?"

Aha, so that was where this was going. "I don't have a girlfriend, Kirsten, I haven't in years. Nobody wants to go out with a man who's exhausted all of the time."

This was true. I knew this because the daughter of the editor of the society page for the local paper had told me so after I had fallen asleep during our date. She had been extremely courteous about the whole incident, as she had been properly brought up, but she was quite definite that she expected more action on a date than her guy falling asleep. Even before the sex.

"Why don't you take a vacation? Why do you have to work so many hours?"

I put a stop to this at once. "Kirsten, let's not talk about work. It's bad enough I have to work the hours I do, I don't want to talk about it when I'm not working."

She nodded agreement. There was an awkward silence for a moment.

I picked up the conversation. "So tell me, how often did you fly the thing?"

She thought for a minute. "Just a few times. By the time I learned to fly it, the Air Force had equipment capable of tracking it in flight. Sven used to fly it once in a while up to the 1970s, but after that, only to teach me."

"Did you ever get caught?"

She nodded, raising her eyebrows as she remembered. "We were picked up and tracked by a military interceptor once. But it couldn't match us for speed, and your uncle got us out of there. "

"Did they shoot at you?"

"Yes, but not with missiles or bullets – the fighter had some sort of beam which interfered with the ship's controls, but Sven maneuvered out of the way and got us home."

Yeah, you couldn't beat Sven for evasive action, not after Korea. What was interesting, though, is that the Air Force had developed some sort of energy field that disrupted the function of the craft. There was only one way they could have done that, and that was by testing it on the real thing. So the rumors were true.

Well, good for the Air Force. They had a lot of smart people, apparently they were putting them all to work on these problems. It made me proud. I wondered if the USAF was flying these things around on recon missions. Then again, why bother, when you had satellites and Predator drones.

"How did you fly it?"

"It has a headset you wear. You think about where you want to go, and the ship goes there."

That must have been amazing beyond description.

"Can you fly conventional aircraft?" I asked her.

"Your uncle taught me. I am licensed for multiengine jet. Up to a Gulfstream V."

I wondered if it was her way of getting closer to her dead husband, who was a jet pilot.

"Jeez, Kirsten, you can fly jets?"

"Sure. You can fly, can't you?"

"Well, sure, but just single engine piston planes. I fly, like, twice a year in a rented Cessna!" I had learned to fly just in case I needed to in wartime. It came in handy more than once during my military career.

"Then you understand." She raised her glass. "To flying!"

I raised my glass to toast, and we clinked glasses. I wondered how many bottles of wine we were going to kill tonight.

She sipped her wine, running her tongue around the glass, watching me as she did so. I could tell she was thinking.

"James…why did you never call me?"

Nothing like getting put on the spot. I thought fast.

"Kirsten. I never call anyone. I have no friends, no hobbies and very little time to myself.

The only one I see on a regular basis is a stray cat who insists on sleeping on my convertible when I park it in front of my house every night."

That made her smile. It was true. The cat liked the soft leather top.

She nodded. Then she put down her glass and reached her hand across to mine.

"Dance with me, James."

She got up from the table, pulling me into the living room of the cottage, and she turned on the stereo. She picked an instrumental selection, and then came to me, putting her hand in mine and sliding her hip next to me. I listened to the rhythm, and led her in a gentle waltz.

She put her hands around my neck and kissed me, and I kissed her back, enjoying the music, the quiet of the cottage, and the distant sound of the surf crashing onto the beach. Then she laid her head on my chest, and we danced some more, together, but each alone in our thoughts and memories.

After a few moments we slid to the floor and lay down in front of the fireplace, fumbling with each other's clothes. We pulled a blanket from the couch and curled up next to each other, watching the fire in the darkness.

"James." Her voice was getting sleepy.

"Yes?"

"I'm glad you're here."

"I'm glad you're here too." And I kissed her neck.

I held her for a while, and she fell asleep in my arms. It had been quite a day, and we were both suffering from jet lag. I, on the other hand, rarely get to hold a woman as beautiful as Kirsten in my arms, so it took me longer to fall asleep, but eventually, with my arms around her, I drifted off, and dreamed of another time when we were both young and innocent and problem-free.

CHAPTER TEN

We awoke slowly the next morning. The events of the past few days were finally catching up to us. I got up before she did, still running on West Coast time, and went into the kitchen to get some sort of breakfast ready.

English muffins, tea, eggs and bacon were the order of the day. There were frozen waffles, but no whipped cream, so I passed on the waffles.

The thing about the cottage is the absolute silence of it. Almost no one lives in the little beach town in the winter, so there is no noise – no cars, no airplanes, no lawnmowers. When the windows are open, you can hear the surf in the background. After what we'd been through, it was pretty restful.

Kirsten finally got up, wandering around the cottage as she usually did in the mornings, nude, warm and sleepy, so I abandoned the eggs and scooped her up in my arms, feeling her body against mine. She draped her arms around my neck, laid her head on my chest and purred like a kitten.

She kissed me. "Your eggs are burning."

I regretfully left her and attended to our breakfast. I usually used paper plates, but William had the place stocked with china, so we were eating upscale today.

She sat at the table and I put food in front of her, which woke her up and she selected an English muffin.

Well, we weren't getting much done today. I felt slightly guilty, but then again, I had not had a vacation in years, so I suppose I deserved a few days off with a beautiful woman.

"What would you like to do today?" she asked, looking at me expectantly.

This put me in something of a spot. When I have a day off, I don't "do" anything. I loaf around the house, watch the occasional football game, sleep, but I don't actually do anything productive. Especially not when I had persuaded a girl to spend the weekend.

She must have seen me hesitate, and she smiled. "OK, aside from sleeping and sex, what ELSE would you like to do?"

I thought a minute. "Well, there is something that I have to do."

"What?"

"We need whipped cream for the waffles. I'll have to go to the store."

She laughed, probably expecting a more ambitious agenda from me for the day. It was good to see her happy.

"All right, so we'll go to the store. What else is there to do here?"

I remembered the local wildlife sanctuary. "There's a Nature Conservancy refuge near here…if you'd like to go for a hike. Lots of critters live there."

The Boy Scouts would probably shoot me. I used to know the names of all of the wildlife in the refuge, but that was twenty years ago when I was a Cub Scout, now they were all just "critters".

I sipped my tea. Earl Grey, good stuff. "We could go sailing, if you wanted to."

That perked her up. "Sailing?" She looked hopeful.

"There's a small harbor in town. It's got a museum of sailing. We could rent a boat or something."

Actually, it did not remotely resemble a sailing museum. What is was, is a yacht collection, which some old salt had talked a lawyer into incorporating as a museum, for which they charged tourists to sail around the bay in the summer.

Only in Connecticut can you find a yacht museum. The yachts were actual sailing vessels from the nineteen thirties and forties, when men raced their sleek hulls for fun up and down the coastline. Over time, the trend moved toward motor powered yachts, and nowadays the local millionaires used a yacht with an engine capable of thirty knots, outfitted with marble baths and king sized bedrooms, not forgetting a well stocked wine cellar.

So they donated their old yachts to this sailing museum for a tax break, and now you could rent one of the fastest sailing vessels in the world for a leisurely spin around the bay. I remember that they had one of the America's Cup defenders in the collection. I mentioned this to Kirsten.

Her eyes brightened. "Great! Let's do that!!"

Now, nothing against the Navy, but I have a healthy respect for the ocean, which is why I served in the Army. My idea of a good time does not involve pitting myself against the sea off the New England coastline, but if that's what she wanted to do, I suppose I could dust off my sailing skills for a few hours.

I nodded. "I'll call over and see what's available."

"Thank you, James." She paused, then said seriously, "it would help me relax. I know you don't like to sail."

I shrugged. I would survive a trip around the bay. If it made her happy. It would take my mind off things for a bit.

Suddenly I remembered. The cottage was normally closed this time of year. "I'll have to get the Jacuzzi turned on."

The hot tub took about half a day to get warm, so I'd have to go out and get the temperature turned up. It would be ready by the time we got back from the ocean.

That settled, we finished our breakfast. The cottage had been wired for modern appliances, which meant there was a dishwasher, so cleaning up afterwards was easy.

She headed off into the shower, and I resisted the temptation to join her, since I would probably distract her from her mission of getting cleaned up, and instead went outside to check the garage.

Driving a Silver Wraith was very nice, but in the tiny streets of the little coastal town a Rolls-Royce was not the most practical option. I remembered that William sent his old used cars to the cottage, so I went to find out what our transportation options were.

There was a Morgan convertible parked in the garage. Keys were hanging on the wall. Well, I couldn't complain, except we were going from the gigantic Rolls to a tiny Morgan. Not a problem. I pulled the picnic basket off the back, and went into the kitchen and stuffed it with all the portable food and drink I could find.

Next I located beach blankets, towels, hats, sunscreen and a collapsible beach umbrella, and stuffed this all into the tiny boot of the Morgan. I added Helly Hanson sou'westers, since the weather off the coast can turn in an instant.

Kirsten came out of the shower, in what she imagined was sailing gear. I suppose she wore this to the beach in California, when she did wear anything at the beach, but this was not going to work on a sailing ship.

"Kirsti, my dear," I began, "might you have anything a little more practical?"

She looked down at her tiny bikini, which I remember was called a sling bikini. "I can't sail in this?"

I shook my head. "You might get a bit chilly. I'd recommend something a little warmer. Where did you get that, anyway?"

"I got it for free, from a modeling shoot." She retreated into the bedroom, and in a few minutes came out in shorts and a pullover. This was more like it.

We piled into the Morgan, and drove down the short distance to the shore, and pulled up at the museum.

I had called ahead to see what was for rent, and learned that among the collection of luxury playthings there was an actual racing yacht, an America's Cup defender, the *Columbia*.

I had sailed her once when I was a teenager, so I knew her fairly well, and had made a reservation for her.

The counter man today was the guy who had gotten the museum started. His name was Charles Edgerton IV, but everyone called him Chaz, and he had been a very good naval officer at one time, having eventually commanded a carrier battle group, I think built around the USS Midway. Nowadays Chaz spent his time tending to old yachts and sailing around the bay for fun.

Almost everyone who owned a sailing vessel hereabouts paid Chaz to keep an eye on their boats, so Chaz would make his rounds every day, ensuring everything was shipshape and Bristol fashion for the boats he cared for, which is a Navy way of saying they weren't going to sink today.

He was wearing the same hat I had seen him in ten years ago, in faded denim jeans and shirt, and he was working on some boat part which I could not identify if my life depended on it. It was good to see him.

"Hello Chaz," I greeted him, "and how is the Navy today?"

"Oak bottomed and copper sheathed!" he replied, which is another one of those Naval sayings I do not understand, except that it means "good". He came around the counter and shook my hand.

"Good to see you, James! What brings you to our little corner of the world?"

He caught sight of Kirsten, and understood instantly. "Doing a little pleasure cruising?" he asked.

That is how Navy people ask you if you're dating the girl you're with, so you have to know what "pleasure cruising" means. I swear, if you want to understand Navy people, you have to learn a whole new language.

"Why yes," I replied dryly, "may I introduce my friend Kirsten? Kirsten, this is Chaz; Chaz, this is Kirsten."

He shook her hand with a courtly elegance I had never seen him display until now. "Welcome, Miss Kirsten, to our little town. I hope that you will enjoy yourself here."

Kirsten warmed to him at once, as did most women, which did not surprise me. When you're in the Navy and at sea for long periods, you have to learn how to impress women in a very short time because they only give you, like, one day off every hundred years.

"Thank you, Mr. Chaz," she replied, "thank you very much."

I cut this off before the old barnacle stole my girl. "Chaz, we'd like to take out the *Columbia*."

He looked up, remembering why we were here. He waved at the yacht slip where she was tied up. "She's all yours, my boy, have a good time."

And she was indeed. I looked out the window, and the *Columbia* rocked gently at her slip, as beautiful as the day I first saw her. I smiled at the memory.

I took out my credit card to pay for all of this, and Chaz looked affronted. "No need, my boy, no need. You've earned your trip today."

I knew what he was referring to. When I was a teenager working at the museum, a particularly bad storm had hit the coast. I had more guts than brains at the time, and while the rest of the state hunkered down to weather the storm, I had driven across the state and had gotten to the museum just as the storm hit. For a full day I had rescued drifting ships, repaired snapped lines, boarded up windows and pumped out leaky vessels. Chaz was impressed by this, which was difficult to do as he was a retired US Navy Captain, and now he refused to charge me whenever I wanted to take one of his yachts out.

I grinned and went out to see my new command. Chaz was busy watching Kirsten as she bounced along beside me. He leaned up against a piling to make sure I remembered my basic seamanship.

This was a good idea, since I had not sailed in, like, fifteen years. I did remember to get in, load our picnic supplies, and get the hatches open and the sails ready.

With some trepidation, I ordered "cast off" and Kirsten scampered about freeing the lines, and off we went. The yacht is supposed to have more crew, but we weren't going to race, we were just going to circle slowly around the bay. That had been the original plan.

Once we were underway, I slowly guided the magnificent twelve meter yacht along the coastline.

I decided to let Kirsten man take the wheel so I could manage the sails.

"K," I snapped out, as she came instantly alert, since I only called her "K" when I was in a real hurry, "take the wheel."

Kirsten was at my side instantly and took over, and I took over the job of ensuring we did not sink the museum's priceless irreplaceable yacht. She was as responsive as ever, the museum having kept her in perfect shape.

For a moment we relaxed. It was quite cold out, but sailing in the cold is preferred by some as preferable to getting broiled by the New England sun in the summertime, and I liked winter sailing.

The sea breeze washed over us. It was great. You get such a sense of peace and freedom when sailing. It usually lasts until the first wave washes over you, and then you get a sense of being cold and wet.

Kirsten had learned to sail from one of her uncles in the old country. Sweden is host to a lot of coastline, so a lot of Swedes can sail pretty well.

It's always erotic for me to watch a woman sailing...the wind blows their hair back, and they handle the boat with such skill and determination, you can't help but wonder what it would be like if they were handling you in the same way. Regrettably, there is no autopilot for a twelve meter yacht, so there would be no romantic interludes today.

Still, I could talk to her. That was something.

"Do you sail a lot?" she asked me.

I ignored this. I did not want to talk about sailing, when I had her all to myself.

Instead, I asked, "Am I ever going to see you after this is over?"

There was a long silence, only the sound of the waves slapping against the hull. She was thinking.

"No."

Well, her mind seemed pretty made up on this issue. I sensed some deep emotion here, something Kirsten was keeping from me, and again I felt uneasy and concerned about her.

"Is it my cooking?" That got a smile out of her.

"No, silly, it's just that you live in California, and I don't, and you're going to leave, and I'll never see you again."

I thought about this. She was probably right. "You could come out and visit me, if you're ever in California."

She shook her head. "Enjoy me while you can, James. Let's not talk about the future. We have too much to do this weekend."

The sails filled, the yacht surged forward, and the moment was lost. But she was right. When this was over, we were going to go our separate ways, and we would not see each other again.

Kirsten took us on a course around the bay, and for a brief time, we were seventeen again, our only worry in the world consisting of navigating a yacht. It felt pretty good, actually. The sea air recharged our lungs after a day of travel in the uncomfortable cabin of an airliner. I actually felt myself relax, something I had not felt in years. It was very comforting.

For her part, the *Columbia* performed like the thoroughbred she was, caressing the waves as she raced around the bay. I had my hands full with her, as always, but we were only cruising the bay, not the ocean, so I managed not to sink her. As we navigated the bay, onlookers stood onshore watching us, wondering why we were sailing around in the middle of winter when most sane yacht owners have their boats laid up.

As we completed our first circuit, Kirsten shouted "do you want to go around again?"

"No, let's make for shore!" I yelled back from the bow. I liked to sail, but I also liked hot showers, hot chocolate, and hot sex, all of which were known quantities waiting for me at the cottage.

"Are you sure?" she yelled back. She pointed at the dock.

I looked to where she was pointing. At the dock was a dark colored sedan, and three men in suits were talking to Chaz.

That could not be good. Nobody wore a suit in the village. Men with suits could mean only one thing, and that would be the government.

Things had certainly moved fast. I was not expecting uncle William until tomorrow. Barely twenty four hours had elapsed since our meeting in the Columbia Club. If men with suits were looking for me here, that could mean only one thing...they had found The Thing in The Barn.

They must have found The Diamond Room crates under the farmhouse, and then must have decided to dig under all of the buildings to see if there was anything else he had hidden.

I should have thought of that, but it was too late now.

Kirsten did not wait to be asked. She spun the wheel over, and the *Columbia* heeled sharply, and Kirsten steered for the open sea.

"Are they who I think they are?" she shouted.

I moved beside her. "I'm afraid so."

"Do you think they're from the Air Force?" she asked hopefully.

"Not unless the new Air Force uniform is a black suit," I replied.

We thought a minute. "What do we do now?" she asked.

The sound of an outboard motor carried over the waves. I looked back at the dock, and the three men in suits had gotten into the Museum's Scarab speedboat, and were headed our direction.

A Scarab is one of the world's fastest boats. It is really just a fiberglass hull wrapped around an engine, but the design is the work of genius, and they are an absolute joy to captain.

The DEA had gotten the Scarab during a drug bust, and the museum had gotten it at an auction sale. Chaz used to take it out occasionally to remind himself that he was a powerboat sailor.

And now it was headed at us.

A Scarab versus a twelve meter yacht was not much of a contest. It would be across the bay in less than two minutes.

I felt sick to my stomach and sat down.

"This is not looking good," I said to her.

And just as suddenly, the sound of the motor stopped. I picked up the field glasses, and looked at the Scarab.

The men with suits were pounding on the engine cover. The boat had stopped in mid-bay for no reason I could see. It wasn't sinking, so it had to be the motor.

I looked back at the dock. Chaz was there, and he was looking at me through his field glasses. He gave a slow wave.

So Chaz had engineered our escape. The Scarab had a fuel cutoff, which you had to know about. If you did not disable it, the engine would cut out and leave you adrift. Apparently, when the men in the suits had commandeered the Scarab, Chaz had somehow neglected to tell them about this feature.

And now we had a chance.

There was really one option. I took the wheel.

"Where are we going?" Kirsten asked, concerned.

The only place we could go.

"The Mansion," I said, and steered a course for Pilgrim's Bay.

C

CHAPTER ELEVEN

Pilgrim's Bay is not actually a bay. It's a cove. And its name is not actually Pilgrim's Bay.

The history of the cove is somewhat scandalous. Bluntly put, the cove over the years has been a refuge for smugglers, pirates and privateers.

It didn't start that way. From the sea, it looks to be a perfect harbor, and indeed it is, if you can get in. The original settlers of the area, Pilgrims coming down from Massachusetts Bay Colony, attempted a landing at the cove in 1632.

What they did not know, is that there is a reef at the entrance to the cove. Their ship, the *Providence*, sailed directly into the reef and gutted her bottom in seconds. The passengers did not even have time to get out of bed as the ship, still under full sail, was driven down into the ocean. There was only one survivor, a child thrown into the sea by a desperate mother. The incident has been immortalized in the classic poem "The Scourge of Pilgrim's Reef" taught to schoolchildren all over New England.

As it turned out, if you can avoid the reef, which is easy to do, the cove is a very nice and protected refuge for a sailing ship. Over the years this fact became known, but no one in their right mind would use the cove if an alternative was available.

So the only people who used the reef were those who had no alternative...like people who were wanted by the law.

Kidd is rumored to have used it. Privateers in Queen Anne's war used it. But it really came into its own during Prohibition.

Just about everyone involved in shipping in the 1930s was involved in smuggling liquor. Connecticut was no exception. Pilgrim's Bay, as it came to be called, was the perfect place to drop anchor unnoticed, offload a quick cargo, and be gone in short order.

Some say that half of the liquor in Connecticut came in through Pilgrim's Bay. The smugglers even built a jetty and a wharf. A lighthouse was added, the real purpose of which was to station a lookout during unloading.

Then Prohibition was repealed, and Pilgrim's Bay was abandoned.

But Connecticut became a preferred place to build a summer house due to its proximity to New York City. Developers bought up the land surrounding Pilgrim's Bay and built monster "summer homes" that dwarfed castles in Europe. Old money from all over the country located there.

The reef served to keep out the riff raff, i.e., those with less than a zillion dollars, and the dock and jetty served as convenient yacht slips for the homes that had beachfront on Pilgrim's Bay.

Over the years the tragedy that had given the area its name was forgotten, and most of the locals in the area assumed the name "Pilgrim's Bay" referred to the respected founding families of Connecticut, and not the horrific deaths of a hundred innocent men, women and children.

I do not know how it got promoted from a cove to a bay. That had to be the work of the real estate developer.

Regardless of what is was or how it came by its name, for us it meant safety and shelter, and we would be there shortly on present course and speed.

We spun the *Columbia* out of the bay and headed to Pilgrim's Bay, which was right up the coast.

"What mansion?" Kirsten wanted to know, when I told her our destination.

Kirsten did not know much about my mother's family, so I filled her in. After the Revolution, the family got into manufacturing, everything from locomotives to munitions. After the Civil War, great-great uncle Benjamin built a family "beach cottage" of fifty rooms or so here in Pilgrim's Bay. It was one of the three homes fronting the Bay itself, the other two being the one of the early railroad fortunes, and the other one of the new fortunes based on oil.

All three families shared the jetty, but each of the mansions had its own dock. This is where we were headed now.

After the stock market crash of 1929, these colossal buildings were repossessed by the city for back taxes. It cost far too much to maintain them as homes, so the city rented them out for gala events, and ran tours through them on the weekends.

For our family, the end had come much earlier. During World War I, Benjamin's son and principal heir, Douglas, had been killed when the troop transport he was in was torpedoed as it attempted to cross the Atlantic. He had actually gotten off the ship, I was told, but the U-Boat crew had machined gunned the survivors.

Without his guidance, the family business foundered, and did not survive the Great Depression.

When I was a teenager, I had also worked for the city, giving tours through great-great-uncle Benjamin's little fifty room beach getaway.

As a result, I was familiar with the back entrances, secret passages, and underground access tunnels in the place, and that was where I intended to go now.

I turned the yacht into Pilgrim's Bay, and she raced to the jetty. It was going to be hard to hide a twelve meter yacht, so we tied it up and left it there.

Kirsten stood on the jetty, taking in the sight of the Mansion, an enormous stone building overlooking the ocean.

"Let's get moving," I said, "we won't have long."

"Your family built this?" she wanted to know, but I cut her off and we ran up the jetty and onto the beach in front of the house.

The seawall in front of the Mansion was a natural stone barrier, at least it looked that way. A lot of money had been spent to give that appearance. In reality, a tunnel ran from the beach to the house, and the entryway was concealed behind a protruding rock wall. In seconds, we were in the tunnel and out of sight of the beach. Unless you knew it was here, you weren't going to find it.

"What is this place?" Kirsten asked, pulling her Helly Hansons over her head to avoid the dripping water in the tunnel.

I found the hurricane lanterns and matches where they were kept in a panel cut into the wall, and lit one. The lamp cast long spooky shafts of light down the tunnel.

For the first time, I felt safe, and smiled reassuringly at her. "This, my dear, is our secret escape route to the beach."

"What's it for?" she asked.

"Smuggling booze," I replied, and took her by the hand, and led her up to the house.

Despite her nautical knowledge, I don't think she had a lot of experience with smuggling. The tunnel had come in very handy over the years moving cargo back and forth in private.

The tunnel also made for a very nice beach passage during stormy weather, of which there is a lot in New England. You could come out here and sit warm and dry by a fire while a sou'wester tore across the shore. The power of the storm was incredible to watch.

Of course, that was before cable TV and the Internet. This is why I was pretty sure no one would be using the tunnel, and I was right.

The tunnel let out into the basement of the house, where food and supplies were stored. In short order we let ourselves into the basement through the entry hatch, which from the room appeared to be ordinary paneling, and we were now dry, warm and safe. The question was, what to do next.

Kirsten sat on a stack of boxes of canned peaches. "Who were those men in the speedboat? What did they want with us?"

I found a bottle of whisky, but could not find any Coke, so it was straight whisky for me. I took a swig and let the smooth liquid fire warm up my stomach.

"I would guess, my little blonde friend, that those men in suits are representatives of our wonderful democratic experiment in Washington, and that they wish to converse with us regarding something they found under my uncle's barn, for example, an alien spacecraft."

She stopped smiling. "You think they found the UFO?"

I nodded. "Could well be."

She thought a minute. "Did your uncle William send them?"

"Probably," I replied, "he must have moved very quickly."

"Has he called you?" she asked.

This is when I remembered that I had a cellphone. I really do not know how all of the features work. It is a phone, and can play video games, and you can watch video clips on it, but most importantly, it can receive text messages.

William would never leave a message about anything so important, at least I thought at the time, but it was worth checking, so I pulled out my cellphone and sure enough, there was a message from the old boy.

Well, well, well, I keep underestimating my uncle. He's in his eighth decade, but he knows how to send text messages. That was really annoying. I don't even know how to send a text message on this phone.

And of course, the blonde had thought of it, which was even more annoying.

"As it turns out," I admitted, "it seems uncle William has indeed been trying to contact me."

"What does it say?" she stood by me and read the tiny screen.

In case you are wondering, if you are ever being pursued by men in dark suits, and a beautiful blonde stands next to you, can you forget your desperate situation and be completely distracted, the answer is yes.

I felt her next to me, and the scent of her made me completely forget for a moment what I was doing.

One of the things I have always loved about this woman is how comfortable she is with her sexuality, and how aware she is of her impact upon me, and how easily she deals with it.

In this case, she sensed my hesitation, and put her arm around me and kissed me on the top of my head, and with her other hand pressed the "display" key on the cellphone.

My concentration returning to reality, I turned my attention away from her soft blonde hair and looked at the cellphone.

Yes, there was indeed a message. When Kirsten hit "display", it said:

HELLO NEPHEW—GOOD NEWS—JOB COMPLETE. CAN WE MEET?

I composed a message and sent it back. I wrote:

AM OTHERWISE OCCUPIED. CAN YOU HANDLE ARRANGEMENTS?

Kirsten looked on as I wrote. "What does that mean, 'otherwise occupied'?"

I smiled at her. "Between gentlemen,' I elaborated, "the phrase "otherwise occupied" means that your attentions are focused on a lady."

She digested this. "You mean, you're on a date and don't want to be disturbed?"

Actually, it meant, "I've a liaison with a totally hot babe, leave me alone", but she was close enough.

"Yes," I lied convincingly, "that's what it means."

William must have been standing by, because almost immediately another message came in. This one was a shocker. It read:

HOST COUNTRY WISHES TO THANK YOU BY INVESTITURE. MUST TALK.

Kirsten's face clouded over. "What does this mean?"

Well, you could have knocked me over with a feather. This was absolutely not what I had been expecting. It also meant that I was as totally wrong as it was possible to get. I would have to tell Kirsten.

"It means," I began, "that I may have been wrong about our situation."

She cocked her head at me the way she does when she's thinking.

"As it turns out," I continued, "those men in the suits may have been working for my uncle William after all."

I looked again at the cellphone, where a reply was indicated. I punched in a message.

MEET ME AT THE MANSION—GRAND BALLROOM—TWO HOURS

I hit "send" and it went sailing through cyberspace to William's phone. While I waited for confirmation of our proposed meeting, I explained further to Kirsten.

"You remember that William went to Sven's ranch to recover the crates holding the gemstones that made up the paneling for The Diamond Room."

She nodded, following so far.

"Well, it seems than in less then twenty four hours, that he has found the crates and recovered them. Apparently, they did not dig under the barn and find the UFO; they stuck to the plan and dug under the coal chute, and found the crates that carry the paneling for The Diamond Room." I thought a minute. "He must have flown out of Maelstrom Air Force base in Montana."

Wow. If William had that kind of clout, he must be very highly connected indeed.

"What does he mean, the host country? What is investiture?" She stumbled over the last word.

"He means the country to which The Diamond Room originally belonged." I remember there was some controversy. The Grand Duke's home country claimed rightful ownership, and so did the Princess' home country. If the US ever admitted it had ownership, there was going to be a monumental legal battle.

"Investiture," I went on, "is the process by which a European country recognizes a particularly noteworthy public service. The person involved is given a title."

Even for a Swede, it did not take long for her to realize what I was talking about.

"You mean," she said, "you're going to be knighted?"

"That's what it usually means," I admitted, "but don't read anything into this."

"I think that's incredible!" she said, excited, "that's great! See, you helped them, and now they want to say thank you!"

"Not really," I said, breaking it to her gently, "what it means is that one of these countries wants to establish its legal right to The Diamond Room, and by giving me a title, it will put me on their side in the upcoming legal fight. It's actually a pretty smart legal move on their part."

"Well," she said, a little disappointed at the reality of European politics, "it's still pretty neat!"

Actually, she was right. It was a classy thing of them to do.

William sent another message.

WILL SEE YOU IN TWO HOURS—MAKE GOOD
USE OF TIME---CHEERS

She read the message. "What does that mean, 'make good use of time'?"

"It means," I said, standing up and gathering her into my arms, "that we have two hours alone together in this beautiful old mansion, and William knows it. I guarantee, he will not be early. Would you like a tour?"

"Love one!" she said, and kissed me.

I would have taken her right there, but I had other plans.

The Mansion is closed during the winter. The security system I am well acquainted with, and had it turned off in short order. We went up the stairs, there being no elevator in the basement, only a dumbwaiter, and emerged after some effort onto the main floor of the building.

I located the light switches and the darkened building came alive with light. The original chandeliers had been retrofitted with fiber optic lighting, which was advisable, since they had been supplied by Louis Comfort Tiffany himself.

Sure enough, as soon as she saw the lights, she asked "Are those Tiffany lamps?"

I nodded, amazed that a young woman would be able to recognize Tiffany's work from decades ago, but the New York firm has a cult-like following among women.

""Is this the ballroom?" she asked, swirling about the hall.

"No, this is the entryway...the ballroom is straight ahead." I walked ahead and pushed open the massive hand carved doors.

They did a good job on the ballroom when it was built, not too ornate, quite functional, could either be used for dancing or dining. She ran ahead of me and stood in the center, taking in the vaulted ceilings and rich mahogany paneling of the walls.

She put her arms up to be held. "Dance with me!"

So I did. I had attended every single debutante ball in the area when I was young, for the simple reason that you could meet a zillion beautiful young women in less than an hour. For this reason alone, I could perform an acceptable waltz, and so I led my beautiful blonde friend in graceful circles around the huge dance floor, humming "The Blue Danube" for effect as I did so.

We spun around the floor until we were dizzy, laughing with the effort, and came to a halt underneath our family crest, carved here a hundred years ago, still visible on the ceiling under a layer of dust.

I had a moment, there, standing in my family's old home, with my own parents dead, realizing that in fact, that I was now the head of the family.

Like a friend of mine who made brigade commander at twenty eight, it was for no other reason than I was the last member of the family left alive except for uncle William.

I was brought back to reality by Kirsten, who kissed me. I kissed her back, and then we wrapped our arms around each other.

"Show me the bedroom," she whispered, and I did.

The bedroom, designed a century ago, had a nice king sized bed. There was no plasma TV or

WiFi connection, since the Conservation Committee that supervised the house was pretty strict about authenticity, but we weren't there to watch TV.

I pulled the bedcovers back, picked Kirsten up and deposited her on the bed, then gently pulling her top over her head, The shorts followed, and then I had her alone, undressed, in a king sized bed.

I got similarly unclothed in seconds, and bounced in to the bed after her. The bed itself was made out of mahogany, so it did not so much as creak under us.

The room has a commanding view of the bay, which means the ships in the harbor could theoretically see in the window with their telescopes, but other than us, there was no one insane enough to take a sailing vessel out in the middle of the winter, so we were unobserved.

I never seem to get tired of having sex with Kirsten, probably because of her uninhibited Scandinavian approach to sex and her endless energy, and she never seems to tire of me, so it worked out pretty well today, as it usually does whenever we hook up. We had sex until we were exhausted, and then I wandered into the shower and let the water revive me.

It occurred to me, as I showered, that we had just made love in the bed where much of my family had been conceived. I laughed, and she noticed the look on my face.

"What's so funny?" she wanted to know, but I just gave her a totally hot kiss, and that seemed to satisfy her feminine curiosity.

"Let's get cleaned up," I said, releasing her from my grasp, "Uncle William will be here shortly."

We had only the clothes we'd gone sailing in, but they would have to do. In short order we were cleaned up and reasonably presentable.

She waited by the bedroom door for me.

"The Grand Ballroom," I said, with a sweeping gesture, "awaits us."

And so it did.

We ambled down the enormous staircase, through the foyer—I had not actually known what a foyer was until I saw this place—and into the Grand Ballroom.

Before movies, television, and the Internet, there was "The Season", which was an endless series of dances, balls, and formal events to which the cream of society attended on an annual basis. To accommodate a few hundred of their closest friends, Benjamin and his wife had built into the house a ballroom suitable for a proper soiree. It was really very nicely done.

I pulled a table from the reception area into the center of the ballroom, and a few Louis XIV chairs over so we could all have a place to sit.

CHAPTER TWELVE

And then we sat down, and waited for William.

I noticed that Kirsten was quiet, something she was not normally.

"What are you thinking about?" I asked her.

"Your uncle William…what's he like?" She was smoothing her hair, a sign she was worried.

That got my attention. For what reason would this little blonde be worried? Particularly about my uncle.

"Why do you ask?" I said, intrigued, putting my feet up on the table.

Her face grew expressionless. "Just curious."

Ha. Just curious, sure. But she was, of course, telling the truth…she was like a cat that way, always checking around to see what was up.

"William. Oldest brother of my mom. Went to Princeton, then the Army, then law school. Private practice."

She cut me off. "I'm not interested in his career…tell me about him."

I switched gears. "His passions are the law, his country, and his family. He is also known to be partial to Napa Valley wine, beautiful women, and skiing."

"Why doesn't he just retire? He sounds like he was pretty successful."

"He did! He did retire...he got bored about three months later, and then resumed working. Of course, now he only does jobs he enjoys."

"Why is he helping you?"

For a blonde, she is pretty smart. She had gotten right to the heart of the issue. For that matter, why was William helping me?

I reasoned it out for her aloud. "In William's community of intelligence officers, information is the currency of the trade....it puts the owner in a position of power to negotiate for information from other people. In this case, it will give him power and credibility not only with his agency, but other governments as well."

"As far as my role in all of this, William knows he can trust me implicitly...since I'm family. It gives him a stable position from which to negotiate with the government, since my credibility is assured."

Kirsten just sat there and looked at me very carefully for a full minute. It kind of made me uncomfortable. Finally she nodded and gave a sigh.

We both looked out the window at the same time, where we saw William driving up the half mile of tarmac that passed for a driveway in these parts.

William was in an Aston Martin today, one of their later models, so I guess his 401K was ticking over comfortably.

He parked the car in front of the portico, which is a series of columns that would make any Roman emperor proud, topped by a massive roof, so your guests can get out of their cars in the rain and not get wet.

We rose to our feet and went to the front to meet him, and I swung open the massive oak doors.

"Hello, nephew," he rang out, "good to see you!"

I grinned and shook his hand, but his attention was already elsewhere. "And who is this angel?"

Kirsten offered her hand, and William kissed it, in European fashion. "Uncle William, may I present a friend, Kirsten Vorra, and Kirsten, this is my uncle William."

"Pleasure to meet you," she said, blushing as he kissed her hand.

"Likewise, my dear," William responded, and you could see the old bastard meant it.

"Shall we sit for a few minutes?" I asked, breaking up the moment and gesturing toward the ballroom.

"You two go ahead," William said, "let me join you."

Kirsten and I resumed our seats in the ballroom, where after a few minutes William joined us. I had thought he was going to use the restroom, but he appeared with some fresh apples and a bottle of White Star, which I assumed he had liberated from the kitchen.

He gently handed one of the apples to Kirsten and another to me, and kept one for himself, and as we munched on fresh fruit, William broke open the White Star and poured us all a glass.

"So, my dear nephew, shall I give you a report?" William was smiling, something he did rarely, so the recovery must have gone well.

"Tell us all about it," Kirsten replied, and William forgot all about me and turned his full attention to the beautiful young blonde across the table, for which I could hardly blame him, as I liked to stare at her myself.

"Well, it all started after our meeting in New York," he began, "after which I placed a telephone call to a former employee of mine, who is now a highly placed official with a certain agency in Virginia."

We both knew better than to ask which agency.

He sipped at his champagne. We all took a moment to savor the White Star. It really is remarkable.

"I asked him to assemble a team of young, strong men and women who could be trusted for their absolute discretion. I also asked for the use of some earthmoving equipment, and an aircraft with suitable cargo capability."

Well, now, this was interesting. William never disclosed operative details. I shot a warning glance at Kirsten. There had to be a reason he was telling us this. She gave me a quizzical look.

William continued. "I met the cargo aircraft and the team at Newark Airport, and we then flew directly to your uncle's ranch in Montana."

Well, that must have been some pilot. He had not flown out of Maelstrom Air Force Base as I had originally thought. And he had landed directly on Sven's ranch.

The ranch was certainly large enough to fit a dozen runways and cargo airplanes, but it was not an improved road surface. Airplanes were made for landing on rough terrain, but how William had gotten hold of one on short notice made for interesting speculation.

"We then proceeded to your uncle's coal chute, and you had directed, and removed the contents, and then excavated the floor."

You could do that, I suppose, if you had your own earthmoving tractor that you had driven directly off of the airplane.

"The crates were still in their original World War II packing, but they had been placed in metal ammunition casings, and were thereby protected from the elements."

William here paused. I was dying to know if the contents had survived, but I wasn't going to press for details, I let him tell the story instead.

Kirsten was not nearly as inhibited. "What happened? Did the diamonds survive?"

William smiled again, the expression of a man who has completed a job well done. "It all survived, my dear, and in near-perfect condition. Every single crate. A quick inventory showed that The Diamond Room panels are all there."

I was thinking ahead. "Where does it go from here?"

Finally, William turned his attention to me. "That all depends on you, nephew, it all depends on you."

Aha. Now we were getting somewhere. I knew there was a reason William was filling us in on what should have been secret operational mission details.

"And how exactly," I asked slowly, "do I have anything to do with it?"

William held his champagne up to the light to watch the golden light filter through it.

"You can have as much, or as little, to do with this as you like, James."

He was using my Christian name. That meant he was now speaking to an equal, and since I wasn't in his league, I was flattered.

I was also worried, because it meant he wanted something from me.

But Kirsten broke in, and even she was aware that the dynamic in the room was shifting. "What do you mean, Mr. Fletcher?

That was my mother's maiden name. Our family name.

"You must call me William," he said to her gently, raising his glass.

She smiled, aware of the effect she was having on him, and raised her glass in return. "So, William…what exactly do you mean by that? Why do we have anything further to do with any of this?"

He put his glass down, placed his hands in his lap, and leaned back. I had a bad feeling about what was coming next.

"As it turns out," he said quietly, "something of an opportunity has come up."

What this meant, as I remembered my uncle William, is that he had figured out how to turn this situation to his personal advantage.

This is not a bad thing, usually, since the United States of America, whose interests William is constantly advancing, usually benefits from the transaction, but make no mistake, what was coming next would benefit primarily William.

"And how is that?" Kirsten pressed.

This was going to be interesting. William was an old fox who had faced down Nazi Germany and the Soviet Union and had decades of spycraft under his belt, but up against Kirsten, he was out of his element.

"This may take some explaining," he said.

Kirsten looked around. "I don't have to be at work until Monday," she said, and pulled her champagne close and curled up in her Louis XIV chair.

William smiled again, thinking he had baited the hook, but he had a big surprise coming if he thought he could use Kirsten as a pawn.

You can't beat these little family get-togethers for sheer entertainment value.

"You may recall," he began, clearing his throat, "that The Diamond Room was originally from an Eastern European country."

We both nodded, remembering the story of the Grand Duke and the Princess who had loved each other so much.

"What you may not know," he continued, "is that after the Second World War, this country became a Soviet Republic."

I had served in the Cold War, but for the benefit of those who do not appreciate the full horror of what had taken place in 1945, the term "Soviet Republic" meant a European country invaded and occupied by Soviet forces, who promptly murdered the democratically elected government, enslaved the people and looted the country, destroying the industrial base and impoverishing the populace for five decades.

Ronald Reagan had put and end to all of that, but an entire generation of Europeans had lived out their lives under a despotic government.

"As a result, as you might imagine, after the fall of the Soviet Union, this country became a strong supporter of the United States and the North Atlantic Treaty Organization."

Kirsten shot me a look, not recognizing the name. "NATO," I said in a whisper.

"NATO, indeed," William acknowledged, "and in recent years, as the Russian Federation has changed somewhat, the United States has suddenly become much more interested in monitoring its activities."

That was an understatement. The current Russian president had stolen so much private wealth from individuals, and put so many business leaders in prison, that most of Russia's wealth had fled to England.

The Russians were intent on restoring Russia's position in the world so as to have a greater influence on world politics. Lately they were practicing national blackmail by threatening to cut off gas supplies to Ukraine and western Europe, but they were willing to entertain any method to do this.

"Toward this goal," William continued, "it has occurred to certain government officials that more intelligence monitoring of the Russian Federation is in order, and the budget for these activities has been accordingly increased."

I was wondering where all of this was going. I did not have to wait long to find out.

"The question then becomes," William said, stretching out his legs, "is where to put such an intelligence monitoring station. Naturally, it should be situated in the most advantageous location."

The beginnings of a plan were becoming evident here. The US wanted to listen in on the Russians, they needed a place to put their listening station, and had the budget to do it. I wonder what William's role was in this transaction.

"A review of the optimal sites," he went on, "has included the possibility of locating the listening station in the country which originally owned The Diamond Room, Valthringia."

There was a long pause while that sank in. From the look on Kirsten's face, it seemed like a done deal. Approach the home country, propose to rent some real estate, put in the spy station, and all set and done.

I, on the other hand, knew that it was not going to be that easy. If it was that easy, it would already be done.

"So, what's the problem?" Kirsten wanted to know. "Can't we just rent some land from them?"

"Ah, the problem," William replied, steepling his fingers, "is that Valthringia is somewhat dependant on its fuel supplies from the Russians, and are reluctant to take any risk which might anger or otherwise irritate them, and thereby run the risk of ruining their economy."

And the USA, of course, did not have any abundant fuel supplies to sell to Valthringia.

Of course, there was one energy source which the USA had in abundance, but surely they weren't thinking about that.....

As usual, I was wrong. Of course, I don't feel bad about that, since international geopolitics is not my area of specialty.

"And we don't have any oil to give them," Kirsten said, thinking aloud, "since we import all of our oil from the Middle East. So we have no way of solving their energy problem."

William did not say anything. He leaned back in his chair with a thoughtful expression, fixed on Kirsten.

Kirsten looked back at him. There was a silence while we all thought about the unthinkable.

"Unless," she said slowly, "unless…you're thinking about….other energy sources."

William smiled a chilly smile, the rictus of a wolf about to devour his prey. I suddenly realized that William had drafted a policy solution to this entire problem.

"My God," Kirsten said, "you're thinking about the nuclear option."

Nuclear energy, of course, was a specialty of the United States of America. Both France and Japan were over 75% nuclear powered. An entire new generation of reactor design was being perfected at the US laboratory in Idaho.

"I am, indeed, thinking about the nuclear option," William confessed, "as it has worked so very well in France and Japan. A series of reactors would not only give Valthringia a sufficient power supply, but would allow it to sell electricity to an energy-starved Europe, thereby adding an important component to its economy, and bringing in foreign currency reserves."

Yeah, right, I was overwhelmed with admiration for Uncle William's compassion for the poor bankrupt Valthringians. For once I had the upper hand in our little discussions. I knew something about a project called Tube Alloy from 1945, something the English had gotten started, and the Americans had finished under the name Manhattan Project.

"William," I said, breaking in to the discussion between the spy and the blonde, "just as a matter of historical reference….wasn't one of the original scientists at Los Alamos named Dimitri Vlaxon? And wasn't he from Valthringia? Didn't he work on the Manhattan Project?"

I caught the old boy off guard. To his credit, he recovered quickly.

"Why, yes," William said, trying to maneuver out of this, "I think you may be right about that."

I knew I was right. William knew I was right. I pursued this.

"Two other questions, uncle.....didn't Dimitri Vlaxon have a son, who was in fact born in the United States, and who is now one of our most prominent nuclear scientists? And furthermore, isn't Dimitri Vlaxon a relative of the current royal family there?"

William gave me a dirty look. He had obviously not expected me to know about this connection.

Kirsten, on the other hand, was surprised to hear about this. But with a historical recall not usually found in blondes, even Kirsten knew what the Manhattan Project had been.

"The Manhattan Project...that was the original atomic bomb project, wasn't it?"

Well, there was no denying this, so William just nodded.

Another long silence. Eventually she figured it out.

"So if you put civilian nuclear reactors in Valthringia....it would be an easy matter for them to process the uranium for use in a nuclear weapon."

William pretended to be interested in his champagne.

Kirsten went on. "And this Vlaxon guy…he is related to the royal family….could easily do the work….and then you'd have a nuclear capable country directly bordering the Russian Federation."

William shrugged, tried to look innocent.

But she was not finished. "That would give them a permanent deterrent against the Russians, not only economically, but also militarily, since the Russians would be vulnerable to nuclear attack if they ever chose to occupy Valthringia again."

Ten points and a cigar for the blonde. Her grasp of world politics was up to date.

"I cannot deny that this could happen," William said indifferently, "but, of course, our role would be to simply supply the reactors."

That would be like handing a match to an arsonist. A nuclear capable former Soviet satellite country would be a permanent headache in Moscow, and it would make William's whole year if he could irritate the Russian bear that way.

Privately, I resolved never to get William angry, because I didn't want him plotting revenge against me if this is what he was going to do to the Russians.

But I had to smile, because although he was retired, William was putting together a plan which would impact the balance of power in Europe, and even among the amazing group of men and women who make up America's intelligence community, this would be a coup of historic proportions.

"Where do we come into this picture?" she asked, clearly understanding the politics, but not understanding our role in it.   She would regret asking.

"It would facilitate matters tremendously," William responded, "if the US could provide some… incentive, or motive, to begin moving the process forward, a good faith gesture, as it were."

Kirsten caught on instantly.   "And you think The Diamond Room is the answer."

William was actually forthright in his response.   "Yes, I do.   The Diamond Room has captured the imagination of the world.   If the royal family could restore this, it would give them the widespread popular support they would need to begin the process of building an energy independent nation, and they would also be more inclined to accept the risk of having an American intelligence gathering station on their soil."

"So, give it to them!" Kirsten said. "We don't want it." She thought the problem would end right there.

When you discuss a political problem with uncle William, bring at least three cigars and an entire bottle of whisky, because that is how long it will take.

"Ah, yes, an admirable solution," he said, "and one which we are currently considering."

"And the problem with that would be....." Kirsten prompted.

"As it turns out," William explained, "this solution might create another problem."

He sighed. "The Diamond Room was, of course, a gift from the Grand Duke of Valthringia to his bride. She, in turn, was a princess of the Duchy of Staatfort. You may recall this name from the current news reports."

Yes, we did indeed. Staatfort was a tiny principality in Europe, which was making international news for its unconditional support for the American position during the current war. They had gone so far as to allow a temporary Air Force base on their territory, which allowed the US to refuel their aircraft and transfer logistical supplies more easily to their fighting forces. Apparently the Prince of Staatfort had been commissioned into the American Army during the Second World War, and had personally led the forces which liberated it from the Germans, using a motley collection of British, French and American irregulars to kick out the remaining German troops in his country. Unlike Valthringia, Staatfort had asked the Americans to stay after the war, which ensured they were never occupied the by the Soviets.

The currently monarch had a very long memory, and whatever the Americans needed, they were going to get from him.

"The Duchy of Staatfort has long held that The Diamond Room was a wedding gift to the Princess, and thereby, is the property of Staatfort."

Yes, and you give me enough lawyers, and I'll find a way to make a claim that says the state of Oregon owns The Diamond Room.

As always, I was glad I didn't have William's job.

"So," I expanded on this thought, "if you give The Diamond Room to Valthringia, you have an edge on the Russians, but that will irritate Staatfort, and you'll probably get your Air Force base kicked out of their country."

William looked resigned. There had to be a solution, but he hadn't figured it out yet.

Neither had I. "So what are you proposing, William? Your text message said something about investiture."

He took a deep breath. "The Valthringian government has been officially notified of the possibility that elements of The Diamond Room may be recoverable."

"You mean," I said, "that you have not told them that you have it in your possession."

William waved this little subterfuge off. "It is on the other side of the world, James, there has not been time to update them on events."

Sure, right, in a world of instant Internet messaging, no one has been able to find the time to email the friendly local Valthringian embassy, which was in Washington.

He went on. "Accordingly, their embassy has requested a meeting to discuss the possible recovery of the artifact, and its transfer to their government, where they propose to replace it in its original home, the chapel the home of their Royal family."

"In addition," he added, "their ambassador had conveyed to us the message that the person responsible for the discovery of the artifact is to be invited to Valthringia to meet the royal family."

"Why would they do that?" Kirsten asked.

I turned to her. "It means that they want to say thank you officially."

William confirmed this. "This would be, in fact, the single most important event in their history since the fall of the Soviet Union. It would provide a strong link to their past, and a visible sign of continuity of government. They are, of course, looking for a way to provide recognition for the person who could do this for their country."

I laughed at this. The Valthringian royal family had been caught in England during the Second World War, and when the Soviets occupied their country, had moved to the south of France, where they maintained a government in exile in comfort while their countrymen were oppressed for half a century. No wonder they were looking for a way to prove their usefulness to their citizens.

Kirsten pressed him. "So what are you going to do?"

William drummed his fingers on the tabletop. "I have several options, my dear; it depends on how willing you are to help me."

She looked curious. "How would I be able to help you? I don't have anything to do with this."

I knew if William had anything to do with this, it would be a fairly complex plan, but since they usually worked, there was no harm in hearing him out.

He looked at me. I, frankly, could care less what became of The Diamond Room, the Duchy of Staatfort or the entire nation of Valthringia, which makes me a cultural barbarian, I suppose, but if these two countries were willing to help in the current war effort, then I could at least listen to what William had to say. After all, a number of my friends were in that war.

Accordingly, I nodded for him to begin, and thus began my first foray into the complex world of European politics.

"Our ultimate goal," William said, "is the furtherance of democratic government throughout the world, wherever there are a free people capable of choosing and supporting such a government."

"As you know," he went on, "we are now engaged in a terrible war in the Middle East, and for the first time, there is hope that in the years ahead, that there is the chance for a real peace in that part of the world."

"To whatever extent that we can," he lectured, as if the two of us were undergraduates, "the intelligence community is working to support that goal. Now we have come to a time and place where we can make a major contribution to the war effort."

"You mean the Air Force base?" asked Kirsten.

"I need them both," William replied, speaking as if he personally represented the United States. This was not too far off the mark, since he was the single largest personal contributor to the campaign of the current President, who at one time had been a student of his.

"I need the Air Force base in Staatfort, and I also need the listening post in Valthringia. If there is any way at all that this can be done, it must be considered. And I believe that the two of you may be able to help us."

"Therefore, I would like you both to attend two meetings. Both will be held in Washington, DC. The first is at the embassy of Valthringia, the other at the embassy of the Duchy of Staatfort,"

"At these meetings, you will meet with the ambassadors of these countries, and gather information from them. Afterwards, you will meet with me, review your conversations, and I will use the information you provide in advising on policy which may be of advantage to the Allied Coalition."

A very long silence while we thought about this.

"Why can't you go?" I asked him.

He smiled at my naiveté. "I am far too well known to be utilized in such a task," he clarified gently, "whereas you are both unknown to the intelligence community."

"Why would they be willing to meet with us?" Kirsten asked. "We don't have any government status."

"Because I will have advised them," William replied, "that the two of you are archeologists responsible for uncovering the evidence which may lead to the recovery of The Diamond Room."

We looked doubtful. "I hasten to add," he hastened to add, "that neither country will be aware of your conversation with the other."

A blonde archeologist was going to raise of a lot of eyebrows, but if anyone could pull it off, it would be Kirsten.

I supposed I could do it. We had both dug up dinosaur bones at a fossil dig one summer in Montana, which believe it or not, is one of the largest repositories of dinosaur bones in the world.

As long as impersonating an archeologist was not a crime, it sounded possible.

William saw us vacillating. "You will both receive appropriate briefings and coaching by an experienced intelligence officer. Afterward you will be debriefed as well. The entire affair should take less than a day."

This meant, of course, that William had already set all of this up, and the plan was ready to roll.

Kirsten looked at me. I shrugged.

So that's how we officially became involved.

As we sat there at the table, I became aware of the unmistakable thwop-thwop-thwop of a helicopter approaching the mansion from the bay.

Since it was winter, in New England, and the Mansion was abandoned during the winter, there could only be one reason that a helicopter was approaching our position.

Sure enough, William looked out the bay window and saw it when we did, and he said "I have taken the liberty of arranging transportation for us all, if you are interested, and we can be in the air shortly."

The chopper sat down on the lawn in front of the mansion. It was one of the new dual jet engine types from Sikorsky aircraft. Limited production. It confirmed, as I had long suspected, that uncle William had a very long reach.

Kirsten stood and walked to the bay window, watching the chopper land. She turned and took a long look at my uncle, who steadfastly returned her gaze.

"Just one day?" she asked.

"Just one day," he confirmed.

She turned to look out the window again. She was clearly thinking about something, I could not tell what. She was quiet for a moment.

"And if I say no?" she said to William.

He looked surprised, not used to anyone turning him down, but like any first rate intel officer he had a backup plan. "I can, of course, arrange alternates in your place, but this affair is far too important to trust to someone I do not know and trust implicitly."

Now we were getting to the truth of it. That's the nice thing about family. If an employee screws up, you can only fire them. But when a family member screws up, you can be a little more draconic in your methods. So William was going to trust a very important meeting to his nephew.

It was nice to know he trusted me to that degree, and I was sure I could do an excellent job for him, but it was kind of worrisome that he didn't have a pool of good candidates to pick from that he could trust totally. Well, the spy business is like that, which is why I served in the Army, not the Agency.

She put her hands in her pockets and faced William, her decision made. When I think of her now, I remember that moment…in faded blue jeans, a pullover top, perfect posture with her face framed by all that blonde hair, wearing an expression of careful thought. It is one of my favorite memories of her.

"All right," she said. "I assume you have something to do with this helicopter."

William smiled, realizing he had won her over. "Of course, my dear," he said, "for you, private transportation only."

We opened the sliding doors that faced onto the bay, and the three of us began walking toward the chopper. Three men in Helly Hansen weather gear emerged and began walking toward the dock where the *Columbia* was moored.

"I took the liberty of arranging for the return of your vessel," William said quietly to me.

I nodded, watching them expertly get the magnificent yacht underway. Sailing against the wind back to the dock would not be easy for them.

One of the chopper crew slid back the door to their craft for us, and I helped Kirsten into her seat. A credit to his professionalism, the chopper crewman kept his entire attention on procedure, never once stopping to stare at her, which is better than I could ever do.

I buckled in next to her, and William stretched out across from us. I noted the seat had a small modified back support he was using. That meant that he used this thing fairly often, since that had to be for his injured back.

They closed the door, and the chopper rose above the grounds of the Mansion. It was the first time I had seen it from the air. It was an excellent way to get a better sense of the size of the place.

Personally, I enjoyed visiting the place, but like so many other places in America, it was somewhere my family had been, not where they were now.

"We shall be in Washington in a few hours," William said. "At that time, you will meet with a man who will prepare you for your meetings at the embassies later today. Perhaps, in the interim, you would care to look at these summaries of the current political situation."

He handed us both a black binder and we settled down to read, Kirsten actually reading the summaries, while I scanned it. It would come in handy later, for what we were about to go through.

CHAPTER THIRTEEN

We arrived in the Washington area that evening, the chopper depositing us at a country home overlooking the city. My knowledge of geography there is hazy, but I am guessing that we were in Virginia.

The farm where we landed had an actual barn, which looked to be functional, with horses in a corral who noted our arrival with little interest. This likely meant that these machines were here pretty regularly.

There was a ranch house, and other than that, not much of anything. There were no neighboring homes as far as I could see.

The chopper wheeled away just as soon as we were out of it, and then there we were, the three of us, standing alone in the middle of a field in Virginia.

"Shall we go?" William held out a hand, gesturing at the house.

Kirsten began a brisk walk toward the house, a painful reminder that she had kept her body in much better shape than I ever had. I was breathing hard by the time I reached the door, but ski bunny Kirsten was already inside.

I walked in after her. The place had huge vaulted ceilings, and an enormous fireplace at the end. It was one of those six foot affairs from the last century, where you could actually cook meals in the fireplace.

Several couches and chairs faced the fireplace, and a bar overlooked the whole affair.

I went straight for the bar. In deference to the fact that we were going to be working, I ignored the alcohol and poured soft drinks for everyone.

"Thank you," my blue eyed friend said to me, and I sat next to her, cheerfully taking every chance to enjoy the feeling of her body next to mine.

William pretended not to notice, properly brought up fellow that he was, and picked up a telephone by the couch as he sat down.

"Hello....yes, we're all here....is there dinner today?"

There was dinner today. In a moment the door at the end of the room opened and a woman came out pushing a restaurant cart. She handed each of us a tray, which held a hot sandwich as well as some chocolate cookies, and then left.

Mine was roast beef, and Kirsten's was an organic burger. William was always the most thoughtful host. If you came to my house, you ate whatever was in the fridge, which wasn't much most days.

For his part, William had a cup of chowder, an old favorite of his.

Silence fell over the room as we all ate for a few moments.

Kirsten delicately wiped her lips. "This is great, William."

He nodded, pleased that she enjoyed her meal. "They have a chef here, he defected from France."

Well, that had to be a story. Last time I checked, France was a democratic republic. I had never heard of anyone defecting from France, but then again, they were socialist, so anything was possible.

It went right past Kirsten, and I decided to ask about that another day, because at that moment, we were joined by a middle aged woman wearing jeans and a sweater.

"Hello, I'm Molly," she said, "and welcome to the Farm. Miss Vorra," she said, addressing Kirsten, "I'll show you the guest bedroom, where you'll be spending the night. If you'll come with me?"

Kirsten leaned over, gave me a quick kiss, and then stood up and followed Molly out of the room. That left William and I alone in front of the fireplace. I had not noticed, but he had come up with two cigars and two glasses of brandy.

When I was younger, I was always hesitant to drink his brandy, because the stuff was so expensive. Nowadays if he offered it, I drank it and was glad when he did.

I lit up my cigar, which, of course, was Cuban, and we sat there for a moment, enjoying one of life's guilty pleasures.

"So, I guess Kirsten and I have separate bedrooms tonight?" I asked him with a smile.

He looked surprised. "Of course, the lady has her own room. But if she should desire your company, you are welcome to join her. We are aware of modern trends in these matters, James."

In his generation, he meant, these things were kept secret, but he was aware that my generation could care less who you were sleeping with and when.

William lit up his cigar. We stared out the bay window.

"Where are we, exactly?" I asked him.

He smiled. "Does it matter?"

I thought about this. "No, not really."

There was a long silence. I wondered how he was getting away with smoking in what had to be a government guest house, then I decided I didn't care.

Then he surprised me. "Thank you, nephew."

For the life of me I could not imagine why he would thank me. "What for?" I asked.

"For your assistance in facilitating my little project," he replied.

I suppose he did have a point. If he solved this problem for the government, he would be untying a Gordian knot, and would be a hero from

Langley to the Pentagon, and everywhere in between. The twin acquisition of a listening post, plus an Air Force base, plus the sale of US reactor technology, would be quite an accomplishment.

"Am I really that much help?' I asked bluntly, as I thought almost anyone could do what we were about to undertake.

He gave a long, thoughtful nod. "Yes, my boy, you certainly are."

OK, if he said so.

Molly returned, presumably from tucking my little blonde friend in for the night. "James, if you'd like to see your room, I can show it to you, or if you like, I can come back after you finish your cigar."

I stood up. "Now is good," I said. "It's bedtime for me."

I turned to William. "Good night, then."

He waved a cigar at me. "See you in the morning!"

Molly walked down the hallway of the ranch house, turning in to what turned out to be a spacious bedroom furnished in the Western motif.

"Here you are," she said. "There's a bath and shower off to the side, and a telephone by the bedside if you should need anything. Is there anything else I can get for you? A nightcap, perhaps?"

I looked around at the room. It seemed comfy enough. "No, I should be OK. Can I get a wake up call?"

She nodded. "You have a meeting at nine, so I'll call you at seven. Breakfast will be in the kitchen any time you care to come down after that time. Do you have any special dietary needs?"

"Steak, bacon and eggs, milk and orange juice," I said.

"I think we can help you there," she said. "Your lady friend is in the room next door, and there is a door adjoining the suites if you should like to open it."

Wow, I guess the intelligence community really was catching up a bit.

Molly left, closing the door behind her. I sat down on the bed.

There was a change of clothes there. A shirt, slacks, and blazer in my size, with socks and loafers. William had undoubtedly provided them with my sizes.

A shower for me, I decided, and in less than a minute was in the shower, letting the hot water cascade over me.

I suppose it was wasting water, but for a full ten minutes I just sat there soaking. My energy levels gradually return with a decent shower, and I took the opportunity to shave as well.

That completed, I dried my hair and brushed my teeth, and now reasonably clean and with the travel grime washed away, now had to decide if it was time for bed, or time to sleep.

There was a time in my life, when deciding between a night with a hot blonde and a good night's sleep would not have even been a decision, but that was back when I was a teenager and had lots of stamina. For the first time that I could remember, I was actually thinking about whether or not to wake up Kirsten for sex or go and get eight hours of sleep.

They say that Duke Ellington died while engaged in sex, and I suppose eventually that will be my fate, because as tired as I was from all of the travel, I still decided to see if Kirsten was awake and wanted attention.

So I knocked on the door adjoining the suites and it was opened instantly.

"I was hoping you hadn't gone to sleep," she said, and wrapped her arms around me.

We didn't actually make it to the bed, so we settled on the floor, but I did drag down a blanket and some pillows for the sake of comfort.

If I had a word to describe our sexual relationship, it would have to be "incendiary", because of the spontaneous ignition that always accompanies our getting together.

Some friends I have who are married tell me that you can get tired of having sex with the same person, but I have a feeling that this would not be the situation with Kirsten. At least, it had never happened to me.

I vaguely realize that often humans form permanent bonds with each other and that their sexual relationship takes on a deeper meaning, but for me and Kirsten, it was just plain fun.

Of course, we are always tired afterwards, because sex with Kirsten takes a lot of energy, and tonight was no different.

Afterward, she curled up next to me and put her head on my chest.

"Kirsten!" I whispered.

"Hmmmmm....," was all she said.

"Let's get onto the bed if we're going to sleep!"

I used to be able to sleep on the floor, the ground, and in airports, but that was also in my distant past. Now I wanted a decent mattress and a pillow.

I picked her up, which was easy, because she weighed, like, a hundred and five pounds, and put her onto the bed, and tumbled in after her, pulling her body close to mine and covering us both with a blanket.

The light was on a remote, so I shut that off too.

Kirsten fell asleep at once. She could do that. She reminded me of a cat sometimes, the way she could fall asleep that fast.

I stayed awake longer, listening to her breathe, holding her and remembering when we were sixteen and had slept the same way. If anything, it was better now, if that was possible.

In a few minutes, I, too, drifted off, the first night I have ever spent as a guest of my country's government since I had left the Army years ago.

CHAPTER FOURTEEN

I do not normally sleep in late, but the next morning I was awakened by the telephone promptly at seven. I answered, but it was an automated wake up call.

"What time is it?" Kirsten wanted to know, stretching her lithe little body to its full length, which is very distracting.

"Ah….," I said, and then tearing my attention away from her, "it's about seven. Time for breakfast."

She nodded, and got up and went to her own bathroom, stopping to give me a wet kiss along the way.

I would cheerfully stopped for an encore of the previous evening, but we did have a meeting, so I went to my bathroom and got cleaned up as well.

In a few minutes we were reasonably presentable. Kirsten returned to my room in an extremely conservative dress, with a high collar and long sleeves, the hem below her knees. It was flattering, but quite modest.

"I assume this is your uncle's idea," she said.

"It's for the meeting," I said, realizing why our hosts had chosen these particular fashions for us. "The Europeans are a little more conservative in their dress codes, apparently."

"Not in my corner of Europe," Kirsten grumbled, and she was right, because in Scandanavia the girls usually go topless just about anywhere they want.

"You look fine," I reassured her, which was the truth, "let's get some breakfast."

So I took her back to the lobby, where a dining table had been set up outside, where it overlooked the valley. Our hosts had set up a steam line for a buffet style breakfast, so we loaded our plates and glasses and sat down and munched on an old fashioned country breakfast. I was eating so much food on this trip, I was going to be months losing all the weight I was going to put on.

William joined us a few minutes later, his breakfast consisting of an English muffin and tea.

"There you are," he said. "I was beginning to wonder if you were ever going to get up at all."

"Actually," Kirsten replied perkily, "we got up at five, but we had sex three times before coming down for breakfast."

William was actually speechless, and then he saw the smile in Kirsten's face, and we all broke out laughing.

"I suppose I deserved that," he said gallantly, sitting down next to us, but Kirsten patted him on the back and gave him a hug.

"No, you're right, we like to sleep in late," Kirsten replied. "We only got up today because we had to work."

"And I do appreciate this," William reassured her. "We have the potential to make quite a contribution today."

Kirsten vacuumed down a sausage, much to my continuing amazement and dismay, as the girl seemed to eat endlessly without putting on an ounce, whereas I could glance at a muffin, and put on weight.

As worn out as I was from this somewhat unusual trip, I was very curious about what the day held for us. "So what's the plan?" I asked William.

He sipped his tea. "Let me introduce you to someone," he said, and picked up the telephone by his side and spoke into it briefly.

After a moment, the door opened, and we were joined by what I assumed was our intelligence officer, a young man in his twenties wearing dark slacks, a blue shirt and tie, and a tweed jacket. He was carrying no materials or books or anything, so I guess whatever he was going to say, he already had in his head. I was right.

"Please don't get up," he said, stretching his hand forward to shake mine, "Jack Caldwell, nice to meet you." We shook hands, and he turned his attention to Kirsten.

I always get a kick out of the effect Kirsten's beauty has on other guys, which causes her to complain, since she says I should get jealous, but the fact is, she's a babe, so of course guys are going to stare at her. Caldwell did a not-so-covert scan of her bod, which I noticed he made sure William did not notice. I wondered what rank structure existed between the two men.

"And you must be Miss Vorra," he said, shaking her hand, and she nodded and let him take her hand in his.

"Kirsten will do," she replied, and they both got seated comfortably.

Caldwell nodded at uncle William, and then got right down to business.

"You'll be in two meetings today, one this morning and the other this afternoon. In each case you will be meeting with the ambassador of the country, first with Valthringia and Staatfort later in the day."

"Our goal today, in each case, is to officially make each country aware that there is a possibility that The Diamond Room could be found. To do this, you will tell the ambassadors that you have uncovered, during your research in the National Archives of the United States, a cargo manifest for a German U-Boat dated April of 1945, which lists the crates containing the original panels for the room."

"To make this easier, this will actually be a true statement."

Caldwell opened a leather notebook, and there was an aged and yellowed document, written in German, from the Abwehr—which was German military intelligence—regarding the capture of The Diamond Room, with additional documents from the Kreigsmarine, or German Navy, regarding their delivery for transportation about one of their U-Boats.

"How did you run across these?" I asked Caldwell.

"It was fairly simple, really. Since we had the actual crates, we discovered they had been stamped with the number of the U-Boat in which they were to be transported, in this case, the U-3531."

He flipped through the documents. "Once we knew the number of the U-Boat, it was an easy matter to go through our records to find the documentation. It took less than a day. If we had been forced to go through the entire list of over a thousand U-Boats, it would have taken forever. Your help in this matter was the key to the recovery."

I did not speak German, but had taken it in college, and had served in Germany during the Cold War, so I was able to stumble through the documents.

"What happened to U-3531?" I asked.

"After her Kapitan surrendered to your uncle," Caldwell replied, "he was ordered to take the boat to England, where, as part of Operation Deadlight, it was scuttled in the sea off the coast of Britain."

"Why didn't anyone ask the Kapitan about The Diamond Room?" Kirsten asked.

"We did not know about these crates at the time," Caldwell said. "We recovered these documents when we overran Germany, but we did not translate them for decades. By that time, the Kapitan was dead, and we were not able to ask him what became of it."

"But you never told anyone," I surmised.

Caldwell smiled. "We're an intelligence agency, Mr. Larson, we never tell anyone anything without a return on our investment."

"And now," William interjected, "is the perfect time to pass this information along."

Made sense to me, I guess.

"What are we supposed to tell the ambassador? There will be a lot of questions." Kirsten was thinking ahead to the meeting.

"You are to tell him that you are going to continue your search of recovered German documents in the US National Archives, and that should you find any further material related to The Diamond Room, that you will call and ask for another meeting."

"That's it?" I asked. "It seems pretty simple."

"The best plans are the simplest ones," William replied, overriding Caldwell. "I do have an ulterior motive."

I'll bet he did. We both looked at him.

"This news will put their countries in a frame of mind to be maximally cooperative with the American government," he said, "and we intend to exploit that opening to further our own interests."

"Which country will you chose to give The Diamond Room back to?" Kirsten asked.

"That will not be my decision," William said, and nothing more.

Aha. That meant, some politician somewhere was going to make a decision. That way, William was a good guy who recovered the priceless artifact, and did not have to make the agonizing decision on which of the two countries would be given one of the world's great treasures, and which would get nothing.

I was glad, again, that I was not an intelligence officer, because I would not want to be the one who had to make that call.

"Valthringia can offer us a listening station in close proximity to the Russian Federation, as well as being potential clients for the American nuclear industry," Caldwell added, "and Staatfort can offer us the ongoing use of Waldron Air Force Base into the future."

Waldron. In my distant memory, I recalled that as the name of the commander of Torpedo Squadron Eight, at the Battle of Midway.

"Is there any danger that Valthringia can enrich the uranium used in the reactors for military purposes?"

All eyes, including Caldwell's, swung to uncle William. He was as impassive as ever.

"There are safeguards for this sort of thing," he said, "I should not be overly worried about it."

Yeah, right. The Valthringian people hated the Russians for what had happened to their country during the Cold War. I'm sure they wouldn't seize the chance to get their hands on nuclear weapons. Yeah, right.

"What do we say if the ambassador asks us any more questions?" I wanted to know.

Caldwell shook his head. "They have been told that the meeting is restricted to a discussion of documents. If anything further is asked, refer them to me."

"You are coming with us?" Kirsten asked.

"I will be your driver, and will accompany you to the embassy, but will not actually attend the meeting. You will be debriefed afterward."

"How long will we be there?" she asked.

"Your commitment is for less than fifteen minutes," he said.

Wow, they were really keeping it short.

My surprise must have shown, for he continued, "You're really there just to bait the hook. We will follow up later through our embassy."

Our big chance at the world of high stakes diplomacy. I privately resolved to not screw up.

"Thank you, Jack," William said, and Caldwell rose to his feet and departed, clearly being dismissed by The Boss. And here all along I had thought that William was retired.

"There is one thing the he has not told you," William said politely. "You will not have to be debriefed."

"Why not?" Kirsten asked, but I already knew the answer.

"Because the clothes you are wearing are bugged," William said. "Everything you say and do will be transmitted to our van outside the embassy."

Kirsten's hands moved over her clothing, but could not find any sort of electronic device. I did not bother looking.

"Where are the bugs concealed?" I asked him.

He chuckled. "Actually, the entire garment is a transmission device. The wiring is built in to the threads that make up the jacket. Miss Vorra's are built into her shoes."

They were high heels, too. Looked like Prada to me.

"But these are Prada heels," she said, confirming my suspicions.

"It would seem suspicious if you wore anything less than high fashion in Washington," William said.

"Will they be jamming our transmissions?" I asked, intrigued, since my knowledge of modern electronics was minimal.

"That would not be possible, with this equipment," William replied.

We sat for a moment. William had finished his tea.

"When do we leave?" Kirsten asked.

"Whenever you finish your breakfast," he replied.

She looked at me. I was trying to limit my caloric intake, so I was already done.

"We're ready to go," she said, looking to me, and I nodded my assent.

"Very well," William said, "I'll have the car brought round." He lifted the telephone again, and made the call.

We stood up and went to the front door of the ranch house, where someone had neatly packed our clothing from yesterday into an airline bag. I opened the door and picked up the suitcase, and Kirsten and I walked outside, William following behind us.

The car appeared from behind the house. This was clearly not William's car, it was a government issue Ford sedan. Still, it had been stretched, so we were going to have the extra legroom.

It pulled up, and Jack Caldwell got out from behind the driver's seat, and opened the door for Kirsten.

"After you," I said, and she scampered into the car, dress notwithstanding. I followed in after her. William waited outside.

"What's our plan after the meeting?" I asked him, rolling down the window.

"See you at the Club for dinner," he said, and went back inside the house.

I wondered which Club he was referring to, but I assumed that Caldwell at least knew what was going on.

Jack put the car in gear, and we stretched out in back, now officially on our way, on our first official assignment, that of impersonating an archeologist. It had been in interesting week, and looked to be more so as we went along.

CHAPTER FIFTEEN

I had no idea of where we were or what freeways were on, but Jack did, so eventually we arrived in Washington, D.C., where he made for Embassy Row.

Washington being the most important city on earth does not change the fact that it was built in a swamp, so the geography can work against it. Now in the middle of winter, it was quite chilly, and a brisk cold wind was blowing.

Still, it is the only modern capital city that was actually planned and built as a capital city, so compared to London or Berlin, it's fairly spacious. At least it used to be, until the freeways are built, and now it's a nightmare getting in and out.

We got there in the mid morning, so traffic was only mildly crazy. Jack maneuvered through the city as only a resident could, and eventually we pulled up at a very nice brownstone with a wrought iron gate in front.

"This is it," Jack announced. "Embassy of Valthringia. Ready to go?"

We were indeed, and said so.

"Final checklist," he said. "Let's run through it. James?"

"OK," I replied, "here we go. The Ambassador is Alexander Zasha. He is an attorney by training, represents energy companies doing business in Valthringia, which is why he got picked to be the ambassador to the USA. This is the guy we are to meet with."

Kirsten picked up where I left off. "We go to the meeting, let him know we are working on the recovery of The Diamond Room, give him one of our business cards, and let him know if anything further develops, we will call him."

Jack nodded. "Right, get in and get out. What do you do if they offer you a free trip to their country?"

I knew this one. "We tell him we would rather concentrate on finding The Diamond Room, and perhaps afterward we can consider a visit."

"That's it." Jack was satisfied. "You're all set. Shall we go?"

I tucked the fake business cards into my pocket. William had set it up so if anyone actually called the number, it went to a voicemail.

Jack got out, and opened our door, and helped Kirsten to her feet. I joined them, and we walked to the gate, where there was a buzzer beneath a speaker.

I pressed it, and the gates swung open.

"See you shortly," Jack said, and returned to the car.

I looked at Kirsten. "After you," I said, gesturing toward the door.

We walked up the little paved pathway to the door. A garden of incredible beauty had been put into the front yard. I couldn't tell an orchid from a geranium, but even I realized that this garden was a labor of love. Odd to find in an embassy, I thought.

I went to knock on the door, but it swung open, and an older man in a suit and tie greeted us.

"Welcome to our home," he said, "please come in."

So we did. We were both wearing jackets, and he helped us out of them, hanging them on a coat rack behind the door.

"My name is Stephen," he introduced himself. "If you follow me, I will take you to the conference room, where you will meet the Ambassador."

Seemed like a plan to me, so we prepared to follow him.

"But first," he said. He then turned to a table by the door, and from a very long box he withdrew a dozen long stemmed roses, wrapped in Queen Anne's lace ferns and closed with a red ribbon. He presented these to Kirsten.

"With the compliments of our country," he said, placing them in his arms, "a gift from our Queen, Sofia."

She actually blushed. "Thank you very much," she said softly, "they are beautiful."

And indeed they were. They had to have been hand selected. I have bought a lot of roses in my time for a lot of girls, and these were the top of the line. If I was not mistaken, they were Emperor roses. Somebody had been doing a lot of prep work for our arrival. There was no faster way to a woman's heart than roses, except for those little turquoise Tiffany boxes.

Stephen smiled back at her. She looked quite elegant, with the roses in her hands.

"This way," he said, and we followed him into a large comfortable room lined with bookshelves, with extremely large leather seats and ottomans. He helped her to a seat, and I sat down near her.

"I shall inform the Ambassador of your arrival," he said, and smiled again, and then left the room.

In the back of my head, I realized that I had seen no security anywhere. This had to have been arranged for our arrival. I hadn't seen any cameras, either, but I was sure they were there.

I looked over at Kirsten. She was smelling her roses.

"They're so beautiful!" she said, and I felt guilty for not sending her any, but I had scarcely had time since we had met.

"And so are you," I said, and she smiled at me, which made me feel guilty all over again, since it made me want to have sex with her, and now was not an appropriate time.

Stephen re-entered the room, this time accompanied by a tall solidly built man in his forties. I always thought of ambassadors as fat guys with silver hair, but this guy looked like a businessman, which he was, of course.

Stephen said, "Mr. Larson, Miss Vorra, may I present Mr. Alexander Zasha, our Ambassador to your country."

I stood up and shook his hand. "A pleasure to meet you, Ambassador Zasha," I said as I did so.

"Please, this is America, call me Alex," he said in perfect English. "And you must be Miss Vorra."

He gave Kirsten a zillion megawatt smile, and kissed her hand in European fashion. "Welcome to our embassy."

A lot of American girls are not used to that, but Kirsten had backpacked all over Europe when she was a kid, so she was as smooth as silk about it.

"Thank you, Ambassador," she said easily, while still maintaining the correct formality.

"And you must call me Alex as well," he returned. "Please sit down and make yourselves comfortable." He waved at the chairs.

We all sat down, and Stephen wheeled over a service cart.

I got a jolt as I saw the silver tea service. It was actually silver. I remembered that I was in the embassy of a European country.

"What can I get for you to drink?" the Ambassador said to Kirsten.

"I am fine, but thank you for your thoughtfulness," she said, repeating what the protocol experts had told her to say.

"Forgive an old man," said the Ambassador, "and indulge me in tea and scones. The tea is native to our homeland; it is one of our most sought after exports. Also, we have real whipped cream for the scones."

Kirsten looked at me, and I answered for us. "Thank you, Ambassador, if it is not an inconvenience."

Stephen poured tea for everyone, and we all got a cup of hot tea and a scone with whipped cream. If you've never tried this, it's worth the trip to Europe.

The Ambassador, who I immediately noticed was not touching his scone, settled back in his chair. So, it was to be straight to business.

"Your government tells me we have only a short time today to discuss this affair, so I hope you will permit me to proceed directly to the purpose of our meeting."

He was talking to me, but staring at Kirsten, which is how all conversations go when she is around, so I let her follow up on this.

"By all means, Alex," she said, using his Christian name. "But tell me, how did you come to speak our language so easily?"

"My father was a pilot in the RAF," he said. "He flew in supplies to the resistance during the Soviet occupation. He met my mother while in my country, and flew her to England to escape arrest by the KGB. I was actually born in England, and after the Soviet Union collapsed, my mother asked to return to her home country. I brought her back, and never left."

"I see," she said.

"But enough about me," he continued, deftly turning the conversation to the topic at hand, "let us discuss The Diamond Room."

As he did this, Stephen brought a humidor over from the service cart and opened it.

It was full of Cuban cigars. Once again, somebody's intelligence service had done a first-rate background check.

In the interests of furthering diplomatic relations, I decided to be polite and took a cigar, lighting it up to Kirsten's astonishment.

"I didn't know you smoked cigars," she said. I grinned at her.

The Ambassador rescued me. "I have been told very little about your work," he began. "I received a message from your government yesterday afternoon. I transmitted this to my government, and this morning have been instructed that you, and your work, are now of the highest national priority."

We both looked at him in surprise. "You must understand," he went on, "the emotional connection of The Diamond Room in our country. It is at the core of our history."

"How can we help you, Ambassador?" I asked him.

"I would like any and all information you can give me on what you have discovered regarding The Diamond Room, where it has been, where it is now, and what your future plans are regarding research in this area."

He looked at Kirsten, apparently hoping since she was a woman she might talk a little more freely, but Kirsten used to buy and sell horses, and she was out of his league in the negotiation business, but she gently directed him back to me.

"James can give you a short summary, if you like," she said, smiling sweetly, and began to eat her scone.

I put down my tea. "I am writing a book on the Second World War," I began, lying through my teeth, "as it relates to blockade and convoy antisubmarine logistics operations against the German Navy."

His eyes glazed over. Good. I didn't know what blockade and convoy operation logistics were either. It was just my cover story.

"While doing my research," I continued with my tale of pure fantasy, "I came across the history of U-3531, one of the long-range German U-boats constructed at the end of the war."

He listened intently.

"I found orders for this particular U-Boat to proceed to the port of Narvik, where it would pick up a secret cargo and proceed to another destination, where it would rendezvous with a Luftwaffe bomber. At that point they were to turn their cargo over to the Luftwaffe."

"And what made you suspect The Diamond Room was involved?" he asked.

"It was the orders for the Luftwaffe. Why would a German Navy submarine be moving cargo for the German Air Force? It had to be the work of Riechmarshall Goring."

He looked puzzled. I elaborated on this for him.

"Hermann Goring was not only the head of the German Air Force, but in fact was in command of the entire German military. To add to that, it was common knowledge that he was stealing most of the art in Europe."

This was, in fact, the truth. At his vast estate in Karinhall, Goring has amassed a huge collection of priceless art, all of it looted from museums all over Europe. He had once even planned to move the Labyrinth from Crete to Berlin.

"So I searched for the cargo manifest for U-3531, and found a single document, which ordered the crew to 'make room for the diamonds.' This, I believe, is a translation error, which when properly worded, translates more accurately as "The Diamond Room."

I paused. The Ambassador had halted his tea halfway to his lips. "And then?" he asked.

I shrugged. "This is all we have at the moment. As you can see, this is not much to go on."

He took a deep breath. "My country is deeply grateful for your work in this area, Mr. Larson."

Kirsten spoke up. "We have not accomplished anything concrete, Ambassador, only a single reference in a single document."

He turned to her. "This is the first information on The Diamond Room since its disappearance in 1941," he said, "and may prove to lead to its discovery."

I put on a noncommittal face. "That may be, Ambassador, or it may lead to nowhere at all."

"Tell me, do you know, what became of this U-Boat, U-3531?" he asked.

Kirsten answered him. We were taking turns, keeping him off balance. "U-3531 arrived in Narvik and took possession of the cargo. This much we have learned."

"What then?" he asked.

I looked at Kirsten, she looked at me. "We don't know, Ambassador," I replied, "we have no information on what became of U-3531."

"What are your plans for further research on this topic?" he asked.

"Actually, I have no plans at all," I replied. "The history of missing art work is not my area of interest. I am going to continue my study of logistics of convoy antisubmarine operations. It was my intention simply to bring this matter to the attention of the Government, whom I assume will follow up on this information."

He looked distinctly unhappy. "Ah, Mr. Larson, Miss Vorra," he asked, making a huge mistake in giving away that fact that he knew Kirsten was a Miss and not a Mrs, which meant he had read an intel report on her background, "our problem is that your government has been searching for The Diamond Room for sixty years and has never found a single clue to its location."

"Perhaps this information on the U-3531 will speed things up," I volunteered, while knowing this was completely untrue.

He stopped for a moment to compose a response. He wanted to say that the US government could not find the Great Pyramids with a satellite scan of Egypt, but he didn't want to insult either us or our government, so he came up with a polite way to say the same thing.

"While this may be true," he allowed, "it is also true that your work is likely to be faster, more accurate and more productive, should you chose to pursue the matter to its conclusion, and find the final resting place of The Diamond Room."

I pretended to think about this. "I am flattered by your confidence," I said, "but I am not a professional archeologist."

Kirsten backed me up. "Surely your country must have a historian who would welcome such an assignment," she said.

He made a wry face. "We have many historians," he conceded, "but as a land locked country, we have no experts in blockade and convoy antisubmarine logistics operations during the Second World War."

Aha, so that was why my cover story was included research into this topic, which I freely admit I did not even know existed until it was given to me as a cover story.

I saw his problem. They needed someone to go through the National Archives of the United States and find out what happened to U-3531. Someone with my background could find it in weeks. A professional historian might take years, or possibly never even find it at all. I could certainly see why his government was taking such an interest in us.

"If it would help," he said hopefully, "my government would be happy to make an official request to your government for your assistance."

Now it was time to tell him what I had been told to say. "I do not work for my government, Ambassador, I am just a private citizen."

For once, the guy was prepared. Clearly, he had been expecting this answer. Someone in his home country had remembered that citizens of the United States are, in fact, citizens, not subjects like in some countries, and could not therefore be arbitrarily forced to do anything.

So, today, they were going to try persuasion.

"I quite understand," he said, "as I am just a simple businessman myself. I am sure you are quite busy in your work and professional lives."

Kirsten stood up to leave, as our time was up. This was, according to our friendly local intel officer Jack Caldwell, when things were going to get really interesting.

"We have taken too much of your time, Ambassador," Kirsten said, "we should be on our way."

Gallant as all Europeans are, he stood up as well when the lady did, and, remembering my manners, so did I.

"Of course, of course," he said. "But before you go, my government has instructed me to say thank you, in a way perhaps more appropriate with the occasion."

He produced a little velvet box and held it out to her.

There is nothing like a little velvet box to get a girl's attention. As cultured and sophisticated as she was, Kirsten was as vulnerable to this as a teenager getting her first set of earrings.

Little velvet boxes usually hold only one thing: jewelry.

And this one was no exception.

Kirsten gently accepted the box, and pulled the top open. It was square, about four inches on each side.

Inside was a silver necklace. Inset into each link in the silver chain, was a tiny, but perfect, diamond.

The jewels caught the light, and sparkled their white fire onto her face. Women and diamonds. It's amazing to watch.

I knew, of course, that the thing had to be priceless, and we could never accept it. I wondered if Kirsten realized this. I did not have long to find out.

"It's beautiful," she breathed, taking it out of the box and holding it up to the light, "I've never seen anything like it."

"It was custom made for the Princess," Ambassador Zasha said, moving behind her and fitting the clasp around her neck. "There are no others like it."

There was a large mirror over the fireplace, which had to have been put there specifically for this meeting, since I was sure our hosts were not going to just hand over an irreplaceable priceless piece of jewelry without something in return. I sighed, and waited for the other shoe to drop.

"What Princess?" asked Kirsten, moving to the mirror and seeing the diamonds around her neck. I was momentarily distracted, as the visual of the blonde and the diamonds was pretty striking.

The diamonds were blue-white, I realized. Once of my friends had been a gem appraiser at one point, and had guided me through purchases of jewelry for my kid sister's graduation from college.

Ambassador Zasha stepped back to allow Kirsten to turn right and left while looking herself in the mirror.

"Why, Princess Marie," he said, surprised, "the woman for whom The Diamond Room was built."

She turned to look at him, captivated. Clearly, this was all a setup, and this was exactly the reaction the Ambassador had been hoping to get.

Well, we had been told to draw them out, so this was as good an opportunity as it was going to get.

"Do you know the story?" he asked.

"Only part of it," Kirsten admitted.

"Would you like to know all of it?" He looked at me. "Do you have time?"

I glanced at my watch, pretended to be thinking hard, a practice I customarily avoid whenever possible.

"We can stay for a few minutes," I said, "but we must be brief."

"Just so," the Ambassador said, and helped Kirsten to her seat. "I believe your time will be well spent."

I sat down too, and for once was really interested. We were going to hear the real story behind the most incredible treasure ever given in the name of love. Since I have never been in love, I always find these escapades funny. Kirsten says I am not a romantic. Oh well.

"As you know," he began, "in our distant past, a marriage was arranged between our future king, Felix of Valthringia, and a young European woman named Marie."

Aha, this was getting interesting. The Ambassador had failed to mention the name of Marie's home country, Staatfort, or that she was of royal blood. So they were going to downplay her entire story.

"Although it was an arranged marriage, the young couple fell in love, and Felix commissioned the creation of a wedding gift for his bride, which you know as The Diamond Room."

"The room was actually the chapel in the royal castle, at Lake Runevald. Craftsman cut mirrors to line each of the four walls and the sacristy. Within each of these mirrored panels were thousands of the highest quality diamonds. The Diamond Room is so well crafted, that a single candle will illuminate the entire room, by use of reflected light from the diamonds."

I was curious. "Diamonds do not occur naturally in Valthringia," I noted. "Where did he get all of the diamonds?"

"It took most of the production of Antwerp for a year," he replied. "The Prince was one of the few countries to assist Antwerp during the Black Plague, and by way of thanks, the city brokered the acquisition of the diamonds for the Prince."

I had forgotten that. Antwerp had been hit hard by the plague; what assistance they received, they reciprocated after the recovery. So that was how it had all come to pass.

"And the necklace," the Ambassador continued, "was the crowning jewel, made from the same lot of diamonds which line the altar of the chapel of The Diamond Room."

Kirsten touched the necklace around her neck reverently.

"The rest of the story you know," he said. "They were married in Runevald, where they spent the rest of their lives. The Prince became King less than three years later, and he ruled for just under twenty years. When the Princess died at the age of thirty four from pneumonia, the King followed her in death in less than six months. They were buried in the Royal crypt overlooking Lake Runevald, where they first met, and they rest there today."

As a romantic story, it was the best I had ever heard. The thing about it, was, it had all really happened. The only documented case of true love I was familiar with.

Kirsten looked puzzled, touching the chain around her neck. "Wasn't the Princess buried with the necklace?"

The Ambassador smiled. "No, she was not. What you are wearing is an exact reproduction, created from the same silver, using diamonds taken from the original Diamond Room, which were originally intended for the base of the Cross at the altar, but never used."

"Who made it?" she asked, looking at it carefully."

"Why, Tiffany's, of course," said the Ambassador, surprised. "We would have preferred Faberge, but the Russians put his firm out of business."

A very long silence followed. Kirsten took the necklace off and examined it with great care.

"It is a gift to you, from our Queen, Sofia," he said, "to thank you for your kind work helping to locate The Diamond Room, and restoring it to our people."

Ha. Kirsten loved Tiffany jewelry with an obsession, but if he thought she could buy her loyalty with jewelry, he had made a major miscalculation.

"Of course, I cannot accept this," Kirsten said. "Please express my thanks to your government." She replaced it in its little box, and pushed it across the table to the Ambassador.

To my surprise, he didn't bat an eye. Someone had prepared this guy for everything.

"I will do as you ask," he demurred. He carefully put the jewelry box aside, from his jacket withdrew a thick envelope. It turned out to be a sheaf of papers, carefully folded in thirds.

"Of course you are aware of what happened next," he said, telling the rest of the story. "During the Second World War the Germans overran our country, and The Diamond Room was stolen and transported to Germany. No news of its existence has surfaced for sixty years until you came across these documents."

"Has your government asked the German government about where it might have been shipped?" I asked.

"In the late nineteen forties," he replied, "our ambassador to Germany was able to establish that The Diamond Room was to be shipped to the estate of Hermann Goring, the head of the German Air Force. Unfortunately, it was shipped by rail through the city of Dresden on the night of February 14, 1945."

"Oh," I said, and that was all there was to say.

Kirsten, however, didn't follow us. "What happened in Dresden?" she asked.

The Ambassador leaned forward. "The rail yards at Dresden were bombed that night," he said, "by the Allied Air Forces. It was assumed that The Diamond Room was destroyed in the bombing."

Actually, the Dresden bombing was the first time humanity had seen a firestorm. The city was quite old, and many buildings were wooden. That, coupled with the fact that many of the homes had underground tunnels connecting them for evacuation, enabled the fire that engulfed the city to grow out of control. The temperature had risen to 1500 degrees, and survivors had seen trees burst into flame at a distance, and concrete melt.

"But now we know, from your work, that crates which contained the paneling for The Diamond Room were to be shipped on U-3531, one of the Kreigsmarine's long range U-Boats. What became of it from there, no one knows."

The tension in the room was palpable. I was beginning to get an idea of just how much pressure the Ambassador was under to get us to help him.

"At any rate," he went on, "my government would like to thank you as well, Mr. Larson, for your role in restoring our country's heritage to us."

So saying, he handed me a single folder paper. I opened it and read it.

It was not long, just three paragraphs. It was an invitation, signed by the current monarch of Valthringia, Felix IX, inviting the two of us to visit his country as his guests, specifically to Castle Runevald, where The Diamond Room had originally been installed. It was written in English, so I read it quickly and handed it to Kirsten, who read it as well.

"What does this mean?" Kirsten asked the Ambassador.

"It means, my dear, that King Felix wishes to thank you in person for your help, and the two of you are to be his guests for a week in his country."

We looked at each other for a minute. Our intelligence officer, Jack Caldwell, had warned us that we would receive such an invitation, and had asked us to turn it down.

The Ambassador misinterpreted our hesitation. "Your transportation to our country, would, of course, be taken care of by our embassy, via First Class seats on any airline you prefer."

Kirsten took the lead here. "I am afraid, Ambassador, that my schedule would not permit me to take the time for such a trip, but please extend my thanks to your country for their kind and considerate offer."

I chimed in as well. "As for me, I have been away from work too long already, and should be getting back. Perhaps another time, Ambassador."

Ambassador Zasha gave a long sigh. Clearly he had been anticipating this as well.

Then he shrugged, a gesture of a man with few options. He lit up another cigar, and handed me one as well.

"They're Cuban," he said, "you might as well enjoy them."

He took a pull at the cigar, then leaned back in his chair and looked carefully at both of us, as if coming to a decision.

"Well, I have conveyed my government's wishes to you," he said, "so my job here is done. But before you go, may I convey a personal message, not as an Ambassador, but as Alex Zasha, a private citizen?"

I waved a cigar at him to proceed. "Please do."

"Miss Vorra," he said, ignoring me, "my country is poor, but rich in history and heritage. We are at a critical stage in our history, and if we manage our affairs correctly, we will once again be able to provide a bright future for our children."

She looked at me. I had no idea of where he was going with this, so I asked him.

"Where are you going with this, Alex?" I asked, finally using his Christian name.

"I realize your government has probably asked you to decline our request for your assistance."

For an Ambassador, he could sure come directly to a point. It must be his background in the oil business.

"Please allow us to thank you in some way, shape or form, Miss Vorra. It would be humiliating for our country to not even be able to give proper thanks to the woman who gave us back our history."

I thought he was overstating the case here a little, but he was a tough negotiator who would never give up.

Kirsten rose to her feet to leave. "I will give consideration to your request, Alex. Perhaps we can chat later."

He handed her his card. "This is my personal cellphone number," he said. "Please accept our invitation to visit Valthringia, and call at any hour."

He handed me one of this cards, too, because he clearly thought Kirsten was the power in our relationship. Somebody must have briefed him.

"Stephen will see you out," he indicated at Stephen retrieved our coats, "and I hope to hear from you again very shortly."

With that, he gave a courtly European bow to Kirsten, and then left the room.

We got our coats on, and Stephen escorted us to the door, and we walked out through the garden, to where Jack Caldwell sat across the street in the van.

He opened the side door, and we piled in. He started up the van and we drove away, although I had no idea where we were going.

"So, how did it go?" he asked.

"I thought you we able to listen in on our conversation," I said, remembering that our garments were carrying transmitting devices.

"That's true," Jack replied affably, "but there were no visuals. How did he seem to you? Was he worried? Anxious? Bored? Curious? Frightened?"

I tried to remember. "He seemed like a man negotiating a business deal," I said. "Nothing we said seemed to upset him. He seemed very prepared."

"They have a very good intelligence attaché here in Washington," Caldwell mused. "I suppose they've been working him double overtime lately."

"It was a really nice necklace," Kirsten said. "Tiffany's made it."

"That's correct," Jack confirmed. "It was a rush order. No expense spared. They wanted it ready for your meeting with them today."

"How do you know that?" I asked him, but Caldwell just gave me a look, and I realized, the guy was a spy, after all, and knew his business.

"Help us get this deal set up," Caldwell said, "and I'll get you anything you like at Tiffany's."

"It's not the same," Kirsten said, leaning back in her seat. "It's better when it's a surprise."

This was true. If you're going to give a girl jewelry, make it a surprise.

"Why couldn't they get Faberge?" she wanted to know.

Jack smiled. "They could have. As a matter of fact, I understand that the House of Faberge would have been happy to help them. But our best estimate is, that since you are an American woman, you would prefer Tiffany over Faberge."

As ill-informed as I was about jewelry, even I knew who Carl Faberge was. He had been the chief jeweler to the Romanov family, the Royal family of Russia. Each year at Easter, Faberge had presented a jeweled egg to the Czar and Czarina of Russia. These little treasures, when opened like any Easter egg, featured such items as a model of the Imperial State Coach, the royal yacht, and so on. Originally they were keepsakes of the family, but after the slaughter of Czar Nicolas and Alexandra by the Communists, they became some of the most sought after pieces of art in the world.

Still, he was right. Ask any American girl, and she'll go for Tiffany's, every time.

"What happens now?" I asked.

"I take the next step," Jack said. "I'll call him later today, ask for a meeting, and we will begin the negotiation process with his government. Ultimately, I think this will go well."

"But only one country can receive The Diamond Room," Kirsten said. "Who is that going to be?"

Jack only smiled enigmatically. Ignoring her question, he handed us the manila folders with the briefing for our next meeting.

CHAPTER SIXTEEN

"Your next meeting is in an hour, at the Staatfort Embassy," he said. "I have to brief you before you go. I have a conference room available for us."

He pulled up at the Mayflower Hotel and exited the van, and the valet got behind the wheel. The side door popped open, and I helped Kirsten out.

The Mayflower has been the scene of many an intrigue in Washington since its completion, so the choice of venue seemed somehow fitting.

The place was as jammed as ever, and we followed James as he threaded his way through the lobby to the elevators. In a short time we were inside a comfortably furnished boardroom, with half a dozen chairs and a computer set up with a video screen facing the table.

"All right," Jack said, as we all took our seats, "let me bring you up to speed on your next meeting."

He withdrew a CD from his jacket and this went into the computer, and it brought up an image of a map of Europe on the screen.

Jack had a laser pointer. "The Duchy of Staatfort. Established in 1532. It isn't really a country by standard definition, but it is sovereign, and it controls some very strategic real estate, so despite its small size, it is of enormous political importance."

He moved to the next slide. It was a picture of a beautiful girl. "The Princess Marie. A painting done by one of the Masters at the time of her Confirmation. She was twelve at the time."

He tapped the computer, the next image came up. The same girl, in a wedding dress. Looked pretty ornate. She had a long veil and an extremely long train. She was blonde, slender, and petite. I commented on this.

Jack looked over. "Yes, Marie was a small woman. Even by standards of the time, when Europeans were as a rule much shorter, and suffering from poor diets, Marie was a petite woman."

"She looks like a size one," Kirsten remarked, one woman checking out another.

"I'm not sure of that," Jack said, "but she was quite athletic. An excellent horsewoman and archer."

Another slide. A portrait of her with a man in uniform, who I assumed had to be her new husband. I was right.

"Her wedding day, two years later," Jack said. "She was fourteen years old."

"Is that the Prince?" Kirsten asked.

"Crown Prince Felix," Jack confirmed. "He was sixteen. His marriage had been arranged when they were both children, but I am told that they fell deeply in love in the years prior to their wedding."

I remembered back. At that age, I was in junior high school. Of course, neither of these two had ever had to attend a high school class. Reading and writing were pretty much sufficient.

"Where did he propose?" Kirsten asked. Typical girl question. I would not have thought to ask that in a zillion years.

Neither, apparently, had Jack Caldwell. He looked momentarily thrown off track, but recovered quickly.

"I do not have that information," he answered with the typical speech pattern of an intelligence officer, "but if you believe it important, I can get it for you."

Kirsten shook her head. "Just curious," she said.

Nevertheless, Jack noted her question on a pad of yellow legal paper. He moved on to the next slide.

"The Diamond Room," he said, and pressed the computer keys.

It needed no introduction. Even though it was a painting, not a photograph, the sheer beauty of the room took our breath away. Each of the walls of the chapel was covered in mirrors inset with thousands of diamonds.

The painting was just of the room. There were no people in it.

"Painted at the time of its completion," Jack elaborated. "Installed in the chapel at Runevald Castle. Felix and Marie were married in this room."

"What did she say when she saw it on her wedding day?" Kirsten asked.

Jack shook his head. "Legend has it that he showed it to her the day before they married. Like most who see The Diamond Room, she was absolutely stunned."

Yeah, most girls would be, if you handed them most of the diamond production of the city of Antwerp for a year.

"She must have been," Kirsten breathed.

He moved on to the next slide. "Death mask of Marie," he said as he punched it on to the screen. "Prepared after her early death."

Death masks were an unusual tradition, I thought, but Europe is hardly a normal sort of a place.

Her death mask showed her features had changed little. Most of the paintings I had seen of her showed her smiling, so this was the first one I had seen of her in repose, as if sleeping.

"Felix commissioned it when she died," Jack said. "He kept it together until after the state funeral, when by all accounts he went entirely mad. Died less than six months later. Cause unknown."

"A broken heart," Kirsten mused, and as unlikely as it sounds, I knew of many older couples where, when the first had passed on, the other followed soon after.

As for going mad, I was guessing Felix suffered from pathological grief, and had not recovered from the death of the woman he loved. I was very uncomfortable with this, for two reasons. The first was, that I had never loved anyone that much, so I could not comprehend it, and second, that my little blonde friend Kirsten I knew to be suffering from exactly the same problem, as she had never recovered from the death of her fighter pilot husband.

Even Jack noticed the intense concentration Kirsten was focusing on the painting. He hurriedly brought up the next slide.

"The royal family of Staatfort," he said, and the next slide showed four people, and older couple and what had to be their children.

"From left to right, they are King Harold, Queen Catherine, and their children, Princess Jennifer, and Prince Erik."

They looked like any American family, except that they were all pretty skinny.

"Needless to say," Jack went on, "the government of Staatfort would very much like to have The Diamond Room returned to their country."

"What do you want us to tell them?" Kirsten asked, which is exactly what I was thinking.

He turned away from the computer and faced us. "Much the same story," he said. "That you came across the cargo manifest of the U-3531, and that you realized its importance, and so you notified the US government."

"Why can't you just tell them that?" I wanted to know.

"We did," Jack admitted. "They asked for a formal meeting with you. Actually, they pretty much demanded it."

"And why did you agree to their demands?" I asked, curious.

"Because they are allowing us overflight privileges, at a time when our country is at war, and because of their location, it is something critical to our war effort," Jack replied.

"What do they hope to accomplish at this meeting?" Kirsten asked.

"Our experts tell us they will attempt to bring you around to their way of thinking," Jack replied, "which is that The Diamond Room is their rightful property."

"What possible use could we be to them?" Kirsten asked.

Jack looked uncomfortable. "As the discoverers of The Diamond Room, you have a certain legal position in this matter, and therefore could be of considerable legal value to their position."

"And how, exactly, do they plan to sway our thinking in their favor?" I asked, with Kirsten following closely.

"There are several options option to them," Jack said, steepling his fingers, "each of them interesting."

"Of course, they could simply tell you their version of the story, but in all likelihood they would realize that more persuasion would be needed."

Clearly the analysts had been working up this scenario for some time. Jack was in his element.

"To be more persuasive, they will likely use techniques that have worked for them in the past."

"And those are?" Kirsten prompted.

"They have already indicated that investiture is an option," Jack said, looking at me.

Investiture is the process of being knighted. In most countries nowadays, it involves having performed some service in the public sector which benefited the host nation on a large scale. It used to be reserved for the warrior class, but then the English began knighting merchants and businessmen. By the twentieth century there were quite a number of soldiers knighted after the Second World War, but when peace came the fastest path to a K, as it is known, became public service.

"Why do they think this will help?" Kirsten asked. "We're Americans. We don't have titles."

Jack nodded. "As a matter of fact, the Constitution forbids it for certain jobs," he responded. "But many Americans have been knighted."

I recalled that each outgoing American president is knighted.

"Do they think this will appeal to us?" I asked.

Jack looked thoughtful. "Actually, we think it's being offered because it is one of a very few options open to them. They have little else to offer you that might be of interest. If they offered you a villa in the country, for example, you would not likely leave California to live there."

Personally, I would not leave California unless it got radioactive, so he was right about that. I've gotten addicted to the surfer girls.

"This process would involve your being received by the royal family, who perform the ceremony, as well as an invitation to the castle."

Long ago, during the days when I was a soldier, I personally promised myself that I would never again cross the Atlantic, unless in a spacecraft which could make the crossing in a few minutes. Being cramped up in a long aluminum tube for five hours was not my idea of a good time.

Too bad they had retired the SST.

Jack caught my grimace at the thought of traveling to Europe. "They would likely be aware of your aversion to air travel," he noted. "Toward this end, you would likely be offered passage on the Queen Mary 2."

Now that, was something I would have to think about. The QM2 was the latest offering from Cunard, and it was the most palatial and luxurious hotel in the world, either on land or at sea. The Cunard line knew how to ease the pain of traveling.

OK, that had got my attention, I started to think about it.

"There is one other option open to them," Jack continued, "which usually works on Americans."

We both looked at him, but I already knew what it was.

"They may try to bribe you," he said. "Of course, it would be very subtle, and tastefully done, and it may be masked as a finder's fee or reward, but they are well able to offer a cash bounty for your cooperation, which of course, their opponents in this matter, Valthringia, cannot do."

Kirsten looked at me, I looked at her. "What kind of numbers are we talking?" she asked.

"It will most likely be in the millions," Jack said. "But they will approach you with great care on this issue."

"Why? " I asked.

"Because many Americans have a very moral sense," he said, "which is often mistaken for naiveté around the world. So they would be aware that you may be offended by such an offer, and therefore, may offer to donate the reward to your favorite charity."

We all thought about these issues for a moment.

"Jack, why is The Diamond Room so important to these countries? Isn't it just an art work? I mean, a really nice art work, but still…"

For the first time, Jack smiled and relaxed. "The reality comes down to heritage," he explained. "The Diamond Room is ranked as one of the top ten art treasures of the world, along with the Mona Lisa, or the statue of David."

OK, sure, I thought, but hardly worth the hornet's nest its potential recovery was stirring up, I thought, but then Jack brought it all into perspective.

"Once recovered and in a museum, The Diamond Room would become one of the must-see items in the art world, worth millions upon millions of tourist dollars to the host country, in perpetuity."

Now it was sinking in. I was beginning to realize everyone's interest in our little discovery.

"There are tourists and then there are tourists," Jack continued, "and it is a simple fact that cultural tourists spend proportionately more per capita than regular tourists. Our analysts project that this will be the situation with The Diamond Room."

"So that's why they want it so badly," Kirsten said.

"Yes, that's pretty much it," Jack confirmed. He turned back to his presentation. "Let's talk about the meeting."

Another slide on the screen. "The embassy of Staatfort." It was a very nice Georgian building. "I will bring you there, but as before, will not actually attend the meeting."

Next slide. "This is Pamela Melanson, social secretary to Queen Catherine of Staatfort. She is Canadian, educated at Dartmouth. She, not the Ambassador, will be your contact at the embassy."

"Why not the Ambassador?" I asked, sensing it was important.

"The royal family is approaching this on a person to person level, rather than government to government affair," Jack replied. "Their view is that The Diamond Room was, after all, a wedding present, and belongs to them personally."

Must be nice, to have that kind of wedding present.

"The meeting, as before, should take you no more than fifteen minutes. Get in, explain how you found the information on the German U-boat, and then leave. Tell her that our government will contact her if more information comes up regarding The Diamond Room. If you are offered any reward, incentive or recognition, our advice is to turn it down."

We both nodded. Neither of us was anxious to get in the middle of a prolonged and nasty argument between the lawyers for three countries, no matter how much money we were offered.

I did stop to think about the money for a minute. I am a working man, and the possibility of becoming a millionaire in the next hour as a reward for finding Uncle Sven's buried crates in Montana suddenly seemed tantalizing.

Then I thought about all the GIs who died in the Second World War liberating Europe from tyranny, and had second thoughts. Better just to hand it over to the original owner, whoever the courts determined that to be.

Jack stood up, and we followed him. He closed his computer, and we headed back to the elevator bank. He called on the house telephone and ordered the car brought around.

"All set?" he asked us as he got into the elevator.

"No problem," Kirsten answered for both of us, and she was right.

If all went well, in less than an hour, this problem would be out of our hands. It would be interesting to see how the US government brokered the recovery, but we would be content to watch the whole matter unfold on cable TV news.

The car was waiting for us, and after we got through the crowd at the lobby, Jack once again took the wheel, and raced off at what seemed to me to be far too fast a speed through the city.

I have no idea whatsoever of Washington geography, so if you asked me where we would up going, I would not be able to tell you. Kirsten, for her part, concentrated on her makeup mirror, getting her hair and lipstick done perfectly for the meeting.

Personally, I have no idea why the woman wears makeup. She's perfectly built, has a flawless complexion, and the face of a model, so she had no need to look any more beautiful than she already is, but I guess some women don't feel dressed unless they have lipstick on. Today she was wearing pink lip gloss, which drives me crazy, so I was going to have to concentrate on the job.

Eventually we pulled up at the Georgian mansion which served as the Staatfort embassy. They were clearly waiting, and the gates swung open.

Unlike our previous meeting, Jack was able to pull into the embassy grounds and head up the driveway, and parked in front of the door. He got out and opened Kirsten's door for her.

"Right, so I'll see you again shortly," he said as I got out of the car, and he got back into the driver's seat and pulled away.

We looked at each other, and then I took her arm in mine in a formal grasp, and we headed up the steps. There was a brass knocker there, so I went ahead and knocked on the door.

It opened immediately, and we were greeted by a trim young blonde woman in a business suit. Her hair was cropped short, pixie style, and she was all business.

"Hello, you must be James and Kirsten," she said, shaking our hands in turn, "I'm Pamela. Won't you come in?"

After the stiff formality of the Valthringian embassy, her breezy and casual manners were a breath of fresh air.

She led us into a reception area furnished with couches and wingback chairs.

"Sit down, relax, put your feet up," she said, waving at the chairs, so I took her up on her offer, sat down and relaxed.

Kirsten was a little nervous, sinking slowly into the couch and looking around.

Pamela picked up a telephone. "Hello? Could we have some coffee and snacks? Thank you."

Almost as soon as she hung up, a waiter wheeled in a beverage cart equipped with coffee, tea, water and soda. It also had a basked of fresh fruit, and a stack of cinnamon buns.

I don't drink or gamble, but cinnamon buns are a known weakness with me, so I made certain I got my hands on one of them.

"Tea?" she asked Kirsten, and when she nodded, Pamela poured her a cup of tea, added lemon on the side, plus two chocolate cookies and handed it to Kirsten.

The waiter held out a coffee mug, which I accepted, and in short order I had a cup of fresh coffee and a cinnamon bun, which made me ready to face almost anything.

"So, welcome to our embassy. Glad you could both come, and thank you both for coming on short notice. Your news is of major interest to Staatfort, and things have been pretty busy here since they received your message."

Kirsten asked, "Are you from Staatfort?"

"No," Pamela responded, "I'm actually from Montreal. I'm studying international diplomacy at Georgetown, and took this job while I get my master's degree. It's a pretty cool job."

As cynical as I am, I knew this meeting had been meticulously planned by the Staatfort diplomatic team. They must have thought that our initial contact with a young person of our age and interests would put us at ease. They were right. Pamela seemed pretty non-threatening.

She sensed Kirsten would ask her more questions about herself, so she took command of the interview immediately. I noticed she was not having anything to eat or drink.

"I know we have very little time today, so if it's all right with you, I'd like to get started right away."

We both nodded our assent.

She moved ahead. "So that you don't have to repeat yourself, I'd like to introduce you to my boss." So saying, she pressed a button on her cellphone.

The doors at the end of the reception room swung open, and a tall slender woman in her forties emerged, wearing a conservative long sleeved dress. I recognized her immediately.

"James, Kirsten, I'd like you to meet Lady Catherine. Lady Catherine, this is James, and this is Kirsten." She came forward and shook our hands.

This was an extremely informal way to introduce a member of a royal family. Lady Catherine was, in fact, Queen Catherine of Staatfort. I had a fast thought, wondering why the laid-back and informal introduction, but then I realized their protocol people must have told them this was the best way to put Americans at ease.

"A pleasure to meet you, Kirsten," she said, shaking her hand, "and you as well, James. I hope Pamela has made you welcome."

"She has indeed, Lady Catherine," I replied, frantically trying to remember any protocol lessons I had ever read about conversing with royalty. What was I supposed to call her?

She solved the problem for me. "While in America, we do as the Americans do," Lady Catherine said. "Please call me Cathy, everyone does."

"Of course," I replied, as if I did this everyday. I had been expecting informality, but this was informal even in California.

She sat down, and I suddenly remembered from some long forgotten class on protocol that one follows the hostess' lead, so I sat down myself, and Kirsten did the same.

"So, James, please tell us what you know of The Diamond Room," she said, looking at me expectantly.

Well, she sure wasn't wasting any time. Of course, this was supposed to be a fifteen minute meeting, so it was understandable.

"As it turns out," I began to recite my well-planned cover story, "I ran across a reference to The Diamond Room while researching blockade and convoy antisubmarine logistics operations against the German Navy."

"You are a submariner?" she asked.

"Actually, I am an occasional consultant for ocean borne logistics," I said, this statement being as far from the truth as it was possible to get. "The Second World War remains the most complex logistical enterprise in history."

"Please go on," she said, and I was glad she did, because I had just stated all that I knew about logistics, and could not discuss it much further.

"While reviewing the transport of materiel for the German Navy, I found a reference to diamonds regarding one of their long range U-boats, the U-3531. I believe that this may indicate that the crates containing The Diamond Room were placed aboard this U-boat."

"And what became of this U-boat?" she asked. I noticed her assistant, Pamela, was taking notes.

"I have no information on the ultimate fate of the U-3531," I said. "Perhaps the German government might have more information."

She sat for a moment and thought about this. "Would you be willing to research the matter further, James?"

She looked so concerned, I felt sorry for her, but my instructions were clear. "I regret that my work would not permit the needed time to complete the research, but any competent historian should be able to finish the job."

She responded immediately. "No historian has found even a trace reference to The Diamond Room's location in sixty years," she said. "You are the single best hope for its recovery."

An awkward silence followed. She waited until I felt extremely guilty, and then she switched gears. You had to hand it to her staff, for what she came up with next, I was entirely unprepared for.

"James, Kirsten," she began, "since we received word from your government on this issue, we have searched for some way to indicate our gratitude for your work. I believe we have found a solution, which will allow us to thank you properly. I would like you to meet someone."

She gestured at Pamela, who was already in motion, and had gone to the door of the reception room and swung it open. As she did so, an athletically built man in his twenties strode into the reception area. I recognized him at once, as well: it was Erik, their Crown Prince, which meant he was to be the next King of Staatfort.

"Hello, Mr. Larson and Miss Vorra," he began, striding up to us and shaking our hands, with particular attention to Kirsten, "my name is Erik. Welcome to our embassy. I hope you are comfortable."

"'Yes, thank you, your highness," Kirsten replied, as formal and correct as she always was, using the appropriate form address for royalty.

"Please, call me Erik," he said breezily, "everyone does."

I knew this was not true, it had to be for our benefit. European royalty does not run around encouraging people to call them by their first names. Well, it was their show today.

"I just wanted to say thank you for your help on what will probably be the biggest news in our country in decades," he said. "The Diamond Room is our single most important treasure, and any help you can give us is of inestimable value."

He had to be up to something. I wondered what it would be, and did not have to wait long to find out. I also noticed that he said The Diamond

Room was "our" treasure, asserting his country's rights over Valthringia.

"Our diplomatic corps insists on thanking you formally, but I wanted to come here and say thank you in person."

"We are glad to be of help," I said, wondering what to say next.

"So, I understand our meeting is a short one, so with your permission I will cut directly to the heart of the matter. You have helped us enormously, James, and I think I have found a way to reciprocate in kind."

"That would not be necessary," I replied.

"Really? Not even if I offered to extend our government's assistance in your country's ongoing work on the Aluminum Trail?"

My blood ran absolutely cold. I felt my heart stop briefly, and became physically aware that the blood was draining from my face.

Well, well, well. Somebody in the intelligence section of the Staatfort embassy had done a first rate preparation for our arrival.

The Aluminum Trail. There was not a pilot alive from the Second World War who did not recognize the name.   Even among the aviation community born after the war, an awareness persisted of this horror story of the air.

During the German occupation of Europe, the single largest problem had been how to dislodge the entrenched German Army.   When planning an attack against an entrenched force, you usually have to plan a three to one balance of forces.

This means that for every entrenched enemy soldier, you have to have three soldiers to attack and drive him out.

By the middle of the war, the Allies had successfully gotten their armies onto the field, and had even learned how to fight and defeat the Germans. There was just this one little problem.

Logistics. An army in the field is incredibly consumptive of supplies, everything from gasoline to bullets to medical supplies.

The German Army had commandeered the high ground all over Europe, and this meant the Allied Army had to go up there and drive them out. Needless to say, their supply line had to follow them.

Only one country in the world had a freeway system before the war, and that was Germany with her autobahns. The rest of the world was using worn out railroads. Staatfort was no exception.

Since trucks could not be used to completely supply the Allied Army, the only logical alternative was by air.

America was turning out tens of thousands of aircraft and pilots, and they began to use DC-3s to carry cargo to the army in the field.

On paper, it looked like a good idea: the DC-3s didn't even have to land, they could just parachute the supplies to the armies on the ground.

In reality, flying across some of the mountainous terrain in Europe, in some of the worst weather, led to the highest losses of aircraft in recorded history: more than enemy action by far.

These mountains cut directly across Staatfort, and as the war ground on, the aircraft losses mounted.

I actually personally knew some of the pilots who had flown these missions. They told me that the sudden and freakish changes in the mountain air would literally rip the wings off of the aircraft.

The wrecked and mutilated fuselages of the aircraft began to litter the landscape of the European mountains.

It gained the grim nickname "the Aluminum Trail" for the glint of the reflected sunlight on the crashed aircraft, flickering back up to the pilots far above, who were able to see the graves of their comrades as they flew, an ever-present reminder of their possible fate, in the fickle, unforgiving and ever-changing air.

Even today, no modern jet flies over the Aluminum Trail. Far easier paths exist to get around Europe. The Pacific theater of war had a similarly treacherous flightpath over the Himalayas.

For Erik to bring this up was a testament to his intelligence operatives, for this meant they had gotten a great deal of information about me in a very short time.

Those who have not served in uniform, will likely not understand how strong the bond is among soldiers who have served together. It's hard to put into words, but in short, there is a common credo that no soldier is ever left behind, even if he dies; as a matter of fact, especially if he dies. More than any country in the world, the United States of America believes in this motto, and they back up their beliefs with men, equipment and support.

The US government has an office that goes around the world, investigating reports on the recovery of the remains of their soldiers. Every month, there are missions in the field searching for the final remains of soldiers from every war since World War One.

And they have been amazingly successful, especially since the advent of DNA analysis.

When I had served in the US Army in Germany, one weekend the chaplain came around and addressed our morning formation.

They were looking for six volunteers to assist an MIA/KIA team which would be working in the area to recover the remains of a number of Allied airmen whose crashed B-17 had recently been located in a nearby forest, after having been missing for fifty years.

Since the Oktoberfest was that weekend, the chaplain had little hope that any of us would volunteer, especially since the work was grunt work, mainly carrying supplies and digging. He thought since our unit spent nine months of the year in the field, few if any of us would volunteer to spend another week in the field, even if it was to help our fellow soldiers.

They needed six people. Over four hundred people showed up.

That was, and is, the kind of spirit that motivates American soldiers. You can't get them to clean their barracks, or keep their hair trimmed, but if you need help for their fellow soldiers or families, consider it done.

I was one of the volunteers. I'd spend the weekend excavating the wrecked B-17. Four of the original nine crewmen were still inside. We removed the bodies, notified the families, and arranged identification, caskets, and transport to the US.

After that first weekend, I spent one weekend a month on this project. During the Reagan years, it went from being a volunteer arrangement to a regular MOS [military occupational specialty].

But I'd never lost my original interest in it, and now here was Erik from Staatfort, offering to help our government.

Erik was watching me carefully. "Much work remains to be done on The Aluminum Trail," he said. "Hundreds of aircraft were lost there over the course of the war. There are thousands of bodies still up there on the mountain."

I tried very hard to look casual, but I was dying to know what he was willing to do to help. For every American soldier missing, there is a family somewhere that waits for him.

"We have a Mountain Division in our Army," Erik continued, "which each year performs annual climbing and acclimatization training in the mountains. It would be an easy matter to arrange for the Mountain Division to bivouac in the area of the Aluminum Trail, and if your government could provide satellite imagery of the area, real progress could be made on body recovery and identification."

He wasn't kidding about that. Imagine having an army at your disposal for a month to recover bodies. That would pretty much finish the job, and provide closure for many families whose loved ones had made the ultimate sacrifice in the name of freedom.

I took a deep breath. Orders or no orders, there was simply no way I was going to turn this offer down.

"Your Highness," I replied, using his formal title deliberately, "this is an offer of incredible generosity. While I cannot speak for my government, I am certain that the US would be extremely interested in your offer of the use of the Mountain Division in its ongoing body recovery operations in the mountains of Staatfort."

Erik smiled, sensing victory. He had found something I was extremely interested in, and could be used as a lever.

Then, with great sadness because I knew it to be true, I added, "Of course, any operations of this type would be subordinate to the current wartime operations."

As bad as it sounded, it was reality. The US was currently in a terrible war in the Middle East, and every man was needed on the front. If it had to, the US would have to balance the needs of the current war against the opportunity to recover the bodies of the fallen, and I knew how that would play out. Not a single man or truck would be diverted to the recovery effort on the Aluminum Trail.

Erik had been clearly expecting this, but he seemed quite at ease, which he could be, since it put him in the catbird seat.

"Of course, of course," he said. "I am sure that one way or another, this can all be worked out. I shall have our Ambassador contact your State Department."

I stood up. I did not know what to say, so I shook his hand.

"Thank you," I said, and meant it.

He shook my hand, and then in that easy informal way of his, smiled and reached into his breast pocket and withdrew an envelope.

"Paperwork, paperwork," he said, opening it. "Can't let you go without the paperwork."

I had no idea what this was all about, so I just listened.

He read from the paper. "By proclamation of King Harold IX, and Lady Catherine of Staatfort, James Larson—that's you---and Kirsten Vorra---and that would be you, Kirsten---are hereby named as members of the Order of the Wolf, dated this day at

Runevald, Staatfort…and it goes on, but you get the idea."

Kirsten was not following this, exactly. "I'm not sure what this means," she said.

"It means," Lady Catherine said, "that you are now Dame Kirsten Vorra." Catherine opened a small mahogany box that had been sitting on the side table, and from it withdrew a small medallion, which hung from a circle of ribbon. She draped the decoration around Kirsten's neck.

While I was watching this, Pamela put a similar decoration around my neck. Erik watched my surprise with amusement.

"There is actually a more formal ceremony," he said, "so when you come to Staatfort, we'll get that set up for you." He handed us a copy of the proclamation.

Well, I was surprised as could be, since they had arranged for it to happen so fast we could not possibly object to it.

Pamela continued to move the meeting forward. "I see our time is up," she said. "Let me take you to your car."

Erik shook my hand again. "A pleasure," he said. "See you in Staatfort."

Catherine followed him, shaking my hand and Kirsten's in the manner of a professional politician. "Excellent work, both of you."

With that, the royals swept out of the room, and we were left alone with Pamela.

"This way," she said, and indicated the door.

Of course we followed her, and she kept the pressure on as we headed out the door.

"Many thanks again for all of your work," she said. "I certainly hope I will be working with you again in the future. Our Ambassador will be contacting your government today or tomorrow to begin the process."

"Glad to be of help," Kirsten replied, as she ushered us down the steps of the embassy.

"Likewise," I said, somewhat overtaken by the turn of events in the last fifteen minutes.

Kirsten proceeded to the car, where Jack Caldwell got out to open the door and let her in.

Pamela pulled at my arm and held me back. "James, here is my card and personal cellphone number.   Please call me if I can answer any questions or be of any help."

I took her card and slid it into my jacket. "Thank you, Pamela, I'm sure my government will take it from here."

She whispered into my ear, "This is not official, James. I'm single. Call me if you're in town and would like some company."

She smiled and turned, bouncing up the steps to the door of the embassy. For the first time, I realized what a beautiful young woman she was.

CHAPTER SEVENTEEN

Then I turned, and walked down to the car, opening the door and let myself in. Jack started the engine and we pulled away.

"So, how did it go?" he asked. "Any surprises?"

"How much were you able to hear?" Kirsten asked.

"Actually, I got it all," Jack said. "Your transmitters got every word. The only thing I didn't catch is what Pamela said to you there on the steps, James."

Kirsten looked at me. "Yes, what did she say?"

Nothing like being put on the spot. I decided to tell half of the truth. "She gave me her business card to call if I had questions," I replied.

Jack grinned, but Kirsten was not fooled. "She thinks you're hot," she said. She seemed unhappy someone was interested in me.

"It's the job, not me," I said. "She probably had orders to get me interested in her." I had been reading too many spy novels.

"No, she thinks you're hot," Kirsten repeated. "She wants to go out with you."

It was flattering to think so, but this was not likely. There were lots of better looking young men in Washington than I.

"She's more Jack's type," I said, deflecting the conversation.

Jack laughed at this. "I'm spoken for, don't get me into trouble," he said.

Kirsten continued her questions. "How did you think it went?" she asked.

"Of course, I didn't see the meeting, I only heard it," Jack answered, "and so much of diplomacy depends on the interpretation of body language and expression, but overall I'd say you accomplished what you were sent to do, and that is to start a dialogue between our government and theirs."

We all thought about this a minute. Jack threaded the car through traffic.

"Where now?" I asked.

"To meet your uncle William," he said. "He's at the club."

The "Club", as he turned out, was actually a private club in downtown Washington. There were no labels, or signs on the door, just double oak doors which were opened by a uniformed doorman.

Jack let us out and went to park the car, and we walked in. There was a desk in a wood paneled lobby, in front of another set of doors.

A hostess at the desk greeted us.

"Welcome to the Black Eagle Club. Are you expected?" she asked, which meant that she knew all of the regulars and therefore knew we did not have a reservation, and were therefore someone's guest.

"James Larson and Kirsten Vorra," I responded. "We are expected."

She ran her finger down a list and apparently, found our names.

"This way," she said, and got up to lead us into the club.

We went through the next set of doors, and she led us into a spacious book lined room, filled with overstuffed leather chairs. It looked like it had been built in the last century. A few elderly gentlemen sat reading the latest copies of the

Washington papers. In the corner was a well stocked bar, behind which a bartender slowly washed glasses. It was a very quiet, very peaceful place.

I saw William sitting in a corner. He saw us about the same time, and got up to meet us.

"Hello, young lady," he said, quite properly ignoring me and turning all of his considerable charm on the hot blonde, "how good to see you again."

Turning to the hostess, he said, "thank you, Julia, that will be all."

The hostess turned and left, and he led us to a private conference room in the corner of the library. We sank into the plush leather chairs.

"Can I get you something?" he asked, and buzzed a button for the bartender.

"Diet Coke for me, and peach water for the lady," I responded.

Kirsten looked at me with a new respect. Flavored water is a favorite of models everywhere, since it makes for a great tasting drink without any calories or carbonation. Plus, in old line society, a gentleman always orders for a lady, which of course means that he already knows what she prefers. I was taking a chance here, but Kirsten had told me she modeled clothing, so I thought it was a sure bet, and I was right. Two points for me.

"Thank you, James," she said softly, and I felt good inside.

William watched this little interplay with interest. He was an inveterate snoop.

"So, I hear it went well," he said. "What was your impression?"

Well, that was fast. Jack must have briefed him over the radio while we were still inside the embassy.

"Hard to say," I responded. "It seems they're willing to talk to the US government, much past that it's hard to say."

He nodded. "And you, Kirsten?"

She thought a moment. "I'd say they will do whatever it takes to recover The Diamond Room," she said. "You're probably in a very strong negotiating position."

William was instantly intrigued. "Why do you say that?"

I was curious myself. Intelligence analysis is an incredibly complex task, far beyond my own abilities, so I was surprised to hear Kirsten offering such a definite opinion. Still, she was an excellent judge of character, so I was going to listen to whatever she had to say.

"I saw Queen Catherine's face when she talked about it," she said. "She is entirely committed to this project."

"That's a good point," I added. "What is the Queen doing in Washington? Was she here on business?"

William thought a long moment before responding, obviously he was deciding how much information to give us. Finally he decided to fill us in.

"No, she was not in town," he asked. "She flew over last night on British Airways. She must have left within an hour of hearing about the recovery effort."

"So, Kirsten is right," I surmised. "It's a very high priority for them."

"None higher," William admitted.

Our drinks arrived. William was having iced coffee, which meant he was working. The bartender left, and we resumed our conversation.

"What is this place?" I asked.

"The Black Eagle Club," he said. "For persons in our, ahem, business," he answered.

"What's a Black Eagle?" Kirsten asked. "I've never heard of one."

I knew that the Black Eagle is a native of Asia, but I suspect the name of the club had nothing to do with any birds found in a book from the Audubon society. I wondered how William would handle this.

"I've long forgotten," he said. "I shall see if I can find out for you."

"Not that important," Kirsten said. Her short attention span came in handy sometimes.

The Black Eagle Trust was formed near the end of the Second World War, when the Allies began to recover enormous amounts of priceless art and valuables from Axis countries. The numbers ran into the billions, and the monies were used to finance anti-communist efforts for the next fifty years.

It was of strategic decision of the US government to use the money in this way, and like most of the postwar intelligence efforts, it had heroes and villains, and that is putting it mildly, but it all paid off on November 9, 1989, when the Berlin Wall was taken down, and communism collapsed all over Europe. I wondered if the name of the club had anything to do with its membership, who were likely involved up to their eyebrows in that operation.

I didn't pursue this, quite naturally, moving on to other things.

"What next, William?" I asked.

"We take the next step," he said. "and prepare a cover story which will account for the actual recovery of The Diamond Room, and then begin negotiations with both governments, which we will turn to our best advantage."

"That will be interesting," I said, which is an understatement.

William just smiled, and I knew he had to be enjoying this.

"I wish you the best of luck," Kirsten said.

"You have been of invaluable assistance to your country," William said, "and this will never be forgotten."

I thought differently. The sacrifices of American soldiers, especially in the intelligence community, where victories are never disclosed, are usually not even remembered. At our last Veteran's Day, the only people in attendance for the wreath laying ceremony were a few politicians and the surviving veterans themselves. Mention Tarawa, or Verdun, to a high school senior and you'll get a blank stare.

There was no point in pursuing that line of thought, it would only depress me.

Kirsten smiled faintly. "It was my duty, nothing more," she said. "Of course I was glad to help."

Mine is the first generation of women in combat in large numbers. American women have been serving in combat since the Revolution, and as a matter of fact there is even one female Medal of Honor winner, Mary Edwards Walker, but with every passing year more and more women are becoming veterans. It is still rare, however, to hear anyone so young speak of duty so matter-of-factly. It makes my veteran's heart beat faster.

"I promised you one day's work," William said, lighting a cigar, "and true to my word, your work here is finished. I thank you both for your help in this matter, and assure you it will all be handled discreetly from this point on."

"Excellent." I was tired and wanted to go home. Let the professionals handle it from here.

"How do we get home?" Kirsten asked.

"I have tickets for you on the New York shuttle," William said, in fact producing the tickets. "And for you, James, home to California on American Airlines."

We each took our respective tickets, Kirsten's going into her purse and mine into my jacket pocket.

"The tickets are dated tomorrow," William said. "I've arranged rooms for you at the Mayflower tonight, and a car to take you to the airport in the morning."

We nodded. A night at the Mayflower, with a decent dinner, would be just the thing before beginning the long cross country trip. It would also give me time to wrap up things with Kirsten.

"What will you be doing?" Kirsten asked, which demonstrated her inexperience in dealing with intelligence officers, who can't even discuss the weather without making up some sort of cover story.

William lit a cigar. "My work is just beginning," he said. "There will be much to do."

I stood up, and Kirsten followed. William got up and walked us to the door.

"Again," he said, "many thanks for all of your work."

"Will you call me and tell me what happens?" Kirsten asked.

"I'm afraid not," William said, "I'll have to refer you to the newspapers."

Kirsten smiled, and then she gave the old boy a hug and a kiss, during which, despite his decades of managing women, it was clear that he was not entirely used to the informality of our generation.

"Good luck," she said, and released him.

"James," he said, taking my hand in his, "as always, many thanks for your help."

I shook his hand, and William opened the door for us. "I've had a car brought around for you," he said, "have an enjoyable evening."

We walked through the door, and he closed it behind us. At the curb was a quite passable Cadillac limousine. I was not aware Cadillac was in the limo business, so perhaps this one was a custom stretch.

I opened the door, and Kirsten got in, and I followed. The driver division window as down.

"The Mayflower," I said to the driver.

"Yes, I have been given that destination, sir. We shall be there shortly. Will there be anything you require?"

Not that I could think of, and I said so.

"Very well, sir," he replied, and pressed a button to raise the division window, which was darkened, so Kirsten and I were alone.

"Well, that was quite a day," I said.

"You're not kidding," she responded, brushing her hair back and sinking into the plush leather seats. "Glad I don't have to do this every day."

I had nothing to add to that, so I simply scooted over to be next to her. She laid her head on my shoulder.

"Thank you," she said, and closed her eyes.

So I let her rest, she had certainly earned it, as we motored sedately through the Washington traffic back to the hotel. The limo had water, soft drinks and alcohol, but we just chilled out for a bit.

At length the car pulled up in front of the hotel, and the Mayflower staff opened the door. Kirsten exited, and I followed her.

"Welcome to the Mayflower," the bellman said. "Will there be any luggage?"

The driver had already opened the trunk, and he brought over our two carryon bags, which I was assuming our clothes had been packed into.

"For Mr. Larson," the driver said, handing our luggage to the bellman, and he was gone before I could tip him.

"Of course, Mr. Larson, this way, please," and the bellman led us into the interior of the hotel.

We bypassed the registration desk, which I thought was unusual, and commented on this.

"Per Mr. Fletcher's instructions," the bellman responded, referring to my uncle William. "You have been pre-registered."

We proceeded to the elevator, and he led us to a suite on one of the top floors.

He let us in, I tipped him, and he left, with a reminder to let him know if we needed anything.

And then I was alone, with Kirsten, in a suite in one of the best hotels in the world, with nothing on the schedule until tonight.

"I want a shower," she said, and peeled off her clothes as she headed for the bathroom, scattering her underwear all over the floor.

Seemed like a good idea to me, what else would you do, except follow the beautiful naked girl into the shower?

Kirsten was already getting drenched in the shower, letting the steaming hot water run over her, so I gently and carefully got in behind her, making sure I did not slip on the wet marble and thereby turn our rendezvous into a fatality.

She leaned back into my arms and for a long moment we just stood there and relaxed.

"What do you suppose your uncle William will do?" she asked, which demonstrates the difference between us, because while holding a beautiful blonde in my arms I do not usually concentrate on matters of international diplomacy.

I sighed, because there would be no sex until this matter was cleared up in her little blonde head.

She turned and pressed her body against me, wrapping her arms around me, and I tried very hard to concentrate on her question.

"I have no idea," I said, which was the truth, "and I am glad I am not the one who has to decide." It would be a painful decision, since one country would receive The Diamond Room, and the other would not.

Then I realized I really did know. It would have to be a political compromise. There was no other solution.

A political compromise, by definition, means a partial settlement by all parties. If properly executed, it meant that no one would be happy with it.

However, such compromises often yield the result of strategic advantage, which, since we were at war, was going to be the key to the answer.

The only question was, would the US go for the short term advantage, in the form of Waldron Air Force base in Staatfort, or the long term gain, that of the sale of reactor technology to Valthringia and the addition of a key ally against the interests of the Russian Federation?

Somebody very high up would have to make this call.

That's what I thought, at the time, which would not be the first time, or the last, that I had underestimated Kirsten Vorra.

"Why don't they put The Diamond Room at Schloss Alphenhof?" she asked.

For the record, it would turn out later that no one, not me, not William, not any of the analysts at the Agency, nor anyone at State, had thought of this. It was wholly, entirely, and completely, Kirsten's idea.

"What the heck is Schloss Alpenhof?" I asked her, since I didn't know.

"It's where Prince Felix proposed to Princess Marie," she replied. "They went on their honeymoon there. It's on the border of Staatfort and Valthringia."

For the first time in my life, I completely forgot about the naked blonde woman pressed next to me in the shower. The simplicity of the solution hit me with full force, to where I focused entirely on the consequences of what could come of this idea.

It got better. Kirsten noted my astonished look, and added, "It was a wedding present from Marie to Felix."

So that is what happened. He gave her a room full of diamonds, she gave him his own personal castle.

A border castle. Located literally on the meeting ground of both countries.

Half in Staatfort, half in Valthringia. With a strong emotional connection to both ruling families, as Felix and Marie had spent their honeymoon there.

Put The Diamond Room at this location, and you would make both countries happy. Literally, a perfect solution.

"You didn't know this?" Kirsten asked, and I could only shake my head.

"Well, I think it's a good idea," she said, resting her head against my chest. "You should tell your uncle William."

"How did you find out about this?" I asked her, amazed that a woman who couldn't tell you who fought in the Civil War would know such a detail.

"Google," she said.

Now I was really embarrassed, since I had not thought to look up any further information on Felix and Marie. I had relied on our intelligence officer to brief us.

It figures. A woman had concentrated on the important details, like where they spent their honeymoon, whereas the intelligence officer could tell us where they were buried.

I cursed under my breath for having missed the obvious, and disentangled myself from Kirsten and got out of the shower.

"Let me make a phone call," I said, getting into one of those fluffy white robes they keep in these hotels, "while you finish your shower."

I dried off and sat down at the telephone. Even though it was late in the day, William took the call immediately.

"Hello, young James," he said cheerfully. "Everything going well? Can I get you anything?"

"It's more of what I can do for you," I responded. "I may be able to be of some further assistance. I realize that it is getting late, but is there a chance you might be available to meet tonight?"

"Of course," he responded instantly, "I am not far away. I can be there in fifteen minutes." He hung up, a custom for people in his line of work who don't like to go into detail on the telephone.

"Kirsten!" I yelled. "Better get dressed, William will be here in fifteen minutes!"

I was hungry, but not for anything like actual food, so I ordered champagne and chocolate éclairs sent up, which for me would keep me going for the rest of the night.

As fast as I could, I got into clean clothes, which turned out to be a good idea, as William knocked on the door within a quarter hour. By that time the champagne had arrived and I was working on depleting the excellent bottle of White Star the staff had brought up.

I opened the door, and there was William with a very interested look on his face. "What do you have for me, my boy?" he asked, and I led him into the room to a comfortable chair.

I explained what Kirsten had told me, and laid out a possible alternative scenario for the management of The Diamond Room, which would include contacting both governments and agreeing to return the artifact conditional upon its placement at Schloss Alpenhof, which was on the border between the two countries.

This would enhance the credibility of the United States, solve a fairly knotty diplomatic problem, and present an acceptable resolution to the governments of both Staatfort and Valthringia.

"Brilliant," he breathed when he had heard our proposal, "just brilliant. I believe you may have found the optimal outcome for our situation."

Kirsten, ever casual, had gotten out of the shower and sat down next to us, wearing only a towel. It is a tribute to William's concentration as an intelligence officer that he didn't stare at her. I, regrettably, did not inherit his powers of concentration so I enjoyed the view.

Kirsten noticed, smiled, and got up and found a fluffy robe in the bathroom.

"Actually, it wasn't me," I admitted. "It was all Kirsten's idea."

William looked fairly surprised, but then, in his career, he had dealt with all kinds of people. "You don't say," he mused.

I shrugged. She's blonde, so people are always underestimating her intelligence.

She rejoined us, a little more dressed this time, in a robe.

"James has been filling me in on your idea," William told her, "and it may just be the ticket out of a dilemma."

She looked thoughtful. "It's the smart thing to do," was all she said.

"How did you think of this?" William asked, curious.

"It was a political marriage," she said, as if it was obvious, "it only made sense that they would have spent their honeymoon there."

Well, none of us had thought of it. William just looked at her for a moment.

"So what happens now?" I asked, snooping around.

William turned to me. "I'll put this idea in front of our State Department, who are occasionally of use from time to time, and they in turn will contact the governments of the two countries. If all goes well, by next week, an agreement will be reached, and it will be announced in the press."

"What story are you going to tell?" asked Kristen somewhat cynically. William had clearly been waiting for that question. "As a matter of fact, young lady, that depends entirely on you."

Her eyes narrowed. "What would I have to do with it?" she asked.

William paused for a moment, to light a cigar, as we both waited for his reply.

"I have been told my media consultants," he said, "that you are somewhat....what is the word they used....photogenic."

Kirsten knew that word. "So what?" she asked.

I understood immediately. Kirsten was, after all, a model, a young and beautiful blonde in perfect physical shape. Of course she was photogenic. That's what she did for a living, get photographed.

And if you're going to break a story about an archeological discovery, if you have a beautiful blonde archeologist, you'll get media coverage all over the world.

"I remember from your profile that you spent some time in Montana, digging up dinosaur fossils," William said.

She nodded. "Under Dr. Adamson, from the University. But I was an amateur, and that was when I was eighteen years old."

"But you do have a documented history of working in archeology," William continued.

Kirsten caught on. "You want me to be the one to discover The Diamond Room," she said.

William made a gesture with his hands. "You are the most camera-friendly individual available to us," he said.

We all sat and thought about this. I knew that with all of that media coverage, it would be of incredible help to Kirsten's career. You can't buy that kind of exposure.

"What would I have to do?" she asked.

William smiled, sensing victory. "Have you ever been to Scotland?" he asked.

CHAPTER EIGHTEEN

William left later that evening, after extracting a promise from Kirsten that she and I would agree to a meeting in the morning with his intelligence staff. By that time, he assured us, he would have a fully formed plan ready to put into action.

This meant, of course, that he was simply going to overwork his intelligence staffers all night long.

But, knowing the spooks as I do, this was the kind of job they lived for, that careers were made on, and I am sure there would be no shortage of volunteers to help William on this project.

I made the call to California, and let my job know I was going to need another week off, and Kirsten made similar arrangements.

Afterward, I poured her a glass of the White Star, and we put our feet up and looked at each other.

"You sure do have an interesting family," she said.

"That I do," I responded, "they were a lively bunch."

"So far, I'm happy about the way this is being handled," she said. "But we'll have to see before we decide…"

I clamped my hand over her mouth. I would not put it past Uncle William to have put a bug in our suite, and I did not want to discuss our next project, which is whether or not we could trust William to arrange the recovery and transfer of the crashed lander in Uncle Sven's barn, which is what I was pretty sure Kirsten was about to discuss.

I made a "shush" motion with my finger to my lips, and Kirsten nodded, so I released her and sat back.

"Enjoy the champagne," I said, "to our success."

"Success," she said, and returned the toast, and we both drank.

"So where is this Loch Ryan?" she asked me.

"I have no idea," I replied, since my knowledge of Scottish history was limited to stories of the old country from a grandparent and the occasional attendance at the Scottish Games. "We'll find out tomorrow."

"What do we do now?" she asked.

I just looked at her. It was late, we were alone, we had the suite overnight. Seemed obvious to me.

She smiled at me. "Do you ever think about anything but sex?" she asked.

"Not when I'm around you," I said truthfully.

"Take me then," she said, lying back in her chair, and so I did, and so we enjoyed each other all over again, instead of getting some sleep, which is what we needed. We were going to be exhausted tomorrow, but it was worth it. It was always worth it with Kirsten.

The next morning came too soon, and we got a wake up call at seven, and met the car at the front door at eight.

As usual, I have no idea of where we went, except that it was in downtown Washington and the building had an underground garage. We were met, as usual, by Jack Caldwell.

We rode up in an elevator to the 11th floor of a building with fourteen floors, and he led us to a windowless conference room. I tried to look around the corridor for some idea of where we were or what we were doing, but there were no labels anywhere on anything.

We sat down at a conference table, and Jack, as usual, had no computer, no PowerPoint display, or visual aids, he just gave us the story from memory. This is how we learned all about Loch Ryan.

Loch Ryan is located in Scotland, where it is and has been a busy sea port for quite some time.

In addition to its history as a center of the herring industry, during the Second World War much of the antisubmarine activity of the Royal Navy was operated out of the loch.

It is so large that flying boats can operate out of the Loch, and often did.

The Loch today has little vestige of its military activity, but one item has recently become much more important: it is the final resting place of much of the German U-Boat fleet.

At the conclusion of the war, when German U-boat commanders were ordered to proceed to English ports and surrender, the boats were simply scuttled afterwards. This was called "Operation Deadlight."

This turned out to have both positive and negative consequences.

On the negative side, virtually no examples of the German U-boats survived the war. It took the United States almost a national effort to agree to spare one of the boats, the U-505, and the Germans managed to save one of their boats, the U-995, but of all the classes and types of U-boats, few remain to tell the tale of the terror that stalked the seas.

On the positive side, Operation Deadlight had an entirely unanticipated outcome, and it has to do with the birth of the Atomic Age.

Apparently, all metal cast after the detonation of the first atomic bomb, at the Trinity test site in New Mexico, is contaminated to some degree by radioactivity.

Researchers, however, have to perform their tests on uncontaminated metal.

This has created, in the past decade, a market for ever-more-scarce uncontaminated metal, and the search has widened for large sources of this increasingly rare and more precious substance.

As it turns out, the largest source of uncontaminated metal is from ships that were built before 1945, that were not exposed to radioactivity.

And where can one find a ship not exposed to radioactivity? At the bottom of the ocean, where the airborne radioactivity cannot penetrate.

The largest numbers of such ships lies in the hunting grounds of the U-boats, which is the middle of the Atlantic, where the water is so deep, it is not practical to salvage such vessels.

But the U-boats themselves are in such shallow water, that an overhead crane can pull one out in a matter of hours.

And as it turns out, one of the U-boats interred at Loch Ryan was the one we were interested in…the U-3531.

Add to which, the British Ministry of Defence had recently granted a contract to salvage the U-boats from Operation Deadlight, so the cranes for the salvage operation were already on site at Loch Ryan.

All Kirsten had to do, was to go to Scotland and be photographed at the salvage operation for the U-3531. She would announce the "discovery" of the crates which contained The Diamond Room, and the US Government could then broker the transfer of the priceless artifact to its new home on the Staatfort-Valthringia border.

I would tag along too, to add credibility to the story. My family history of the loss of family member in a U-boat attack would play well in the press. I wasn't sure about this, since cousin Douglas had been killed in World War I, not World War II, but I wasn't in charge of this little caper.

"When would be leave?" Kirsten asked.

"Any time," Jack replied. "You'll be traveling by private jet, so whenever you're ready."

We were moving up in the world. A private jet.

Jack saw my look. "It's not a government jet," he explained, "we have arrangements with certain Fortune 500 companies for the occasional use of their aircraft for certain discreet missions."

I hoped it was a Gulfstream V. I had a friend who made a zillion in the Internet boom, he had a "G-5", as he referred to it. The plane was unbelievable, and each one came equipped with its own stewardess, usually a blonde direct from Sweden.

That's what he told me, anyway. I once asked another jet owner about this story, and he said for enough money, an aircraft manufacturer will put anything you want into an airplane, blondes included.

"We'll need clothes," Kirsten said. "I didn't pack for a trip to Europe."

"All arranged," Jack said. "I have a car waiting, to take you to the mall. Buy whatever you need for a two day trip. I'm afraid there is a budget for this."

He handed Kirsten a credit card, which he produced from an envelope in his breast pocket.

"I'll need receipts," he said. "Accounting is pretty strict nowadays."

"What about me?" I asked.

"I took the liberty," he said. "Your uncle supplied your shirt and slacks sizes. You've been set up with jeans, work boots and heavy sweaters. It's in a suitcase downstairs."

Seemed reasonable. Kirsten needed fashion, I needed function.

"How soon can you be ready?" I asked Kirsten.

"Meet me here in four hours," she said. "I have only one question. I don't have my US passport."

Neither did I, I suddenly remembered. I mean, I do have one, and it's current, but it was in California.

"Updated passports," Jack said, producing them from his jacket. "Courtesy of the US State Department." He handed them to us. The picture had been taken from our drivers licenses.

"Who do you know at the State Department, to get these so quickly?" I wanted to know.

Jack smiled. "Don't ask."

And I didn't. In this business, never ask a question you might not want to know the answer to.

And that is how we came to be at Loch Ryan. True to her word, Kirsten completed her shopping and was packed in under four hours. She showed up in a white silk blouse with a high neck and long sleeves, with an above the knee skirt that was beautiful without being revealing, which was easy because of her long, tan, California Girl legs. She had on silk stockings and sensible shoes, with her hair swept back and tied with a silk bow. She was dressed every inch the American Executive, and she was sexy as hell. We took a limo to Andrews Air Force base, boarded an executive jet, and took off for Scotland.

It really was a Gulfstream V, so for once in my life I got to live like a truly relaxed person and stretch out my legs in the airplane.

We had to work on the flight over the Atlantic. Jack, who accompanied us, handed us briefing summaries, and we memorized a great deal of information about the German U-boat fleet, stolen art from the Third Reich, and something called provenance, which is a fancy word for the history of an artwork, like, who owned and when they sold it.

Apparently the Germans had stolen a lot of artwork during their twelve year Reich, and now it was surfacing all over Europe, and a lot of unethical people were buying it with no questions asked.

The recovery and return of The Diamond Room would hopefully focus world attention on this problem, and turn up new leads on much of the still-missing works of art that were never recovered in 1945.

I thought that was a pretty ambitious agenda, but I wasn't a cop or an art expert, so I did not offer my opinion on this to Jack.

When we got tired of reading about stolen art and missing U-boats, we took a nap. It was going to be a busy day.

The stewardess woke us up as we came in for a landing. They really are cute and blonde. I tried not to stare, but it was hard not to.

I bucked up my seatbelt, and looked out the window as we landed. It was overcast, gray and gloomy outside. The runway was wet, but it wasn't actually raining.

The jet pulled up next to a large unmarked van. I noticed uncle William smoking a cigar, leaning against the van.

I wondered how he could have survived to this age while smoking cigars.

The stewardess let down the stairs, and Jack assisted Kirsten out of the aircraft, and I followed them.

"Hello, my dear," William said, and Kirsten gave him a hug. "Thank you for coming."

I walked over and shook his hand. "And you, young James, has Jack been taking good care of you?"

"Absolutely," I said, becoming aware that in some fashion, Jack reported to William, although William was supposed to be retired. "We're all set to go."

"Then let us go," he said. ""Our transportation awaits."

Jack pulled open the side door of the van, and we stepped into a nicely furnished corporate shuttle van.

As soon as we were in it pulled away, and I noticed we had a police escort, clearing the road ahead of us.

"We'll be there shortly," William said. "Jack will take you to the site of the U-3531 recovery. You'll be given a short orientation, and then you will meet a reporter from one of Britain's major networks. He will conduct a short interview, and take some pictures."

"I hope not very difficult questions," I asked, "since I know nothing about U-boats and less about art."

"He will stick to a prepared script," William said, "which I prepared for him."

A prepared script. Reporters hated those. "How did you arrange that?" I asked.

William looked surprised. "It was not difficult," he said. "Reporters will do anything for a story."

I laughed, since it was true.

"Besides," William added, "Kirsten will be taking the questions. "You'll be in the background, stacking the crates."

"Are the Diamond Room crates here?" I asked.

"The crates are here," he replied. "But the contents are sitting safely in Virginia."

"Do I have a script?" Kirsten asked, ever the modeling professional.

Without a word, Jack handed it to her. She calmly took it from him and began scanning it with a speed I was unaware she possessed until this moment.

The van moved swiftly from the airport to the seaside.

The final resting place of the German U-boat fleet was in a neglected corner of the Loch. There was nothing to mark the location, except a huge overhead crane on a barge at the site.

I noticed the cables were in the water, presumably wrapped around the hull of U-3531.

"Everything's in place," William said. "Shall we proceed?"

The van parked, we all piled out, and Jack led us to the shore by the barge.

A media van was parked nearby, satellite dish on top folded down. I realized that they would not be broadcasting live, just making a tape.

"Let me introduce you," William said, and walked over to the media van.

The reporter was a man, very young, powerfully built. He had sharp intense eyes, and ordered his cameraman about without mercy.

"Kirsten, James, may I present Mr. Taylor," William said. "Mr. Taylor, may I present Ms. Kirsten Vorra, and Mr. James Larson, the team that discovered the clues to the resting place of The Diamond Room."

"Pleasure to meet you," Taylor said,

"Likewise," Kirsten responded, shaking his hand.

"Mr. Taylor," I said, shaking his hand in turn, "how can we be of service to the media today?"

He instantly became a focused media professional. "The crane is ready to begin the raising process," he said, gesturing behind him at the overhead crane whose cables ran into the water. "When they're ready, we'll start filming. We'd like to get a shot of the U-boat breaking the surface. Afterwards, we'll take some shots of the recovery team opening the hatch and checking for the crates. Finally, I'd like a short interview with one of you about your work."

"I'll defer to my colleague, Ms. Vorra," I said, pointing at Kirsten, "she's more comfortable with the media than I am."

"Of course," Taylor replied, not bothering to disguise his glee that he would be able to get the cute blonde in front of his camera.

"I'll meet you later, then," I said to Kirsten. "I'll get over to the U-boat."

She nodded, and off I went, while Taylor set up his cameras to record a short interview with her. She had her cover story rehearsed and was set to go.

This was probably going to be the only chance I ever had to get near an actual U-boat, so I wasn't going to miss my opportunity, even if the U-Boat in question had been sitting on the bottom of the sea for sixty years.

I strode over to the recovery site, and took a position on the beach a hundred yards inshore directly opposite the cables.

A loudspeaker echoed over the Loch. "Overhead crane now in operation," it said, "all personnel take safety positions."

William stood behind me as I watched. It was a very slow process. The crane made a slow hum as the cables slowly tightened in the water.

"How deep is she?" I asked him.

"You should ask someone who knows," he said. "Let me introduce you."

He turned, and behind us was an elderly man with white hair dressed in a thick sweater and peacoat.

"James Larson…may I present Oberleutnant Carl Bergsten, last surviving officer of U-3531."

I was absolutely stunned. I had no idea that any U-boat officers were still alive, let alone able to make the trip to England. I faced him and shook his hand.

"Mr. Bergsten," I said, unsure of whether to address him by his rank, "it's a real pleasure to meet you."

"Thank you," he said in perfect, unaccented English. "I appreciate the invitation. I have not seen U-3531 in sixty years."

"Where did you learn English?" I asked him.

"I studied in England before the war, and of course afterwards it was quite useful," he replied.

"So you were one of the officers of the U-3531?" I asked.

"Oh yes," he said. "I was not on board for her last cruise, as I could not return to the base as the railroad lines were bombed out. My last cruise with her was in April of 1945."

I was awed. "What can you tell me about her?" I asked.

He smiled, like someone remembering an old girlfriend. "She was a Type XXI," he said.

I didn't even know there were different types of U-boats. I had thought they were a mass production run of the same type. I guess my Army service leaves me pretty ignorant of submarine technology.

Offshore, the cables had tightened, and the motor revved up as it picked up the load of the massive submarine hull under the water.

"What is a Type XXI?" I asked him.

"An Elektro boat," he said, surprised, as if everyone in the world was familiar with U-boat types. "She could do fifteen knots, submerged. Maximum depth over nine hundred feet. Range almost three hundred miles, submerged."

Wow. Good thing there were not a whole lot of these things running around in 1945. The outcome of the war would have been entirely different.

The crane motor slowed. The cables were visibly moving. The water began to bubble at the surface.

"She's surfacing," Oberleutnant Bergsten said simply.

And she was. Slowly, very slowly, the water parted, and for the first time since she sank below the waves for Operation Deadlight, the U-3531 came to the surface.

My only knowledge of U-boats comes from movies, but even I could see that this was a truly advanced submarine for 1945. The deck guns and open railing I had seen in movies were concealed in a sleek and rounded conning tower. There were no obstructions on the deck to impede her passage through the water.

Plus, she was a whole lot longer than I had ever imagined her to be.

The crane slowly lifted her massive bulk until she was clear of the water, and then slowly, slowly, swung to the left, where a temporary drydock had been built on the beach to hold her.

With careful precision, the U-3531 was lowered into the cradle on the drydock, and then the cables went slack. The recovery operation was complete.

William led the way, and we threaded into the drydock, where a team of welders was cutting open the hatch on the conning tower. A safety officer handed us all yellow hard hats.

Oberleutnant Bergsten, despite his quite advanced age, scampered up the ladder like a mountain goat and was on the conning tower in moments. William was not far behind him.

I was fifty years younger than either of them, but I had to take my time up the ladder. I really needed to work out more often.

The dockyard crew took about fifteen minutes to cut the hatch away, but they finally got it clear, and used a cable to winch the hatch clear of the vessel. During this time, the submarine drained massive amounts of water out of her hull through the seacocks.

To begin the exploration of the submarine, I had ordered a video camera and light fitted to a cable, and this was lowered down the hatch while we were able to watch a television screen in the conning tower.

I couldn't tell one end of a submarine from the other, so I had no idea what I was looking at, but Bergsten did.

"It's her," he said. "It's the U-3531."

"How can you tell?" I asked. "I don't see anything that can tell this ship from another."

He nodded. "Only three type XXIs ever made a war patrol," he said. "One is the U-2511, sunk at Moville, and the other, U-3008 was broken up. This is a Type XXI, so this has to be the U-3531."

He pointed at the monitor. "There's our emblem."

On the TV screen, the video camera which had been lowered into the ship showed an image painted on the equipment. It was of a seahorse above crossed tridents.

"That is our ship," Bergsten concluded.

"Thank you," I said to him, as he looked quite absorbed in seeing his wartime vessel again after sixty years. What memories he must be having.

"Let's talk," I said to William, and having positively identified the ship as the U-3531, we descended the ladder and stood in the drydock.

"The next step is to cut open her hull," William said. "Then we'll announce that the crates have been removed, and Taylor will show video of this on his television station."

"And then?" I asked.

"Then the US government will appoint a commission to review the claims of each country as to the final disposition of The Diamond Room, and after a suitable interval, will chose Schloss Alpenhof as the ultimate repository. Our art historians will oversee the transfer and ensure reconstruction of the Room."

"How long will it take?" I asked.

"To actually rebuild the room requires only reassembling the panels, and our experts tell me this will be only a matter of days—as a matter of fact, that process is already underway in Virginia. To convene the commission, hold hearings, and set up the agreements between Staatfort and Valthringia, six months, easily." William grinned at this irony.

Kirsten joined us. "How did it go?" I asked her.

"Very quickly," she said. "He asked me about The Diamond Room, and Prince Felix and Princess Marie. Then he took pictures of the boat, and that was about it."

William nodded. "Taylor has been of use to us before," he said. "And he will be again, if he handles this correctly."

I was surprised to hear this about a supposedly free press, but then I remembered I wasn't in the United States anymore.

Kirsten was looking at me steadily. I knew why. With this accomplished, there was only one other item of business to be completed. It was time to discuss it.

"Then we are finished here?" I asked.

"We are." he said. "And my thanks to the both of you."

Kirsten took his hand in her. Then she looked him squarely in the eye, and with quiet deliberation, she said, "I am glad we have been of use to you today," she said.

William caught her gaze, his interest captured, aware she was making a point.

She went on carefully. "Perhaps we will be again."

With these few words, William said later, he first became aware that we were using him, and not the other way around.

She released him, turned away, and quietly walked to the shuttle van.

William turned to me, curiosity written on his features, a new respect for her developing.

"James," he said, which meant he was dead serious, since it was not 'young James', "what exactly does she mean by this?"

I thought about telling him. I really did. But we were standing in a dockyard, in a foreign nation, even if it was England, and there were plenty of eyes and ears about which should not, and could not, hear what I, and Kirsten, had to tell William.

But I would need him alone, and so I invoked the phrase my family always uses when there is a life-changing emergency pending, and that is when I said," I believed she mentioned to me that she had a legal question for you, so perhaps when we return to America, you might have time to discuss it with us."

William caught on instantly. "A legal question?"

I nodded. That was the phrase, "a legal question."

He went on. "And you would like for me to discuss it with both of you, not just Kirsten alone?"

"Yes. The both of us."

For a long minute, William just looked at me. He was taking my measure, realizing how fully involved we both were, and weighing the benefits our work had brought him, the Agency, and the country.

"Very well, young James," he said, very softly. "I shall make immediate arrangements for our return to America."

Then he turned away, and opened his cellphone to make a call.

CHAPTER NINETEEN

I left the dockyard workers to do their job, and they were already bringing the cutting equipment to open the hull.

The shuttle van was ready, and I joined Kirsten there. The van sped away from the site. Our faithful intelligence officer, Jack Caldwell, did not accompany us.

I took her hand in mine and squeezed it, and she smiled, because we both knew that the next phase of our plan was underway

The driver seemed to know where we were going, which was fortunate, since I did not even know where we were, except that it was somewhere in Scotland, at a placed called Loch Ryan.

We were delivered to the airfield, where the G-5 sat patiently. We re-boarded, where the same briskly efficient stewardess got us strapped in. I do not know how he arranged it, but William was already aboard.

He was wearing an expression like a crocodile in a Florida swamp. He had gotten more than he bargained for, but he just didn't know how deep he was.

"We meet again," he said. "Kirsten, James has told me that you a have a legal question for me when all of this is over."

She carefully studied him. "Yes," she affirmed, "when all of this is over."

There was a long silence. He became aware that she wasn't going to discuss it further.

"Very well," he said, they smiled at each other.

It was going to be a long flight. We raced off the runway, and went to altitude very rapidly. I was pretty sure the G-5 pilot had flown fighters at one time.

The G-5 is actually faster than a commercial airliner, so the Atlantic crossing was shorter than usual. We spent the time in different ways. William read, I rested, and Kirsten retreated into her shell, staring quietly out the window for the duration of the flight.

Her determination to address the unresolved matter of The Item In The Barn, I believe, was strengthened by the pain of her loss of her husband. She had never come to terms with it, but if this would help her deal with that agony, and transition to the next stage in her life, then that, in my opinion, was an option worth pursuing.

Flying across the Atlantic, on the other hand, did nothing but remind her of her husband, who had been a pilot. Flying, I think, strengthened her resolve. Good for her, I thought. The power of flight had liberated other human souls, as the poet said, on laughter-silvered wings.

I had time, on that flight, to reflect on my friendship with Kirsten, something I did rarely, since I thought of her primarily in a physical sense.

My work leaves me little time to devote to my actual friends; I have too often not been there for them, and often am not even aware of the struggles they have faced in their lives. In her case, it was different; Kirsten is a woman who suffers in private. She withdrew after her tragedy; most of her friends, myself included, were unable to reach her, and thereby were never able to provide her the comfort of friendship at a time when she needed it most. But even if we had, she would never have let us help her. She was a very private woman in many ways.

This, I suppose, is why I never feel guilty about our relationship. I lack the ability to manage such a complex woman.

Today I wondered to myself who might. I was the closest thing she had to a friend. I had something to think about on that flight. I would not reach a solution for some time to come.

We ultimately put down at a private airport in Virginia, and a car was waiting for us.

William was the last one into the car. He swung the door closed, and the limo swung slowly into motion. I sneaked a look back, as that was likely going to be my very last ride in a Gulfstream V, or any Gulfstream, in this lifetime.

The car picked up speed. I noticed we were not headed toward the capital.

"Where are we going?" I wanted to know.

William checked his watch. "I have a surprise for you," he said. "We will be there shortly."

Kirsten was instantly alert. "What kind of a surprise?"

William wouldn't give it away. "You'll have to wait," he said. "I set this up for you personally. I'm reasonably certain you'll find it worth the wait."

That was all he would say on this topic. He settled back into his seat, and the car motored quietly into the countryside.

Kirsten looked at me for support, but I wasn't going to upset William. If he had done this for us, I wanted to see what he was up to.

I took her hand, and she relaxed.

I have to confess, I was curious. I had not had any kind of a surprise, at least a good one, in years.

So I tried to figure out where the car was going. As it turned out, we were headed into a light industrial area.

The car pulled up in front of a warehouse. It was fitted with a dozen truck docks, so clearly at one time it had been a shipping facility.

There were, however, no trucks docked there.

So the limo pulled into one of one parking spaces and we all got out. William escorted us to a side door, which was one of those big garage doors on wheels.

He went to slide it open, but the guy was over eighty, so I got it for him. Even fifty years younger, it was tough for me to do—the door was old, rusty and screeched as we opened it.

"They've been using the truck dock to get in and out," William said by way of explanation.

He knew his way around, though, because the interior of the building was in complete darkness. William felt along the side door, and threw a switch.

The lighting system went on.

The building was an empty shell. Overhead, racks of lights illuminated the floor, much like a football field. In the center of the vast space, someone had been working on something.

There were electrical carts scattered about and some of those huge Gladiator wheeled toolchests. Someone had set up bench table saws, and the smell of freshly cut wood filled the air.

A square room had been erected in the center of the floor. It was made of wooden sides, which were reinforced with wooden two by fours.

William held out his hand, indicating that we should go to see it.

Kirsten halted for a moment. "Aren't you coming with us?"

He shook his head. "You have earned this," he said.

I strolled toward the construction site. I couldn't imagine what this might be, which goes to show just how tired I was. Must have been the jet lag.

Kirsten caught up with me.

We got to the wooden framework, which was pretty much what if looked like, a wooden framework. So we went around the sides, and came around to the front.

And there it was.

The recovery team had, in less than four days, reassembled the original panels of The Diamond Room, in a quickly constructed mockup replica of Runevald Chapel.

We just stood there for a minute.

The Room had five sides. There was a floor, a ceiling, the right and left walls, and the floor.

Each of these, even the floor, was inset with diamonds. I have no idea how the craftsmen had done this, for they were embedded in the mirror panels themselves.

The light shining from the overhead grid lit up the interior. The room was shimmering in the reflected, refracted light of thousands of diamonds.

It was like being in the middle of a white fire.

No photograph, no painting will ever do it justice. You have to physically be there to understand the beauty and power of The Diamond Room.

No wonder three different countries were hot to get their hands on it.

We didn't speak, for a moment. We were just visually overwhelmed. Kirsten reached forward and touched one of the panels.

Good idea, I thought, so I did the same. It was cool to the touch, and smooth.

Gently, I took a step toward the Room. I looked over at William, to see if that was OK.

"Go right ahead," he said, walking casually across the warehouse floor. "Our technical experts say the structural integrity is completely intact."

So I did. I stepped onto the floor of The Diamond Room. I was a bit cautious at first, but it seemed as solid as any concrete floor.

I extended my hand to Kirsten, and she joined me. And there we were, standing in the chapel of The Diamond Room.

I pulled her close, and gave her a slow kiss, holding her body close to mine as I did so. She was surprised, but she kissed me back.

"What was that for?" she asked when the kiss was over.

"I just wanted to kiss you in The Diamond Room," I said, "and it seemed to me to be my best chance."

"Silly!" she said, but you could tell she was happy about it.

William coughed behind us. We parted and turned to face him.

"Our technical experts have taken pictures," he said. "I have taken the liberty of making you a set." He handed us a leather bound photo album.

Kirsten took it from him, and went through it. I looked over her shoulder. The pictures were technically excellent, but they did not do justice to the room itself.

"So they stood here," Kirsten said, "this is where they were married."

I remembered why this room was built. Two people had stood here so deeply in love that when one of them died, the other followed within six months of a broken heart.

And here, in this room, the walls still mirrored the incandescent flame of their passion for each other: captured, forever, in the panels surrounding us.

I felt warm. The sight of Kirsten, with the light of diamonds reflecting off her blonde hair, was quite sensuous.

She closed the book. And looked at me, and smiled.

That will always be one my private memories of Kirsten. Standing in The Diamond Room, the light shining on her hair, a smile on her face. Now, after everything that has happened, that moment binds me to her, and always will.

"Shall we proceed?" William asked.

I turned to leave the room, and took Kirsten's hand, and we stepped down from the platform.

We took a final look, and then headed toward the car.

William closed the warehouse door, and joined us in the limo.

"Where shall I take you?" he asked.

"National Airport," I responded.

"Very well," he said, and directed the driver accordingly.

The limo spun away, and we headed to what would turn out to be the most interesting chapter of our lives.

CHAPTER TWENTY

The trip to National Airport was made in relative silence. William was clearly curious, but I refused to consider any questions in this environment. But the time came when we arrived.

I directed the driver to take us to departures, and he dropped the three of us there, and then went off to find parking. William arranged to stay in touch with him by telephone.

We had those cool tickets where you get to go in a separate line for Elite customers, and since we had no luggage, we had our boarding passes in minutes.

William waited patiently for us through all of this, and while I know he was dying of curiosity, he said nothing. Later he would tell me that since we'd brought him The Diamond Room, he would pretty much be available to us for anything else we might need for the rest of our lives, on the chance that we might have something equally interesting to talk about, and like most things in his life, William was right.

We all stepped into the First Class lounge, where they serve all the alcohol you can drink before boarding, William using his official identification to bypass every single security checkpoint, actually taking us to the concourse by a concealed route which was obviously used by security personnel for sensitive and VIP passengers.

We all sat in sprawling chairs by huge bay windows overlooking the runways. I had a whiskey and coke. Kirsten went for champagne. William went for coffee, a sure sign he considered himself to be working.

"So," he began, as the drinks were delivered, "you'll both be going to Montana again."

We both smiled at him.

"Yes, it's a beautiful place," Kirsten said. "You must come visit."

There was a long silence. William was studying her.

She continued. "The fishing and hunting in Montana is truly a remarkable experience," she said. "Perhaps you'd like to come and do a little hunting."

Actually, although William was a hunter, he mostly stuck to deer, which were a real nuisance in Connecticut. Still, we all knew we weren't talking about hunting for deer. He'd be hunting for something a lot more valuable.

"What is there to hunt in Montana?" William said with a measured tone.

"Probably things you've never seen in Connecticut," she said, and wasn't that the truth. "You really must come."

"I shall," he said, continuing the charade as if he was really coming to the ranch to hunt deer, but still using perfect grammar. "When would you like me to visit?"

She looked over at me. I took a sip of the whiskey. Not bad stuff. It was going to be up to me.

I thought for a moment. What had to be done? We wanted to get William on site and turn over The Thing in The Barn. Logistically, there wasn't much to do in order to set this up. We had to get to Montana to Uncle Sven's ranch, but that was about it. And we already had our boarding passes.

We would sleep there tonight. He could then join us there tomorrow.

"How soon can you come?" I asked.

William thought about this. "As you might imagine," he said, "your most recent discovery has made my schedule a bit more hectic."

We weren't sure of where he was going with this, so we let him continue his thought process.

He went on. "How long might you imagine I might stay?" he asked.

Kirsten finished her champagne. "Perhaps this weekend," she said, "then if you enjoy it, you might stay longer."

So there it was. The invitation was open.

"I believe," she finished, "that, like most people, that you will find your stay in Montana to be a unique and unforgettable experience."

"I'm sure that will be true," William responded, "if past experience is any guide."

That was it, then.

It was kind of hard to talk in public, but we couldn't really tell him flat out what was going on in anything except a secure environment, so it was best left up to when he finally got out there to see for himself.

Our flight was announced. We stood up to go, a bit unsteadily, thanks to the alcohol.

"Take care, nephew," the old boy said, shaking my hand. "I will arrange a flight to Montana for tomorrow, and will join you at the ranch in the afternoon."

He went to shake Kirsten's hand too, but she just wrapped her arms around him and kissed him gently on the cheek.

Ever the gentleman, he let her kiss him, and carefully untangled her.

"It has been a real pleasure meeting you," he said, and you could see his courtly manners were having a real impact on Kirsten, who was really just a small town girl.

"And you as well," she returned, and let him go.

He turned, and with a final look over his shoulder, he went his way, and we went ours, off to the gate, destined for Montana.

We got to our gate, and we able to board first, since we had first class seats, which was nice, since everything else about air travel has gotten steadily worse over the years.

As soon as we sat down the stewardess offered us a drink, which neither of us turned down since we going to be flying for six hours, and in a few minutes we were tucked in, seat belted, and quite tipsy.

Alcohol knocks Kirsten right out, since she almost never drinks, so in short order she curled up next to me and fell soundly asleep. When she sleeps, sometimes she'll give off a little purring noise, so she sounds like a kitten, which I think is adorable.

The East Coast airport system is full of delays, and today was absolutely no exception, and we sat on the runway waiting for clearance. I leafed through the airline magazine, hoping to find a decent movie, but I had seen all of the movies before, and they had been edited for content, which means they had cut out all the interesting parts, so there was no point in watching them.

I had not thought to bring a book to read, not that I would have been able to concentrate anyway with everything that had happened recently, so I decided to follow Kirsten's lead.

As soon as we got to cruising altitude, I finished my champagne, handed the glasses to the stewardess, and put a pillow against the window and went to sleep.

When I awoke we were descending in to Salt Lake City, which for once had good weather, and we were even on time, the pilot having poured on the gas to make up for our delay in departure.

This was a good thing, since we had a connecting flight to Billings to catch.

Again we de-boarded first due to our first class status, and caught the connecting flight to Billings. Another departure, another boring flight, and finally we touched down at the Billings airport.

The airport had a decent selection of four wheel drive vehicles. They had a Hummer, which cost extra, but that was an easy decision.

I had thought I'd be driving, but Kirsten gracefully swung into the driver's seat, exposing those magnificent California girl legs under her skirt as she did so. She caught me watching.

"Pervert," she said, but she smiled as she did so.

"Hey, I can't help it if you've got killer legs," I returned.

Kirsten had a personal preference for high performance German sports cars, but she managed the Hummer expertly and effortlessly. Something about watching her push the monster truck around was mildly erotic.

She hit the highway, got the vehicle up to seventy five miles per hour, set the cruise control and sat back, kicking off her shoes to better manage the car. I noted that her toenails were neatly manicured and painted a soft pink.

I couldn't help myself. She was as beautiful as any model in a magazine, and when were alone it was nearly impossible for me to keep my hands off of her.

And since we were alone now, I saw no reason to behave any differently. I reached over and very gently, so as not to catch her by surprise, pulled her skirt slowly up over those incredible legs, as far up as the fabric would go.

She watched this with some amusement, as she always did when I was played with her body.

"What are you up to, tiger?" she asked, not moving my hands from her skirt.

"Just playing," I said, thoroughly enjoying myself, as I was still getting used to the touch of her perfectly toned bod, and never seemed to tire of it.

"OK, but let's not get into a wreck," she chided gently, enjoying the power she was always able to exert over me with a minimum of effort.

I suppose a gentleman would have allowed her to drive in peace, but I have been so tired and stressed out at work recently that the blast of adrenaline she gave me when I touched her was a welcome and rare experience, so I gave in to my more base impulses and ran my hands over her legs and let the feeling of pure pleasure wash over me.

After a moment sanity returned and I withdrew my hands from her legs, which, after all, were operating a high performance automobile at excessive speeds, and I did want to live through the trip.

She flashed a smile. "You're losing your famous self control," she said, and she was right, a long time ago I had been quite restrained about such physical demonstrations.

"More on that later," I responded, and settled back in my seat, allowing her to drive in peace.

With some effort I diverted my thoughts to the project ahead. I had to think of what I was going to do next.

So, we would get to the ranch tonight. Get settled in. Tomorrow William would join us. What to do at that point?

I made a decision at that point. Looking back, it turns out to have been the correct one. I was fatigued and under strain, but I also do a lot of my best thinking under such conditions, and the way I set it up had a definite impact on how the rest of the process went.

I decided that when William arrived, the best way to break the news was not to tell him, but to show him. I would get the backhoe started, and physically excavate the UFO. Then, when William arrived, I would simply take him out to the barn so he could see it immediately.

I thought this would save a lot of time and explanations. I was right.

Before we arrived at the ranch, we stopped off at a supermarket, selecting one some distance from the ranch itself. In this way, we could avoid the gossip that accompanies small town markets. I didn't want anyone to know we were headed out there.

Kirsten, of course, a tall, skinny blonde, got lots of attention wherever she went, and the market was no exception. We loaded up on enough supplies to last us another week, heavy on the steaks and alcohol.

After that, we completed the trip to the ranch, and Kirsten rocked the massive Hummer right up to Sven's door. The groceries were quickly unloaded, a fire started in the fireplace, and Kirsten got busy in the kitchen making us a decent meal.

After running all over Europe, the cold was hitting me pretty hard, so I kept my sweater and coat on until the place warmed up a bit. It didn't take long.

"When will your uncle get here?" Kirsten asked me.

"Tomorrow sometime," I responded. "All we have to do now is wait."

We were both starving, so as soon as the steaks were ready we made short work of them.

It was a little spooky being back at the ranch, where all of this had started. When we finished our meal and had cleaned up, I went downstairs to inspect the coal chute, where the panels for The Diamond Room had been stored.

William's men had dug up the chute, extracted the panels, and replaced it all expertly afterward. It was still possible to notice that the walls had been disturbed, but it was not obvious.

Nothing else to see here, to I rejoined Kirsten on the ground floor.

She was putting on her mittens.

"Shall we check on the barn?" she said.

And so we did. We walked out to the barn and swung the doors open. Apparently there had been some days above freezing, so the snow on the floor had melted. The dirt floor was as hard as concrete, however.

I checked to make sure the backhoe was plugged into the wall so the engine wouldn't freeze. It was all set.

Kirsten, who apparently knew the barn better than I did, plugged in an electric industrial space heater, and it immediately flooded the barn with warm air.

"So that tomorrow the ground will be softer and the barn more comfortable to work in," she said by way of explanation.

She was always a practical kid. Typical farm girl, always goes out the night before and set up for tomorrow's chores.

I had another thought. "We should check the bunkhouse."

Likely William would be accompanied by a team of excavators, I thought, so we would need a place to put them. The bunkhouse had not been used in years, but it was intact, operational and designed to hold a harvesting crew. It would have to do.

We closed the barn door and went over to the bunkhouse. It was in better shape than I had expected it to be. Sven had wrapped electrical heating elements around the plumbing, which guaranteed the pipes would never freeze. The water still ran in the taps—although a significant bit of rust came out when we turned them on.

Other than that, there was nothing to do but wait.

"Let's go to bed," I said, and we did.

Sven's place had a fireplace in the master bedroom, since the building predated central heating, so I stuffed it with firewood and in short order had a decent blaze going. I turned out the lights and got into the huge bed, and in a few minutes Kirsten came out of the bathroom wearing one of those little Victoria's Secret flannel nightgowns. She tumbled into the bed and curled up alongside me.

After a moment she looked up at me, remembering we didn't always use the bed for sleep. "Did you want sex?" she asked.

"Do I ever not want sex?" I returned, and she giggled at that, so before we turned in we had a very long, slow, and comfortable play session.

That was my last night of sleep as a private citizen. After that night, my whole life changed, permanently.

CHAPTER TWENTY ONE

William showed up early the next day. I had expected him to arrive the same way we had, which is to say, fly into Billings, rent a car and then drive up to the ranch.

Instead, bright and early at 7:30 AM—which meant he had been flying all night—he arrived by personal aircraft at Sven's ranch.

Now, the ranch can accommodate almost any size airplane, since, like a lot of Montana, it is flat and very large. However, the landing would be fairly rough, since the road is only gravel.

I was aware that the US Air Force had in the inventory aircraft capable of landing on unimproved or rough runways, but like almost everything else he had done on this trip, uncle William surprised me again.

The clatter of rotors awoke us, since we were quite lazy and had not yet gotten out of bed. Of course I knew it was William, so at first I thought it was a helicopter. This was an entirely reasonable thought, since it certainly sounded like a helicopter and it was a good choice for the terrain.

But it wasn't.   It was something entirely different – it was an Osprey.

The Osprey is an aircraft that can take off like a helicopter and then convert to fixed wing flight. It is a favorite of the Marine Corps, and sure enough, this one had Marine Corps markings.

As far as my limited military knowledge ran, there were no Marine Corps bases anywhere near Montana, so I wondered where he had gotten one of these on short notice.

At any rate, this flying monstrosity clattered down onto the ranch about three hundred yards from the house itself. The door popped open and William strode out, wearing jeans, a thick sweater and a parka, suitable for the Montana cold. He came to the door, where I was gawking at the incredible flying machine he had brought with him.

For her part, Kirsten gave a tiny "EEK!" and ran back into the house to get a shower and do her hair, for apparently it is The Law of the Blonde that you can never be seen in public without having your hair done.

"Hello, young James," William said, shaking my hand. "Good to see you."

"Thank you for coming," I replied. "I appreciate it," and meant it. If William was not my uncle I would honestly not have known how to handle this situation.

"Come in," I continued, "We've got coffee on."

Kirsten had started the fire in the main fireplace and the coffee was brewing. William came in and stomped the snow off of his feet, and looked around.

I looked out the window. "Will your crew need anything?" he said.

He shook his head. "They're not cleared for our conversation," he said, "They'll wait in the aircraft until I need them."

Sure enough, the Marine pilots were hanging out by the Osprey, and they already had their coffee mugs out.

"Kirsten will be here in a minute," I said, "she had to take a shower first."

He smiled. "Women," he said, and I nodded agreement.

I handed him a cup of coffee. It was Sven's coffee, so it was pretty strong.

We settled down on the overstuffed chairs in front of the bay window overlooking the Montana landscape.

"You have my undivided attention," William said. "What is this about?"

It was that easy. It was now or never, so I drank a shot of the coffee, looked my uncle William in the eye, and told him the story.

I told him about Uncle Sven, and the video, and the late night excavation, and my meeting with Kirsten, and how she and my uncle had gotten the thing flying. I filled him in on the history of her husband, killed in the Gulf War, and her commitment to seeing the technology transferred to the custody of the Air Force.

Then I told him my own concerns—that I didn't want to be bothered for the rest of my life by incompetent security staff, that I valued my privacy, and that I thought Kirsten was suffering from the worst case of pathological grief that I had ever seen.

I concluded by telling him the Thing In The Barn was his free and clear, and that all I wanted out of it was a decent doctor to take care of Kirsten's depression.

Throughout the whole story William's expression did not change. He sat calmly and listened intently. When I was finished he rose to his feet.

"We're going to need a different airplane," he said, and walked out the door to where the Osprey sat on the ground.

Apparently, he dismissed the Marine Corps pilots, for in less than a minute they had the rotors turning and the Osprey lifted into the air and made for parts unknown.

Kirsten joined us about this time, drying her hair. "Where's your airplane going?" she asked.

"I'll need a different airplane and crew," he said.

She looked at both of us. "You told him," she said to me.

I nodded.

"Fine," she said.

"You've had quite an interesting time of this," William said to her. "This is the most interesting story I've ever heard."

Kirsten took on a whole different persona. She poured herself a cup of coffee and looked at William with those pale blue eyes of hers and took his measure.

"You will help us?" she asked, staring at him.

"I will," he said.

"You will take possession of The Lander?" she asked.

"Yes."

Long silence here. The blonde and the spy just stared at each other.

"You will give it to the Air Force?" she asked.

A very long silence.

"It will be placed in the appropriate hands," was all he would say.

Kirsten figured it out first. "You've done this before," she stated.

William was wearing his poker face. He might have been carved from stone. He evaded the question.

"Our technical people will have questions for you," he said.

"You have done this before," Kirsten stated, this time not a question, "which means the government has more of these things."

William said nothing, did nothing, just stared back at her.

"I don't care," she said, "and don't want to know any more."

I had a question. "How fast can you get rid of this thing?"

William had his telephone out. "Let me see," he said, and typed in a text message. He hit "send" and closed the telephone.

"Today or tomorrow," he said, "from your perspective, this matter will be entirely closed."

That was the answer we were both looking for.

"Excellent," Kirsten said, speaking for both of us.

"May I see it?" William said.

"Sure," I responded, "I'll have to dig it up first."

"I'll make breakfast," Kirsten said, and I went out to the barn and swung the doors open.

William followed me, curious.

"May I be of assistance in some way?" he asked.

"No, just have a seat, it won't take long," I said, because operating the backhoe was a one man job.

So he went up the ladder to the hayloft, armed with coffee, and I swung into the cab of the backhoe, and started work.

The ground having been disturbed last week on my initial excavation, it went a lot faster this time. In short order, the ground was dug up, and the Lander lay exposed on the floor of the barn.

It was an eerie black color, absorbing the light, its sleek lines as futuristic looking as ever. I parked the backhoe, and turned it off, and William came down from the hayloft to check it out.

"So this is it," I said, with and expansive wave toward the Lander.

William maintained a healthy distance. "Any radioactivity?" he asked.

"None. Checked it with Sven's Geiger counter."

The ranch, like most in the Montana area, had trace deposits of uranium. Sven kept a Geiger counter, and I had swept the Lander last week before I reburied it.

"That doesn't mean it isn't chemically dangerous," I hastily added, "or otherwise toxic, but Sven and Kirsten have both been inside it, and they're still with us."

It was that exact minute that I remembered that Sven had died of cancer, and I wondered if exposure to elements in The Lander had been responsible. If so, it had taken fifty years to kill him.

I mentioned this to William. He nodded his awareness of the risk.

"At this age, my boy, I'm willing to take a few more chances," he said.

He moved around The Lander, taking pictures with his camera.

"How do I get inside?" he asked.

Kirsten, the only person on the planet who knew how to open the thing, arrived with paper plates loaded with scrambled eggs and bacon. She had added English muffins, a favorite of mine.

She heard his question. "I'll show you," she said, and handed us our plates.

It seemed a bit incongruous, seeing the tall, beautiful blonde in white ski clothing scampering over an artifact from another world, but she jumped in to the excavated area and nimbly moved to the front of The Lander. She pushed on a particular area, and a hatch opened.

I could hear it, but not see it; the hatch was that well machined. I moved to the side, to see it better.

"Would you like to come in?" she asked William.

He lowered himself much more carefully into the site, mindful of his eighty years, but he was still a slim person, so Kirsten showed him how to wriggle into the ship, which they had to do by lying down and pulling their bodies into the structure.

That left me outside. I knew it had a two person capacity, so I would have to wait until one of them came out.

So I sat there and ate my breakfast.

There really wasn't much to see from the outside. It was just a long, sleek, flying machine.

I briefly wondered what its range and performance characteristics were. But since I didn't even know what these figures were for any of our own military aircraft, or, for that matter, even a Boeing 747, I wasn't that interested.

I thought I heard the distant ring of the telephone, before I remembered that I had disconnected Sven's phone service.

But it wasn't a phone. It was The Lander.

An almost inaudible humming was emitting from the craft as it lay in the Montana earth.

Someone had turned it on.

That had to be Kirsten, I realized, demonstrating her knowledge of the controls to William, but I hadn't realized she was actually going to fly the thing.

But she did. The sound grew louder, just a gentle hum, and The Lander rose vertically into the air, about six feet.

Just in case, I did a little flying myself, namely, up the ladder to the hayloft.

The Lander hung there in midair for a full minute, silent, not moving, just sitting still in midair. In spite of myself, I wondered what kind of an energy source it must have, to be still operational after sixty years. Had to be nuclear. But then, what did I know about advanced energy technology.

Then, as gently as it had arisen, it lowered to the ground again and settled into its earthen cradle. The earth crunched underneath it, the humming stopped, and The Lander was silent once again.

I guess Kirsten had been telling the truth. She really had been flying the thing. I had not realized it would turn on that fast or fly so easily.

The hatch popped open and Kirsten, ever the human energy ball, popped out, her pure white ski outfit in start contrast to the silk black of The Lander. William followed her a moment later, much more slowly.

For a man who had just flown a UFO, he seemed pretty calm.

"You might have told me you were going to fly the thing," I said, coming down from the hayloft.

Kirsten smiled. This is a girl who loved to fly.

"It was just an impulse," William explained, as I helped him up out of the ditch. "I asked her to show me how it worked, and she just started it up."

Well, the technical people were going to have a field day with this one, I thought.

"What do you think?" I asked him.

"I think you have done your country a great service," he said.

"What was it like?" I wanted to know.

"See for yourself," he said, and gestured at the ship.

I took a deep breath, and handed him my coffee. Then I very gently, very slowly, let myself down into the earthen crater where The Lander sat.

Kirsten exhibited none of this caution. She bounced into the crater like a cat after a mouse and popped the hatch open. She let herself in first.

"Give me your hand," she called from inside. "I'll help you in."

I lay down on my back as I had seen her do, and pushed my head and shoulders into the narrow hatch. Kirsten, already inside, pulled my body until I was all the way in.

It was quite dark and I couldn't see a thing. Kirsten hit her flashlight, and the cabin lit up.

The first thing is, that it is quite cramped. There are seats, if you can call them that, but they more resembled children's chairs. It is hard to fit a human body on them, Kirsten having the advantage over me there, as she was a lot smaller, so I was extremely uncomfortable.

But I wrangled my body into the cockpit so I was facing forward.

I suddenly realized I could see out the front of the craft, a panoramic view which was interesting because if you're outside, you cannot see inside.

There was a flat panel to the side of the seats, which had a number of symbols on them. I did not recognize any similarity to any language I had ever seen or heard of.

Kirsten seated herself in the left seat [there were two, a pilot and copilot configuration] and watched my reactions with some amusement.

There was a headset which fit around the head, much like a band, but worn vertically, not horizontally. Kirsten put it on, and it seemed an exact fit. I remarked on this.

"Their heads were pretty large," she said.

I looked behind me. A walkway led back into the craft. It was featureless as far as I could see, and if I wanted to go back there, I was going to have to do it on my hands and knees.

"What's back there?" I asked.

"Storage," she said. "And a place to lie down. Possibly a medical cubicle."

It did not take long to see the entire inside. It was about the size of a large station wagon.

Pretty elegant and efficient design.

But it got me to wondering. This had to be a short range craft of some sort. It was almost like a fighter plane. It had no capacity for long term assignments. Of course, the range was probably incredible. But there was no place to put very much in the way of supplies for an extended mission.

"Scout craft," I muttered to myself.

Kirsten smiled, watching me think.

Of course, being inside brought more questions than it did answers. What was this craft doing in Earth airspace in the nineteen fifties? More importantly, if was a short range vessel, where was its base, or mother ship, or other similar craft?

"Any records at all?" I asked Kirsten, thinking of a ship's log or flight log.

"Probably," she said, "but I can't read them."

OK, I was impressed. It was a pretty interesting experience, being inside the thing.

But that was about all there was to it. You could see the entire inside in less than thirty seconds.

I wriggled out of the ship, rejoining William by the side of the hole in the ground where the Lander sat.

He eyed me carefully. "It is certainly interesting being a member of your family," he said. "Never a dull moment."

Good point. "A dull moment is exactly what I am after," I said. "I came to Montana for a simple family funeral, and this is what I find. I'd like to go home and forget all about this."

"What about Kirsten?" he asked.

I looked at him. We had just shown him an alien spacecraft, and the only question he had for me was about my girlfriend.

I looked back at The Lander. Kirsten popped out, and began to secure the hatch.

"I have no idea," I confessed to my uncle, 'I haven't even thought about it."

"Think about it," he recommended. "She's quite a girl."

You have to understand just what kind a statement it was for him to make. In the twenty years I had been dating, he had introduced me to just about every eligible woman he knew who might make a decent wife. I had dated debutantes and doctors and Olympic athletes and stewardesses and models, and of all of these, William had never expressed approval of any of them.

Now, after spending time with Kirsten, he had actually recommended that I see more of her, which he had not done for any woman I had ever dated in my entire life. This was quite an endorsement, coming from him.

He noted my surprise. "You're not getting any younger, nephew," he said. "You're all the family there is left."

Well, he had that right. I was it, as far as the family was concerned.

I returned my attention to the alien spacecraft in the floor of the barn, and helped Kirsten out of the crater. She had secured the hatch of The Lander.

"Any idea where it comes from?" he asked her.

"Not at all," she said. "But I've only been in it a few times."

We all sat and looked at the thing for a moment.

"We have a lot to talk about," William said. "Shall we adjourn to the ranch house?"

So we did. I swung the barn doors closed, and we retreated to the warmth and comfort of the ranch house. Kirsten poured us all coffee, and I found some cinnamon sticky buns and put them in the microwave.

We were all silent, wondering about The Lander. Actually, only William and Kirsten were thinking about The Lander. I really could have cared less.

I suppose that the presence of alien life on earth is the biggest news story in history, and that it is exciting, and I should be thrilled to be a part of it, but in reality it wasn't my job to handle this stuff, it was the job of the US Air Force, and the sooner they were working on it and I could go home, the happier I would be.

"When will your friends arrive?" I asked.

"A matter of hours," William said. "The artifact will be off of your property by nightfall tonight."

Now that was fast action. Of course, with his recent track record, William would have very high credibility right now, so they were probably giving him just about anything he wanted.

"Is there anything else your uncle has hidden around the ranch that might be of interest?" William inquired, quite seriously.

I thought a minute. The place was full of military surplus, but it was sixty years old and belonged more in a museum.

"Just military surplus," I advised William. "Nothing current or up to date."

"Just the same, I'll have our people look around when they arrive," he said.

Sounded like a plan to me.

"Will you need us here for anything?" Kirsten asked.

She was right. Now that William was here, there was no reason why we couldn't go home. And pick up our lives.

"You could be of some service," William began, "if you would be willing to brief the technicians on what you know about the artifact."

By "artifact" I assumed he meant The Lander.

"I can show them how to fly it," she said.

"That would be much appreciated," William responded. "May I interest you in a trip to our, ah, laboratory?"

That perked my ears up. I hadn't thought of it till now, but the Air Force would obviously be taking The Lander somewhere to study it. I wondered where that was, then decided I didn't want to know.

Kirsten considered this. "Will it take long?"

William, in turn, gave this thought. "It may be a week or two," he said.

"Yes, I will train them," Kirsten said, and I had a mental image of this blonde with a high school diploma training US Air Force pilots on the operation of an alien spacecraft. Seemed amusing at the time; it became less amusing later.

"Count me out," I said. "I want to go home."

William gave me a long look, but this was not negotiable. I wanted to sleep in my own bed and get on with my life.

He turned to Kirsten. "Thank you, my dear," he said, "I am certain they will find your assistance invaluable."

I finished my coffee and went to work on the cinnamon sticky buns. I could care less.

"What became of the original pilots?" he asked, and we told him, and he was a little shocked to learn that their bodies were interred in our family cemetery.

"We'll have to remove those as well," he remarked, and I suppose that was true.

The unspoken question in the room, of course, was exactly what experience the USA had in the operation of alien equipment and technology, but neither of us asked and had no intention of doing so.

In the distance we heard the sound of an aircraft overhead, but it became louder, and I remembered we were expecting guests.

"That would be our party," William said, and rose to go outside and meet them.

We followed him, and I remember thinking that we would be expecting a small jet or propeller driven craft capable of transporting a small technical team, so I was entirely unprepared for what was descending from the sky when we got outside.

It was an Antonov-124.

These things are hard to imagine unless you've actually seen one.

It is the world's largest cargo aircraft, larger even than the C5-A Galaxy, and with the exception of its cousin the 224, which is used to transport the Russian Space Shuttle, it is the largest aircraft in the world.

As calmly as if they did this every day, the crew flew this monster a few miles away, touching down at the now-abandoned Dolgan Air Force base, which at one time had handled SAC bombers for their B-52 fleet.

We watched it pass overhead.

My respect for my uncle went up several notches. This was the largest cargo carrying aircraft in America. He had real pull somewhere.

He watched it fly overhead with some satisfaction. "They should be here shortly," he said. "They'll secure the aircraft and proceed here by truck."

We just nodded, speechless. Even Kirsten, herself a pilot, knew what the Antonov 124 was.

Nothing to do now but wait. We went back inside the house.

CHAPTER TWENTY TWO

They came in three vehicles, one a flatbed trailer truck, one a bus with blacked out windows, the other a Hummer. The vehicles had been extensively modified for off road work. They swung up in front of the ranch house and William went out to meet them.

I watched him from inside through the bay window. The Hummer door opened, and one man came out, and one man only. He was dressed in comfortable work boots, black jeans and a fisherman's sweater and parka. He didn't look military to me. He was also younger than I had expected.

The two men chatted for a few minutes, and then William rejoined us inside the ranch house.

"They're going to begin working," he told us, "and ask that you remain indoors while they work, and that we close the curtains."

Kirsten immediately did so, and we were closed off from the outside world.

"I shall be assisting them," William said, "and will be in the barn. If you should need me, please call on the cellphone."

He left by the front door, and Kirsten and I were left in the big empty house just looking at each other.

She looked at me for a moment. "Thank you for helping," she said.

I knew how much it meant to her. "No problem," I said.

It was time to think about what to do next. "What will you do from here?" I asked her.

"I'll go with them," she said after reflection. "I'll have to show them how to fly the thing."

"And then?" I asked.

She looked at me over her coffee. "I haven't thought that far ahead." She paused for a moment. "What about you?"

It seemed I was the only person with a well developed plan. "I plan to go home as soon as possible and get on with my life. I have other priorities than hanging around an abandoned ranch."

"What about The Lander?" she asked. "Aren't you even curious?"

"Not at all," I responded. "The Air Force is here, they'll take it to their lab, where I assume they will make good use of the technology they find. Not much need for me on that project. I don't even know how to fly the thing."

Kirsten nodded.

I realized she had not intended to ask me about my career plans, but about what I intended to do about her. That kind of put me on the spot, since I had given the future of our relationship no thought whatsoever.

"So by the next time I see you," she said, "you'll be settled down with a wife, two kids and a mortgage."

"Not likely," I shot back, "I've gone this long without a wife, I doubt that will change."

She looked pensive. "Why did you never marry, James?"

"Because you were already taken," I responded gallantly, "and I've never met anyone like you since."

She waved off this evasive answer. "I wasn't taken when I was seventeen, James, and you passed me by. "

This was making me uncomfortable [since it was true] and she sensed this, and relented.

"We're friends, James, so tell me. Why is it that you have never let anyone get close to you? Why do you deprive yourself of the love of women?"

Well, I had never heard it put quite like that before. It wasn't that I was deliberately avoiding relationships, it was just difficult finding the right person. How to explain that to Kirsten?

I chose my words carefully.

"The truth is," I said, making it up as I went along, "is that I'm not really very good husband material. I wouldn't want to marry someone and make them unhappy because I wasn't a good enough husband."

She thought about this for a moment, and issued her evaluation.

"Nonsense," she said.

So we just looked at each other for a minute.

"Are you going to tell me the truth?" she said.

The truth was pretty brutal, but she was asking for it.

"All right," I said. "The reality is, I've never met anyone willing to work on a relationship. It takes work to make them succeed, and the women I've dated can't be trusted to water houseplants regularly, let alone take on the responsibility for sharing a household, managing financial matters, and building a two person relationship."

This was the truth. All the women I'd ever dated just wanted me to take care of them; none of them wanted the work associated with running a household and taking care of a husband.

"So you've been dating the wrong women," she concluded, and here I nodded.

A long silence while she thought about this.

"So," she said, "What would you do if you met the right woman?"

I had never thought about this, since this was about as probable as the sun blowing up in the next ten seconds.

But it was clear that Kirsten was talking about herself, not some vague future liaison I might have.

So I told her what I would have to tell her when the day came when she and I would have to, once again, go our separate ways.

"She would have to tell me," I said, "that she wanted to be my wife, and that she would be a full partner, and share in the responsibilities, as well as the rewards, for all of the years of our lives."

I felt pretty safe here. Mention work, and the women I dated scattered to the four winds. I should mention I date a lot of what are courteously referred to as "party girls".

Until that moment, I hadn't realized that Kirsten was thinking about taking our relationship to the next level, and it made me nervous, since I was entirely aware of my own deficiencies in long term relationship maintenance.

But this made her smile. "What will you do," she says, "when the day comes, and a woman says this to you?"

OK, back on safe ground. "It hasn't happened so far, and I doubt it ever will," I responded. "If it does, I'll have to ask her why she would want to be involved with someone with so little experience in stable relationships with women."

She sipped her tea, and looked across the table at me.

I was actually cheered by this conversation, for it meant that she was contemplating the next phase of her life, which up to this point had been unable to progress past her widowhood over a decade ago.

Probably the fact that the Air Force was a hundred feet away loading up The Lander was helping to close this chapter in her life, and making her think of a new beginning.

The thought of being someone's husband, however, was making me quite uncomfortable.

There was a knock at the door, and Kirsten went to get it. William entered, shaking the snow off of his boots.

"They'll be done shortly," he said. "There are a few matters left to clear up."

I hadn't realized this meant more work for me, until he went on.

"James, I'd like you to accompany one of our specialists to your family cemetery, to open the graves and retrieve the coffins containing the bodies of the pilots."

I wondered how they were going to do that in the middle of winter, what with the ground being frozen, but said I'd be happy to help.

He continued. "Kirsten, I would like to take you to the Laboratory. You will be needed there for approximately two weeks for a debriefing, and to train Air Force personnel on the operation of The Lander."

She nodded. We all just looked at each other for a moment.

"I will be leaving now," William said, "and Kirsten will accompany me. I shall leave you for a moment for your goodbyes, and James, I will be in contact with you when all of this is over."

He exited gracefully, closing the door behind him, and Kirsten and I were alone, again, in the big empty ranch house.

"So this must be goodbye," I said, not knowing what else to say.

A short silence while she watched me, then she spoke.

"Kiss me, James," she said, and so I did, walking across the floor, gathering her slim athletic body into my arms, and giving her a slow and gentle kiss.

Then I released her.

"Will I see you again?" she asked.

"Come to California," I said, "and we'll do a beach weekend."

"I will," she said, as I had known she would, since she loved the beach, "when all of this is over."

We put our jackets on and headed out the door to the barn.

The barn doors were closed, and William and the man who was obviously in command were chatting outside the door. The flatbed truck was already inside the barn, which meant the recovery team was already loading The Lander onto the truck.

"Meet someone, James," said uncle William, "this is Mr. Smith."

The young man in the black denim jeans shook my hand. "Glad to meet you," he said, "Got any more of these things?"

I laughed, shaking my head. "Mr. Smith, meet Kirsten. Kirsten, this is Mr. Smith."

They shook hands, Kirsten actually offering her hand in the Continental fashion, and Mr. Smith shaking it. I suddenly realized Kirsten was making an assessment of him: by this simple act, she established he was American with virtually no cultural awareness at all.

"Ms. Vorra, I've heard a lot about you," Smith said, "looking forward to working with you in the weeks ahead."

"Glad to help," she said quietly, with her Scandinavian reserve coming to the fore.

Smith turned to me "We'd like your permission to survey your uncle's ranch," he said, "just in case there's anything else here worth knowing about."

I looked around the horizon at the borders of Sven's massive holdings. "Be my guest," I said. "Just be aware he kept a lot of military surplus around here."

"I will, and thank you for the heads-up," Smith said. "Now I'd like you to meet someone."

He spoke quietly into a walkie talkie, and the barn doors opened and another man came out and joined out little group.

He was a squat, powerfully built man with a buzz haircut. He was dressed in dark blue cargo pants and a dark sweater, over which he wore a barn coat. I still have no idea to this day whether these guys were from a military unit or not, but they were going out of their way to appear non-military, since there were no salutes or acknowledgements of rank.

"This is Mr. Jones," Smith said. "Mr. Jones, meet James Larson."

We shook hands. Smith addressed this 'Mr. Jones' person. "James will be taking you to his family cemetery," he said, "where I believe there is something of interest to our government."

I nodded. The names "Smith" and "Jones" in government and specifically military service meant a person who was not to be identified and was on a mission beyond your security clearance, and you're not supposed to ask these people any specific questions, like, what their real names were.

"Shall we get started?" Jones asked, and I nodded assent.

I turned to William. "You have my number," I said. "Call if you need anything."

"I am sure I will," he responded, and with a final look at Kirsten and with very fond memories of the past week, I turned to go with 'Jones'.

He led me to the Hummer, which was parked outside the back end of the barn.

"I understand we have some digging to do," he said as we got in and started the vehicle.

"That will be quite interesting," I said, "since you'll be digging in frozen ground to a depth of six feet.   Got any plans for this problem?"

He steered the Hummer down the rocky gravel road toward the cemetery.   "I have some ideas," he said.

That was up to him, I thought, and said nothing further.

He didn't say anything further, either, until we arrived at the cemetery ten minutes later.

He pulled up to the front gate, and I directed him to where the graves were, and in short order, there we were, standing above the burial site.

"This is it," I said.

Jones pulled a twenty gallon gas tank from the back of the Hummer.   He walked over to the gravesite.

I watched with great interest.

He poured a clear liquid over the graves in an even distribution. It was colorless and odorless. I was mystified as to what he was doing.

Then, he backed up, and from a safe distance, lit a match and threw it onto the graves.

The liquid ignited, and burned for less than a second, and then went out. But I could suddenly hear the ground hissing, as the liquid, whatever it was, gave off enormous amounts of heat.

I actually backed up, the heat was so intense. Clouds of steam rose in great sheets from the ground.

I looked at Jones. "It'll soften up the ground," he said by way of explanation.

It certainly did. The ground actually turned to mud. The chemical continued to do its work, seeping down further and further into the ground.

Steam vented from the site for another ten full minutes before dissipating.

When it was over, the ground above the two graves was quite soft.

Jones pulled a gas powered ditch witch from the Hummer, which can excavate earth in short order, and he fired it up.

He moved it over the first grave, and it went to work.

The coffins were buried at a depth of four and a half feet. It did not take long to find them.

Jones by this time was dressed in a biohazard suit, and he handed one to me.

I had not worn one of these since my Army days, but I needed no encouragement to put one on.

We were digging up an alien life form. There was, potentially, no more greater danger to our lives.

As I dressed, I remembered what had happened when Europeans had come into contact with the Native American population in the early 1500s. By a century after first contact, over ninety percent of the Indian population had died.

It was all due to bacterial exposure.

So I paid enormous attention to getting my biohazard suit on properly.

Jones had pulled an engine hoist from the vehicle, and placed it above the grave. In addition, he had two aluminum containers capable of holding the coffins, in the back of the Hummer. These were placed on the ground at the grave's edge.

The engine hoist, fitted with a sling, easily lifted the first coffin from the ground. It was still sealed and, using the hoist, Jones slipped it into the aluminum container, then closing and sealing it. He had a hand held welder, which he used to finish the job.

I noticed, as he did so, that the aluminum containers were insulated, which meant that they would maintain the freezing temperatures, thereby not disturbing the contents within.

The excavated earth was quickly replaced, again using the ditch witch, and Jones turned his attention to the other grave.

This was also excavated in the same way, and the engine hoist did its job, and Jones quickly sealed the second coffin in the same fashion as the first.

He did not ask for help in loading the coffins into the vehicle, using the hoist to lift them off the ground, and then pushing them into the Hummer.

That was it. The guy had been an excellent choice for the job. Didn't talk much, worked fast, got the job done efficiently.

He took his biohazard suit off, and so did I, and we put them into a container and zipped it shut.

Shortly thereafter, we were inside the Hummer, and he turned it around and headed back to the ranch.

By the time we returned, the place was abandoned.

I got of the Hummer, and checked the barn.

The Lander was gone, the earth filled in and smoothed over. Even the tracks that heavy equipment had been there had been erased.

It was a little spooky, standing there on Uncle Sven's ranch, the house silent and still, the barn closed and locked. It felt abandoned. I suppose it was.

Across the fields in front of the house, I saw an amazing sight: a pair of timber wolves loping across the range.

In 1995 the Federal government reintroduced wolves into the Montana area; it was an overwhelming success, and now they have repopulated much of their original habitat.

With Sven gone only a few weeks, the wolves had sensed that they were no longer in danger, and now felt completely comfortable ranging across the grounds of the ranch.

I watched them as they moved along. They saw me, turned and stopped. They sat, just out of rifle range, the two of them, watching me.

Suddenly I felt somewhat concerned. I was not armed. These wolves were quite wild, and could run like the wind.

Jones got out of the Hummer, and watched me look around. I returned to the vehicle.

"We're done here," he said. A man of few words.

I nodded. There was nothing else to say.

"I'll have to ask you to accompany me," he said, "to Dolgan Air Force base, where the recovery team is waiting for me."

"What for?" I asked, surprised.

"The team will have questions for you," he said.

"Questions? What questions? What do I know about this? Kirsten is the one you ought to ask questions of; all I know about these bodies is that she told me they were here."

"You'll have to come with me," he repeated.

Well, I had to get back to California, and back to work. "I can't," I said, "I'm due at work in two days. If the team has questions, call me or see me in California. My uncle has my address."

"I'll have to insist," he said.

We stared at each other. "It's not negotiable," I said.

"In that case," he sighed, "I'll have to place you under arrest."

I could not believe I was hearing this. "What for?"

"I'll think of something," he said.

"You'll have to explain this to my lawyer," I said, getting angry.

"You don't seem to understand," Jones said. "There isn't going to be any lawyer, or a phone call, or a trial. If I arrest you, you'll just disappear. This is a national security matter."

I just stood there and stared at him.

This is exactly what I had been trying to avoid when I called uncle William to handle this matter. I didn't have time for a bunch of amateur Keystone Cop security types to debrief me for two years after turning The Lander over to the government. I had a life and I wanted to get back to it.

I reached for my telephone to call William, and quickly and easily he caught my arm, twisted it behind me, and put me in handcuffs.

And there I was. Detained for questioning in a national security manner. I had to be at work in two days back in California. No matter how this went, it did not look positive.

"I'll take you there in restraints if I have to, but you're going to go," he said, and shoved me toward the Hummer.

He pushed me into the passenger seat, and slammed the door.

That's when I noticed the keys were in the ignition.

The car automatically locked after five seconds, which meant that Jones had actually locked himself out of his own vehicle, with a prisoner and two alien bodies inside.

With my hands cuffed behind me, I was in no position to drive off with the Hummer, and would not have if I could have, not wanting to add evading arrest to what was already turning into a bad afternoon, but it was funny.

Jones walked around to the driver's side of the vehicle, but when he tried to open the door, it was of course locked.

He did not look happy.

He banged on the window. "Open the door!" he said.

I had not driven a Hummer since my Army days, and the one I had was outfitted with canvas doors. This monster had four inch thick metal doors. I had no idea how to unlock it.

"How?" I yelled back.

"The unlock switch!" he yelled back.

Now that wasn't really useful. Like I would know where the switch was in this car. I did look around, though.

"Hurry!" he yelled, and I wondered why he was in such a panic, but then I looked out the window and realized why.

The wolves were moving.

Now Jones had a very real problem.

Since the reintroduction of wolves to Montana, they had multiplied faster than anyone had predicted. Natural born killers, Sven had called them once, as he picked them off with his Korean War era sniper rifle after he found them bothering his cattle. They had feasted on the elk and cattle that fill the Montana countryside, and now they were a regular menace.

There were no recorded attacks of wolves on humans, Sven had explained to me once, but there were a lot of missing persons reported in Montana, and so Sven was armed, at all times, and always kept a long range rifle in the cab of his truck, after he had found them attacking his cattle, and he did this just in case they caught him outside, away from the house.

Just as they had now caught Jones.

They were moving at very high speed, crossing the space separating them from the car in very short order. I watched them almost hypnotically, marveling at their grace and speed.

I could do this, of course, since I was inside an armored Hummer, and safe from attack, but Jones was in another situation entirely.

He was frantic, smashing on the windows of the Hummer in an attempt to break them open before the wolves got to him. This did not help, since the Hummer had reinforced windows.

He was screaming when they got him, and the pair leapt from the ground in a single fluid movement, knocking Jones off his feet onto the ground, and sinking their fangs into his throat.

That was pretty much it for Jones. It was over in seconds. I had never seen anything like it in my life.

I could hear them snarling outside, as they methodically ripped him to bits.

It was winter, after all, and food was limited, and he had been an easy target.

Lots of people move to the Western states to retire, to enjoy the big sky and the wide open spaces. Too often they fail to respect the elements that make up the ecosystem of the far West, and too often they pay the price for it, whether it be tourists in a rented Honda freezing to death in a sudden blizzard, or in this case, ignorance of the nature of the animals that rule the prairie.

I nervously checked the windows of the Hummer. The car was locked and the windows closed, so I assumed I was pretty safe.

After about fifteen minutes the wolves bolted from the shredded corpse, and raced back across the open range.

I watched them go, making sure they were out of sight before attempting to get out of my predicament.

After a dedicated search, I found the unlock button for the Hummer. With my hands behind me, hitting the switch was some difficulty, but I managed it, and then pulled the door open and exited the vehicle.

Jones' body was lying directly behind the Hummer. Except for the clothing, there was little to identify it as the remains of a human being.

I turned the body over with my boot, and heard the jingle of keys.

Turned out he kept them on the back of his belt, so I reached down and yanked them off.

Handcuff keys are easily identifiable, so in short order I had the cuffs off.

Now what to do, I wondered.

CHAPTER TWENTY THREE

I was in the middle of Montana, in the middle of winter, with a Hummer containing two fifty year old alien bodies, with a dead Federal agent at my feet.

Of course, I called William.

But this time, there was no answer; it went to voicemail.

I tried Kirsten, too, but got the same result.

I remembered they were both flying to some Laboratory the Air Force kept hidden somewhere in one of the big empty Western states, so that meant they were probably in the air, which is why I could not reach them.

What now, I thought.

So who could I call, with my somewhat limited experience in transporting the bodies of dead aliens and Federal agents.

This was somewhat outside of my training and experience.

Well, I could just call the Air Force. Then look forward to spending the next zillion years in detention trying to explain my role in all of this.

Or I could wait until William called back. But the recovery team, and presumably their transport aircraft, was waiting for Jones at Dolgan Air Force Base a few miles away; if he did not show up, they'd come looking for him.

There was one other option.

I had served in the Army. Now I'd been in the first Gulf War, and had been discharged afterwards. But a friend of mine had continued his service afterward, and currently was serving in the Army as a Major in a fairly sensitive position. I wasn't supposed to know what he was working on, but I knew for a fact he was assigned to the anti-matter bomb project.

Anti-matter has to be manufactured; it only occurs in nature in trace amounts, and is instantly annihilated. But manufacture it in quantity, and combine it with matter, which is what all of us are made of, and you have a destructive force of unbelievable proportions.

The creation of an anti-matter weapon is supposed to be a) impossible and b) too expensive to be practical but I also knew that c) neither of these was true and that work on such a weapon was well advanced.

As to how I knew this, well, ask anyone who has ever served in the US military if they have ever seen anything they should not have seen, or if they have accidentally run across something beyond their security clearance, and the answer is usually yes, but they kept their mouths shut.

Like many other veterans, I had been in a shooting war, and when that happens, a lot of the really serious classified hardware comes out of storage. In the Gulf the public became aware of the capabilities of the F-117 Nighthawk fighter, and the stealth bomber, but there was a whole lot of other equipment deployed in that war that was seriously interesting and quite effective.

I had handled some of it, and become aware of a lot more.

During the course of the buildup before the war, and the drawdown afterwards, I had received discreet inquiries from a number of government agencies as to whether or not I might be interested in working with them on this type of technology.

I had given it serious thought, since the technology they were working with was science fiction stuff, extremely advanced, and very exciting.

The problem arose with the working conditions.

The facilities were located in the middle of nowhere, far from any city, or cultural resource, and even if you liked living in the country, which I did, these places were often on lockdown, and security had to know where you were every hour of the day and night, so you were never truly alone or had any fun. Plus, if you were single, you were in real trouble, since young beautiful girls do not hang around top secret US military bases in large numbers.

I, of course, being single, placed a very high priority on living in an area where there was an abundant supply of beautiful young women, which is why I live in California, which has the highest per capita number of hot blondes in the length and breadth of the civilized world.

So I had turned them down.

However, if you were married, this kind of offer was irresistible. It have you the chance to work on state of the art technology, with decent working hours, a good salary, with health care and pension benefits, and there were even decent schools for your kids on these bases.

My friend, whose name was Luke Chivington, had fallen for one of his fellow officers, an Air Force type name of Sherry and whose last name I forget, and after a whirlwind courtship they had gotten married.

They continued their military careers, trying to find a posting where they could serve together even though they were in different branches of the military, and they had eventually wound up finding such a slot in one of these aforementioned high-tech top-security bases out in the middle of nowhere.

The middle of nowhere, Montana.

As I remembered, it was north of Billings. I had even planned to visit them on this trip if time permitted, but time did not permit.

It was a very long drive from here, but a short hop by air.

I did not want to disappear from view for the next two months. I did not want to have to try to explain to the Air Force how it came to be that their guy had been eaten by wolves. I especially did not want to be found driving around Montana in someone else's Hummer with two alien bodies inside.

So I called Major Chivington.

He was in the contacts section of my cellphone, so I had him on the line in less than a minute.

"Luke," I said, "how the hell are you?"

"Great," he shot back, "what have you been up to?"

Luke is an actual smart person. His IQ is way, way, up there, and his wife is probably at his level or even higher, which is why their relationship is still red hot after all of these years.

"Not much…work, work, work…..listen….I have something of a situation here….I'm calling to ask for your opinion on something."

"Shoot," he said promptly. Like most Army people, he was pretty to-the-point.

"Would you be willing to help me with a Question," I asked, putting extra emphasis on the "Q" in 'question'.

As a side note, at one time, one of the highest security clearances one could obtain was a "Q" clearance – it was for really high level stuff.

There was a very long silence on the other end of the line.

The principal way of discreetly communicating a high security problem over a telephone line, he and I had worked out, was this 'Question' keyword.

Like the phrase "a legal question" I used with my uncle William, the phrase "help me with a question" between the two of us referred to an incident early in our mutual military history.

When we were at some briefing during the buildup for the war, I had asked a question, the answer to which was outside of my security clearance.

The briefing officer had replied, "Good question," and promptly refused to answer it, citing security concerns.

I had thought no more about it, until after the briefing, when I was approached by this officer, who had offered me the desired information, if I was willing to consider working in his organization.

I had turned them down, but Luke had taken them up on the offer, and was now working on some pretty high level stuff.

Luke thought about this. "Sure!" he replied enthusiastically. "What can I help you with?"

His family went back to about 1585 in North America, so he had, like, a seventeenth generation security clearance.

"I've found a rare dinosaur," I said over the open phone line. "Would you like to help recover it?"

The "dinosaur" term is a private joke. At one time the F-117 Nighthawk fighter was absolutely Above Top Secret, but we had heard an aircraft designer refer to it as a "dinosaur", so we speculated about exactly what type of aircraft he had to have been working on where Stealth technology was actually obsolete. We concluded it had to be pretty advanced.

There are, of course, lots of real dinosaur skeletons in Montana, so anyone listening on this phone line would assume we were talking about the real thing.

"I'll be there in an hour," Luke said. Where are you?"

"Sven's ranch," I replied. Luke had stayed there over some summers. "How can you be here in an hour?"

"I'm the Base Commander!" he said. "Got my own plane!"

This is a perk of command. Base commanders have their own aircraft.

"Bring something to haul cargo with," I advised.

"Roger that!" he said, and hung up.

I relaxed. Between us, we knew enough generals to manage this problem.

He arrived in less than an hour, in an enormous Sikorsky helicopter. He bounded out of the chopper and I went to meet him.

We shook hands.

"Hey, how the hell are you?" he said. "Long time no see!"

"Tired and overworked," I responded truthfully. "How are you?"

"Great, great," he said. "Lots of work, but that's OK."

Since we were in the middle of a war, that had to be true.

"So, that was an unusual phone call," he said. "What's the story?"

So I told him.

I told him about uncle Sven, and Kirsten, and The Thing in the Barn, and the recovery team, and the bodies in the Hummer, and the wolves, who had partially eaten the guy now lying in the blood stained snow.

Luke handled this like he did this every day.

"Sure," he said, taking the news of extra terrestrial life on earth very calmly, "I got it. Two bodies, alien, in the Hummer. One body, human, partially eaten by wolves, next to the Hummer. You want me to take possession of these."

"That's it," I said, "but the important part is, leave me out of it!"

I had a life, which I would like to get back to. It was a lot of work, but better than hanging around this place.

"Sorry about Sven," Luke said, and the guy was a real officer and gentleman, to take the time at this moment to express his condolences regarding the loss of my uncle, whom we both had admired a lot.

"Thanks, Luke," I said. "I appreciate that."

He snapped his fingers, and two men in flight suits emerged from the chopper.

Luke directed them to take the aluminum cases out of the Hummer, which they did, and they put the mortal remains of the security guy in a body bag, and that went on the chopper, too.

All told, he was on the ground for less than twenty minutes. Luke gave new meaning and breadth to the term "military precision".

I climbed in the chopper with him, and we got airborne. The aircraft swung away from Sven's ranch, and away we went.

The chopper was extremely uncomfortable, and I had to sit on one of those little fold down seats it has, and it was cold, and I was miserable, which is why I had served in the Army, not the Air Force.

Not that I'd ever admit it in public, but the Air Force really is a fantastic group of extremely dedicated and capable people, and I was glad they were on our side. I did wonder how Luke, an Army guy, was able to lay his hands on an Air Force chopper, and furthermore how he got to be base commander as a Major, but I knew better than to actually ask.

The flight took an hour.

Luke handed me a thermos of coffee, which I gratefully accepted. I took a sip of this stuff, and realized I was drinking real Sumatra coffee. This stuff was insanely expensive and difficult to get. Luke always ate well in the field, and so did his men.

For the first time, I was beginning to relax. Luke could handle anything up to and including a nuclear war, so I'm sure he could handle this.

"Got time for a quick debrief when we land?" he asked through the intercom. "Give me one day, and I'll have you flown home by direct military transport."

"Sure!" I yelled back, as it was difficult to hear over the chopper motor.

California was now only one day away. I could hardly wait.

The chopper descended to the middle of the prairie at the base of some low foothills. It really was in the middle of nowhere; I could not see a road anywhere. There were no buildings, no power lines or anything else.

Then the side of the mountain opened up.

Someone had built a hangar door into the side of the mountain. It was so well designed to resemble the mountain, that to the naked eye at fifty feet it was not possible to tell.

An aircraft tug came out and pulled the chopper into the hangar.

The chopper door opened from the outside, and I was helped out by the crew, and I got my first look at one of America's secret military bases.

It looked like any other air base, except that it was built into a mountain. There were a number of aircraft there, all of them modern and declassified. It was pretty much a standard military hangar. Mechanics were running around servicing the aircraft.

Luke bounced out behind me. He is physically fit and trim, and exercises regularly, unlike myself, as I am overweight and do not exercise unless threatened with death.

"Welcome to Shangri-La!" he said, and I laughed, recognizing it as the name Franklin

Roosevelt had given to a mythical secret American base from which Doolittle's Raiders had struck Imperial Japan in 1942.

"This way!" he said, and I followed him.

We left the main hangar area and moved into a corridor leading further inside the base. None of the doors were marked or identified in any way. Military personnel were all about, all wearing US Air Force and US Army uniforms. So there was a lot of security, but these people had to be cleared for this.

Luke opened one of the doors and led me inside. It was a conference room, with a large table surrounded by a number of chairs. An airman stood at one end of the table, pouring coffee into cups. There was a pastry tray stacked with cinnamon buns.

Luke sat down at one end of the table, pushing the pastry tray over. "Your poison is cinnamon, right?" he said.

Well, he had remembered. It certainly was.

I got some coffee, too.

"So tell me," he began, "give me this whole story."

I started at the beginning, and gave him the entire version of what had happened. I finished by telling him that this security guy had attempted to detain me at Sven's ranch, and how he had locked himself out of his own vehicle and had been promptly eaten by wolves. In addition, I expressed my desire to see this technology turned over to the US government for appropriate research.

Finally, I explained why I had chosen to contact him, as I suspected he was working on or at least familiar with advanced reactor technology.

"Am I right?" I asked.

He looked at me for a minute. "Let's just say you came to the right place," he said.

We looked at each other for a minute.

"I can put you in touch with my uncle William," I said, "he knows where they actually took the Lander, and where they're working on it."

Then I received the surprise of my life.

"That won't be necessary," Luke said. "He's already here."

He got up and opened the conference room door, and uncle William walked in.

Of course. It made sense. Where would the Air Force send a nuclear powered artifact? To their most advanced reactor research facility. I had thought it was in Nevada, but Montana made perfect sense.

"James," William said, walking over and shaking my hand, "I see that you are acquainted with Major Chivington."

"William," I said, returning the handshake, "actually, we served together in the Army."

"Glad to hear it," he said. "It will make things easier."

"So this is where you brought The Lander?" I asked.

He nodded. "It is already under study."

Luke motioned out toward the hangar. "The bodies have been recovered and are in the morgue," he said.

"Excellent," William said. "So everything is on schedule."

I just saw there slack jawed, amazed that these two people knew each other.

"Where's Kirsten?" I asked.

"She's getting suited up," William said, "she's scheduled to give an introductory class on the Lander in less than an hour. Like to see her?"

"Sure would," I said, speaking the unvarnished truth.

"Let's be about it, then," William said, and he stood up.

"Major," William said, "I'll have them both on the hangar floor at the appointed time."

"Great!" Luke said, and turned to me. "Good job," he said, and that meant a lot, since he is one of only a few people I respect in this world.

We left the conference room and William took me deeper into the base, to an officers quarters area.

There were a series of small apartments at the back of the base, which I assumed were for visitors. William motioned to one of these doors.

"She's inside," he said. "I'll leave it to you to disturb her. One of our airmen will be here shortly, to take you to the conference."

He gave me a pat on the back, and left.

I stood there for a moment, then knocked on the door.

After a moment, the door swung open, and Kirsten was there.

"JAMES!" she yelled, and pulled me inside and kissed me.

I kissed her back, believe me.

"How did you get here?" she wanted to know.

"Long story," I said. "I'll explain later."

My life was getting more complicated by the minute, which had never been my intention, but getting close to Kirsten made me feel better.

She was wearing an Air Force flightsuit, which is like a big canvas bag, and ordinarily not a very attractive garment, but on her, it was stunning. It's always nice to see a hot blonde wearing the uniform of your country.

It had no rank or insignia, so at least she hadn't enlisted yet.

"Where's the Lander?" I wanted to know.

"It's in the hangar," she said. "Where are the bodies?"

"Also in the hangar," I replied.

"Did everything go OK?" she asked.

Here I decided to leave out the part about the security guy being eaten by wolves. It had been her idea, after all, to turn The Lander over to the government.

"Sure," I said, lying with the ease of the pathologically afflicted, "it all went smoothly."

"I'm glad," she said, and gave me another kiss.

After the long chopper ride, she smelled very nice.

"What are you doing here?" she said. "I thought you were going back to California."

I thought fast. "They needed help with the bodies," I said.

She nodded, accepting this blatant disregard for the truth as fact.

"Thank you for helping," she said, "I know you wanted to go home to California."

"You got that right," I said, for once expressing the truth, "I can't wait to get home."

I looked at her flightsuit again. "Are you going to be flying today?"

She looked down at her perfect figure, neatly outlined by the flightsuit. "I have to give a lecture on how to fly the Lander," she said.

I nodded. Not much else to say to that.

"Would you like to come with me?" she asked.

"Not really," I said. I had no aspirations to pilot the thing any time soon.

"Come anyway," she said, "it will be easier for me to talk if you're there."

I thought about that for a minute. It sounded suspiciously like work.

"I'll make you coffee," she said. "And a steak dinner tonight. Plus anything else you want."

OK, that was officially an irresistible offer.

"Sure, all right, count me in," I said. "I'll be there."

She smiled. "Just give me a minute to finish getting ready," she said.

So I sat down, and she zipped into the bathroom, where she brushed that incredible mop of blonde hair into submission and tied it with a little blue ribbon. That apparently was all that was needed, for in a few minutes she was back again.

"All set," she said, and sat down next to me.

We just looked at each other.

"Hey, I missed you," I said to her.

"I missed you too," she said.

I put my arm around her, and she rested her head on my shoulder.

My heart beat faster, as it always does around Kirsten Vorra, and my whole body relaxed. For a moment I thought about the next two days, when I would leave her and return to California, and never see her again.

Even then, I realized what a special woman she was. California is full of beautiful blondes, you can find a dozen of them on any beach, but no one I have ever dated in my life has ever made me feel the way she does. I wondered what I was going to do about her, but fortunately my inability to manage complex relationships came to my rescue, and I gave up trying to figure it out.

There was a knock at the door. I went to open it, and, as promised, there was an airman to take us to the hangar.

"Mr. Larson, Ms. Vorra, I am Airman Pickford," he said, "Will you accompany me?"

We both moved into the corridor, and as we did so, he handed both of us a single sheet of paper.

"These are your security clearances," he said. "Please keep them with you."

I looked them over. At the bottom, I realized that uncle William had signed them. A chill ran through me. William was the man who handled security for recovery of alien artifacts. This was an entire chapter of William's life about which I knew nothing. I had a sudden newfound respect for the man.

Airman Pickford also handed us security badges, which hung around our necks. Properly attired, we moved back into the hangar area.

The Lander was there, surrounded by a swarm of people. It had been cleaned of the Montana earth in which it had been buried, and was sitting on an elevated platform. For the first time I was able to see it as it would appear in flight. It was spooky looking, with its dark black color and sleek profile.

Yet, it did not seem to be much more advanced in design than a Stealth bomber. Slap a US Air Force insignia on the side and park it in public view in Chicago O'Hare airport, and it would look like any other Lockheed fighter plane.

Of course, it had this design sixty years ago.

A tall skinny fellow with white hair was standing on a ladder, which adjoined the open hatch of the craft. Catching sight of us, he called the meeting to order.

"Gentlemen, ladies," he said, "our guest lecturer has arrived. Can I ask you all to move to your seats and we will begin."

Folding chairs had been set up next to the alien ship, and the crowd of people, approximately twenty of them, moved to their seats.

William was there. He was seated in the far back, and I joined him there.

"Thank you again, nephew," he whispered.

"The credit is all yours," I said truthfully, "we couldn't have done this without you."

The white haired guy introduced Kirsten.

"I'd like you all to meet a remarkable young woman," he began, "who is responsible for bringing to us, intact, the vehicle you see before you. She has rendered our country a great service, and we are in her debt. Ladies and gentlemen, Ms. Kirsten Vorra."

Kirsten gracefully stood and moved to the podium, as the audience applauded politely.

When she has to be, she can be a very articulate speaker, and this was one of those times. She went right to the heart of the matter.

"My husband," she began, "was killed in the first Gulf War when his A-10 Warthog was destroyed by anti-aircraft fire."

You could have heard a pin drop. She had their complete attention.

"It is my intention," she went on, "to turn this craft over for research in order to develop new technologies which will enable the armed forces of the United States to dominate the skies, and in so doing better withstand the threat from enemy anti aircraft weapons."

Looking back, I really don't think the collection of scientists assembled there expected the cute young blonde to have the grasp of aeronautics that Kirsten demonstrated that day.

She had their undivided attention, and continued with her comments.

For my part I was very relieved. The Lander and the bodies were both in the possession of the

US Air Force, or whichever government agency was responsible for this hidden base, so my job was just about over.

I was looking forward to a short technical debrief with one of Luke Chivington's scientific staff, after which I would at long last return to the clear blue air of California, where I intended to take a week off and sleep at the beach.

I remember, later, that this is what I was thinking when it happened.

It started slowly at first, a twinge of muscles in my left chest, a vague feeling of discomfort, as if I'd had something to eat that didn't agree with me.

But then it spread, from my chest, to my left shoulder, and then a surge of sharp electrical pain.

It washed over me in waves, the pain getting stronger and stronger. It went from being uncomfortable to agonizing.

I was having my first heart attack.

What had I expected? A life of hurried meals, too much steak, smoking cigars whenever I had the chance, exercise sacrificed to a busy career, and twenty pounds overweight. It had been just a question of time.

And the time was now.

By this time I was quietly gasping for breath. William, seated next to me, noticed this.

"James," he said, "are you quite all right?"

I shook my head and moved my right hand over my heart. The pain was now like being struck by thunderbolts, like a giant weight on my chest.

William understood instantly. He stood, and then reached over and helped me to my feet.

We were in the back of the room, and we turned so that my condition was not obvious to the people attending the conference. It wasn't actually necessary, all eyes were glued on the hot blonde giving the talk on the technical performance characteristics of the alien spacecraft.

I was not entirely unprepared for this. You can't eat steak everyday and not be aware of the ultimate price tag.

Now, the key to my continued survival was in my wallet.

I always kept two aspirin on hand. It was one of those tiny packets the airport travel shops sell, containing just two aspirin. I had known this day would come, and had prepared accordingly.

I pulled it out of my wallet, tore it open and swallowed the aspirin whole. William grabbed my arm and steered me out of the conference room.

He tried to get me to the elevator, but I got about halfway down the hallway when my clock ran out. I had to sit down, so I pretty much collapsed onto the floor, William's arms locked on mine, making sure it was a controlled crash.

"Wait here," he said, "I'll get help."

He sprinted to a wall phone, and called the base operator. He ordered a medical team to our location, then returned to my side.

"Help is on the way," he said. "Stay with me."

In the corridor where we were sitting, a number of young men and women in Air Force uniform had been coming and going, but now they congregated around me.

"What is it?" one of the young men asked. "Does he need help?"

"Heart attack," William answered quietly. "Help me lift him up."

Help was needed, since William's spine would never be able to handle the load of my uncooperative body, so I sat there like a rag doll while a dozen strong hands lifted me from the floor and leaned me against a wall.

Standing made me feel a lot better, breathing was easier.

"How is it?" William asked,

I realized I was probably dying, but I sure didn't want him to be concerned, so I lied through my teeth and said, "Better."

The elevator doors opened and four Air Force medics with a gurney emerged, swiftly moving to my side.

They pulled me on to the gurney and quickly fitted me with an oxygen mask. I breathed in the pure oxygen, and felt better at once.

One of them gave me a pill to put under my tongue, which was nitroglycerin, a medicine used to dilate the coronary arteries.

It was almost immediately effective, and I felt the pressure on my chest ease and the medication took effect.

The medics worked silently, taking my blood pressure and moving onto the elevator. They fitted an EKG onto my chest, William accompanying them as they did their work.

The elevator descended several levels, then a long trip down a corridor to the infirmary.

I learned later that as an Air Force base with mostly young healthy people, I was the first actual heart attack victim they had ever treated. But the medical staff was calm and unworried, since even though they didn't get a lot of this type of business, they knew what to do when it showed up.

They drew blood and stuck IVs in my arm, and a young brunette woman who looked like she belonged in high school injected medications into the IV. This person, I learned, was the doctor.

"I'm Doctor Windsor," she said. "You're having a heart attack. We're giving you medications to ease the load on your heart. I need you to relax and try to rest. Can you answer some questions?"

I nodded, and she continued. "Do you have any allergies?" No. "Are you taking any medications?" No. "Do you have any other medical problems?" No. "Does your family have any history of coronary artery disease?" I had no idea.

She personally checked my pulse and viewed the EKG. "Lay back and relax," she said. "We'll take good care of you."

Sounded like a good idea to me. I lay back against the pillow, inhaling the dry pure oxygen through the mask, and relaxed.

"What's your name?" she asked, leaning over me.

"James Larson," I said.

"All right, James Larson, you're in good hands. Rest easy."

So I did. There was not much else I could do.

CHAPTER TWENTY FOUR

William stayed by my side for the first few hours. I was concerned about Kirsten, but he assured me he would keep this matter private.

When you have a heart attack, you feel fairly tired, although you are not sleepy. I lost all interest in doing anything at all except looking around the infirmary.

The infirmary was a small clinic, with two small treatment rooms and then a small surgery bay, of which I was now the principal resident. There were not other patients at the time.

As I looked around, I realized that I had friends here. The two aluminum cases housing the bodies brought back from the ranch were on a pallet in one of the treatment rooms.

Seemed logical, I thought, to bring them to the medical clinic. I wondered if they would be opened and autopsied here, but looking around, the clinic seemed unequipped for such a task.

It was, however, equipped with imaging technology. I recognized an X ray unit and well as a portable MRI.

The doors at the far end of the clinic opened. Dr. Windsor entered, accompanied by uncle William, and Luke.

They all looked very serious. I suppose this is because I had suffered a heart attack and would not be able to tell them about the UFO if I died. It made me laugh.

"Hey, man," Luke said with a concerned look on his face, "what happened to you?"

I laughed. It was painful, but it was worth it.

"Change of plan," I said, "the cigars caught up with me."

Dr. Windsor looked distinctly unhappy. "How long have you smoked?" she asked.

I thought for a minute. "Maybe two cigars a month."

Two cigars a month didn't seem that bad to me, but she shook her head, looked even more unhappy, and checked my EKG pattern.

While I had been dozing, someone had moved a crash cart next to my bed. Dr. Windsor noticed me looking at this.

"Just in case," she said,

"How long do I have to stay here?" I asked.

"A few days at least," she said. "I have a cardiologist flying in from Walter Reed to check you out.

Luke raised his eyebrows. The medical staff at Walter Reed is usually reserved for treating Congressmen.

"You're a very important person," William said, "we'd appreciate it very much if could hang in a bit longer."

"Where's Kirsten?" I asked.

"She's working with the technical team," Luke said. "She's be a while. Not to worry."

"Does she know?" I asked.

"Not yet," Luke replied. "Do you want us to tell her?"

Dr. Windsor shook her head. "I wouldn't recommend it."

That was an interesting comment. "Why not?" William said.

"Something like that, you tell a woman in person," Dr. Windsor replied, revealing for the first time that underneath the technically skilled exterior that she was a real living breathing female.

The three of us guys just looked at her for a minute, but she was right.

"I'll arrange it," she said. "Have her come by this evening. I'll make sure the medical staff gives you some personal time together."

She promptly blasted me with more morphine, the first time in my life I had received such a powerful medication. Having a heart attack is no fun, and morphine makes me feel sick.

She left us alone, and the three of us looked at each other.

Something was clearly bothering Luke. "James, the fact is I have some pretty important questions for you about your uncle Sven, your girlfriend Kirsten and what you've been up to the past few days. Are you up to it?"

I felt tired, but I certainly was not in any pain at all, not since they hit me with morphine. "Sure."

Luke sat down next to me and pulled his chair closer.

But before we got started, I had to go over something with William.

"William," I said. "I have a request for you."

He moved closer. I was going to need his help on this.

"I realize I have a medical problem," I said, "but as soon as I'm stable, I want out of this clinic and I want to go back to California. I can recover there as long as needed."

Ever the patrician, William registered surprise. "You didn't seriously think I'd let my only nephew recover from a heart attack in a base clinic, did you?"

Come to think of it, it would not be like him to trust me care to someone he did not know, regardless of their qualifications.

"You'll be taken by hospital jet to California," William said. "You will leave at daybreak. You already have a suite reserved at the Pebble Beach clinic."

That was too funny. The Pebble Beach clinic was a state of the art, extremely private and insanely expensive surgery center and postoperative recovery facility located on the coast of central California. It catered to the truly rich, and protected the privacy of its patients with legendary care.

I was moving up in the world.

"Give Major Chivington all the information you can," William said. "I'll be with Kirsten in the hangar. When you're able, I'll bring Kirsten by, and you can talk to her."

He gave Major Chivington a nod, and left the room to rejoin the conference in the hangar.

So for the next two hours Luke ran through a long list of questions, mostly about uncle Sven and Kirsten, and what she had told me, and what I knew about the craft and its occupants.

It didn't take long, since I knew very little about the ship, the crew or what Sven had been doing with it all of these years. I told Luke, who I had known for two decades, that Kirsten was taking a huge step, giving away her privacy to turn the artifact over to the government, when she could just as easily let it rest under the Montana sky for eternity.

Luke had actually been trained as an intelligence officer, so he got what he needed from me in just a few hours. I had to take a break now and then to relax and take a deep breath and rest, but it was better than just sitting in bed, as the clinic did not even have a TV.

After that, we just sat for a bit in the silence that friends can enjoy.

Luke, however, noticed the aluminum cases sitting on a pallet in one of the treatment rooms.

"Are those our guests?" he asked.

"The very same," I responded. "Sixty years in the ground. That's going to be one hell of an autopsy."

We were both thinking the same thing. There were two bodies in the next room and an X Ray scanner not in use.

Dr. Windsor chose this moment to re-enter the clinic.

"How's the patient?" she asked, watching the monitors as they tracked my cardiac rhythms across the monitor.

"Bored stiff," I said. "Ready to go home."

"Not today," she said. "We've be watching you for a few days."

I didn't have the heart to tell her that I was going to be transferred to a private clinic within twenty four hours.

Dr. Windsor turned her attention to Luke. "Major Chivington," she said. "A question for you."

"Shoot!" he replied, in that casual way of his, which he uses on civilians. When addressing other members of the military, he uses a much more formal conversational pattern.

"It's about your other patients," she said, gesturing at the sealed metal coffins, "I'd love to go over the medical files on them. This would be my only chance to do this kind of work."

Luke looked at the doctor for a moment. She was clearly excited, and in fact no one knew what was in those cases, as no post mortem had ever been conducted: Sven and Olaf had simply put the bodies into the coffins and buried them the next day. There were no medical files. Luke knew this; I had told him.

"There are no medical files, doctor," he said, "as a matter of fact there are no medical records at all on those bodies. There hasn't been time."

Clearly Dr. Windsor had figured this out. "I am at your service," she said, "if you would like those begun immediately."

Well, that was a moment I'm not going to forget in a hurry. I was lying in a hospital bed, with two IVs in my arms, recovering from a heart attack, listening to an Army intelligence officer and a medical doctor discussing the autopsy of two alien bodies recovered from my uncle's farm.

"I'm not sure I'm cleared to give you permission to conduct any sort of an autopsy," Luke said, "and of course there is the question of controlling infection."

She nodded. "This facility sits on a Bio Level 5 laboratory," she responded, "and passive radiographic imaging could be easily done without disturbing the contents."

I was absolutely stunned, but Luke seemed pretty calm.

The existence of the Bio Level 5 facilities has been rumored, but never confirmed. It is the highest level of biological security, and no government has ever publicly admitted ownership of one, because Bio Level 4 facilities are used to control the most dangerous pathogens, such as smallpox or Ebola virus. The construction of a Bio Level 5 facility would be an admission that something more dangerous than smallpox or Ebola exists, and that would have to come from an off-planet source.

That meant that this place was equipped for such an eventuality, and managed such concerns regularly.

Luke obviously knew this, he was not surprised by the news. "What have you got in this clinic, that could image the contents of the coffins without opening them?"

She pointed to a massive machine in the next room. "I have a fluoroscope, and am qualified to use it; I can do a real-time study immediately."

I looked at Luke, he looked at me, we both looked at the doctor. "By all means, doctor," he said, "a fluoroscopic x-ray is certainly justifiable, if for no other reason than to ensure we picked up the right coffins."

She moved immediately into the next room, and pushed one of the coffins into the X-ray chamber.

The coffins themselves were inside the aluminum cases the recovery team had supplied, and the cases were sitting on top of gurneys capable of holding their weight. So it was an easy matter for Dr. Windsor to push them along, even though she was, like, about a hundred and ten pounds herself.

"We perform this procedure routinely," she said, "as we are a receiving laboratory for the POW-MIA laboratory in Hawaii."

She moved with the calm swift movements that doctors often pick up when they work in an emergency room. In short order she had the first coffin in front of the fluoroscope, and got it turned on.

"I'll send you a signal," she said, and with the activation of a number of switches, the X-ray screen appeared over my bed, so I could see what she was doing.

She closed the X-ray lab door, and she went into the control room, which I assume was shielded from the massive amounts of radiation that these machines generate. Luke accompanied her, but they activated a speaker over my bed so I could hear them talking.

"Beginning examination," she said, and her voice lost all expression as the scanner began its work. She spoke aloud, reporting on the findings.

"The following is dictation for patient Alpha, recovered from central Montana as of this date. The subject is enclosed in a standard metal coffin circa 1955, which is itself enclosed in an aluminum alloy biohazard container."

The scanner began to move over the coffin. I was absolutely fascinated. The image of the coffin inside the aluminum container became visible. The scanner was going to move from one end of the coffin to another.

She continued her report. "Initial examination confirms the existence of a skull. Prominently noted is an enlarged cranium and oversized orbits."

It had a large head and big eyes, is what that meant. The scanner was imaging the alien skull on the screen: it was very differently proportioned than a human skull.

"The lack of classical nasal bony architecture is noted," she said, which meant it did not have a normal nose.

"A mandible is present," she went on, "however no teeth or similar structures are noted. No similarity is noted to homo sapiens."

OK, so it wasn't human.

"Extensive fractures are noted in the frontal and temporal aspects of the skull," she said thoughtfully, noting the ghostly x-ray images on her screen, "with similar damage noted to the frontal and nasal sinuses."

The alien has sustained skull fractures in the crash. Not a surprise.

"The survivability of such injuries is doubtful," Dr. Windsor continued, her eyes glued to the screen.

The scanner continued its progress.

"The specimen does have cervical vertebra," she confirmed, "however these too are extensively fractured and broken."

It was a very short body. The scanner moved relentlessly through the coffin. It was awe-inspiring.

There were ribs, and a pelvis, and arms and legs, and hands and feet. But the number and arrangement of the bones were entirely different.

All in all, it confirmed what I already knew: that the pilots of the wrecked ship were small, and they had died on impact.

"I'd love to do a soft tissue examination," Dr. Windsor said, "but the bodies will have to be removed to the laboratory."

"Very well," Luke said, "I'm sure that will be arranged, and I can put you in contact with the medical team if you prefer to work on this project."

She nodded. "Thank you," she said. "I'll do a similar study on the next coffin."

And she did, too. She manhandled the first gurney out of the X-ray lab, and wheeled the next one in, and in short order had the second coffin up on the screen.

The second body was in worse shape than the first, with a number of bones simply shattered from the impact. But the skeletons were complete, and I knew the data they provided would be priceless.

All in all, little Dr. Windsor was a whirlwind of efficiency. It was an interesting day.

Eventually she finished with her alien patients, and when she had returned the coffins to the waiting room, she came to see how I was doing.

"You do realize, you saved your own life," she said.

"How's that?" Luke asked.

"The aspirin you took," she said. "and the fact that you took it immediately, saved your life."

I nodded. My own doctor had told me of the benefits of aspirin in heart attacks, back in the days when I had gone to visit her. I stopped going when she got mad at me for smoking and drinking and eating steak.

"You will be at risk for the next ten days," she said, "so we'll have to keep a close watch on you."

She checked my IV drip, and wrote notes in my chart. Then she left us, and there I was, the heart attack victim, just trying to recover.

"All right, my friend," Luke said, standing up and getting ready to leave, "you've given me a lot to work on. I'd better get at it."

I grinned, and we shook hands.

"Come visit me in California," I said.

"Fat chance," Luke said, "with my schedule. Not with this project going on."

"Give my best to Sherry," I said.

"Will do." He stood there a minute, wondering how to ask the next question. "Listen, my friend, what's up with you and Kirsten? Are things getting serious?"

Like I knew. But he was my friend, and he had a right to know.

"I'm not sure myself," I said. "We're just old friends that met up at a funeral. Kirsten seems pretty focused on getting The Lander and these bodies turned over to you; we haven't really had time to discuss our own future."

Long silence while Luke digested this. He wasn't any better at managing women than I was, however.

"Keep me posted," he said, and I agreed to do so.

Then he turned and left, and I supposed I wouldn't see him again until the next war broke out.

Dr. Windsor, who had been discreetly observing us, rejoined me at my bedside. "New orders," she said.

"What's going on?" I asked.

"You're to be transferred," she said. "'You're going to California by air ambulance."

Uncle William had set this up, obviously. The Pebble Beach clinic.

She was injecting something into my IV line. "What's that?" I wanted to know.

"Sedative," she replied. "You're going to go to sleep now. By the time you wake up, you'll be in California."

She pushed the plunger on the IV line, and a warm comfortable feeling infused my entire body.

"But Kirsten," I asked, as the medicine began to knock me out. "What about Kirsten?"

"Who is Kirsten?" Dr. Windsor asked, but it was too late, I was falling into a very deep sleep.

CHAPTER TWENTY FIVE

I woke up two days later in California, in what I was later to learn was the cardiology center at the Pebble Beach clinic. Seems my heart problem was of concern to somebody, to rate this kind of attention.

I had my own room, with a view of the ocean. It was brightly lit, the sun was out, so it was daytime, and it was reasonably comfortable, as much so as a hospital bed can become.

As my focus cleared, a nurse entered the room, watching me carefully.

"Good morning, Mr. Larson," she said. "How are you feeling?"

"Like I've been eating cotton," I said, speech being difficult. "But my chest doesn't hurt anymore. Who are you?"

"I'm Angela, and I am your cardiology nurse," she said, efficiently checking my vital signs.

"How am I doing?" I asked.

"I'll let the doctor tell you that," she said, and sure enough, we were joined by a guy in scrubs and a white coat, about forty from the looks of him.

"Mr. Larson, I am Dr. Gray. Your uncle, William Fletcher, asked me to look in on you."

I nodded. Figured William was the only one with enough pull to get me in here.

"I'd like to go over your case, if you're ready, Mr. Larson, are you up to this?"

"Go right ahead," I said, wondering in just what kind of shape my heart was now in, and curious to know if I would live through the week.

"You've sustained a mild heart attack," he began, "and you owe your life to the fast response of the Air Force medical team that took care of you. Your condition has stabilized, and we are preparing you for discharge, however you are going to have to make some major changes in your lifestyle, from this point onward."

The good doctor went on to forbid virtually everything that made life worth living, such as whiskey, cigars, steak, mashed potatoes, bacon and eggs, and recommended a diet high is stuff that is supposedly good for you.

However, I was in no position to contradict him, since I had sustained a heart attack, and he was a doctor.

After this depressing lecture the doctor signed my discharge orders and left. Angela had a change of clothes for me, which she put on the bed before she, too, left to take care of other patients.

I got into the shower and got cleaned up, and then shaved. When it was all over, I looked myself in the mirror, and was reassured to see that I looked reasonably presentable.

My medical chart notes were on the bedside, so I read them. Seems the US Air Force had run just about every conceivable test on me, as they were apparently concerned that my heart attack might have been attributable to an exposure to something toxic, and that had been ruled out. No alien exposure had been responsible for my illness, it was the cigars and steak.

I left my room and went to the discharge desk. My doctors had signed me out, so all I had to do was sign the forms. The bill, apparently, was being taken care of my uncle William.

The ever-efficient staff at the clinic had a car waiting for me, and from there I was driven directly to my own home, which is not far.

In the mail there was a single white envelope. It was from uncle William.

It's always interesting to get a letter from him, so I opened it immediately.

He asked me to prepare a journal of the past two weeks, saying it was of important scientific and historic value.

I wondered about that. Kirsten, William, and Luke Chivington had done all the work here. Uncle Sven is the one who had actually recovered the Lander. My role in this whole affair was fairly minor.

But I was not the one to judge; if William said it was important, it was, so for the next ten days, I sat at my computer, typing up this journal, making a permanent record of how it had all began, and what had happened since.

It turned out later that William was concerned that I was going to actually die from my heart condition before I told the story, and that he wanted a record of it written down as soon as possible.

It seemed a reasonable request after all he had done for us, so I went to work on it right away, and this journal is the accurate history of the events of the past two weeks.

When it was complete I called uncle William, and he said he would send a courier to pick it up. This happened in due course, and I felt a sense of relief when the journal left my hands. Now it was William's concern.

I wondered if, when I was seventy five years old, if I would be working as hard as my uncle William, but I doubt that very much.

After the courier left I put the top down on the convertible and drove to the beach.

The beach in California is a kind of unique place. Folks come here to get in touch with themselves, and for a lot of us Californians, it is kind of a second home. I'm no different; I do all of my serious thinking at the beach.

I had my ultra sunglasses on, and parked the car along the road overlooking Big Sur. It was a short hike to the beach.

During the week, the beach itself is fairly empty, so I was surprised to see someone there.

I was even more surprised to realize that it was Kirsten.

"Your uncle told me I'd find you here," she said, walking up to me and taking my hand.

She kissed me, and I instantly kissed her right back.

After a brush with death like a heart attack, kissing a blonde like Kirsten gives you a reminder of what life is supposed to be about. It was a very welcome sensation.

"Nice to see you again," I said, when she came up for air.

"You too," she replied, and we walked for a bit on the beach.

"So what are you doing in California?" I asked.

"William told me you were under the weather," she said, as we walked along the beach, "he said I should come visit you."

I suddenly realized that William had not told her what had happened to me. Secrecy was a part of his character, so he had kept the fact of my heart attack from her.

"How are you doing?" she asked.

"Fine, fine," I said, lying effortlessly, "how did everything go with your...work with the Air Force?"

"Faster than I thought," she said, "now it's all up to them. They have The Lander, and they know how to fly it."

William was true to his word. The Lander was now in the possession of the United States Air Force, where they could study it to their heart's content. Good luck to them. Our part in it was now concluded.

"Where are you staying?" I asked her.

"At the Ventana Inn," she said, referring to the legendary Big Sur resort. "Your uncle reserved me a room."

He sure liked to travel First Class. The Ventana was quite a place.

"Of course, I'm there all by myself," she said.

I wondered what to do next. Kirsten lived in New York, not in California, and there was no reason on earth why she would come to this isolated beach except to see me. And there could only be one reason for that, which would be to continue our relationship.

I've never been good at long term relationships, and have never been in one. Furthermore, I've never been faithful to one woman at any time in my entire life.

"What are your plans?" I asked her bluntly.

She took a long time answering. I took advantage of this to rest my gaze upon her perfect body.

Then she stopped, and drew a heart in the sand with her toe.

"I wanted to ask if you would marry me," she said.

But that is another story.

AUTHOR'S NOTES

MEET THE GIRL! - If you would like to meet the actress who may play the character Kirsten in the planned movie version of this book, go to www.http.downfallpress.com and check the schedule for the live chat! Check the website for updates as the book is developed into a motion picture.

The Office of Strategic Services: created in 1942, the OSS was America's first formal intelligence service. Commanded by William Donovan, a law school classmate of Franklin Roosevelt, it conducted a number of successful operations. The men and women of the OSS were often recruited from elite American colleges, such as Columbia and Princeton.

German U-Boat 3531: . During World War II, Germany built 118 type XXI boats, by Blohm & Voss, F. Schichau, and AG Weser, but only three of them made a war patrol. One survives today, the U-2540. The type XXI U-boats were faster, quieter, had greater range, and carried much more armament than the more common Type VII.

German WWII Intercontinental Six Engine Bomber: Germany actually had two six engine bomber plans, the Ju-390 and the Arado 555 Flying Wing "Amerika" bomber. Of these, only the Ju-390 was built, and rumors persist one of them reached the city of New York late in the war.

The A-10 Warthog: The A-10 is an actual jet ground attack aircraft operated by multiple branches of the by the American military. It is popular for its ability to stay aloft for long periods, its near-indestructability, and the fact that it carries a large and varied ordnance package.

The Douglas Skyraider: this exceptional American aircraft began as a carrier based dive bomber but met is full potential as an armored ground attack aircraft, and was in service for over 30 years.   It is true that Skyraiders, a piston powered aircraft, are known to have destroyed jet MIG fighters during the Korean war.

Operation Alsos: The highest priority of the European theater of WWII, Operation Alsos concerned the recovery of the German Atomic Bomb project.   Considered a success, it is now believed that the Germans were altogether too close for comfort in their efforts to build a nuclear device.

www.ingramcontent.com/pod-product-compliance
Lightning Source LLC
Chambersburg PA
CBHW070751280626
47162CB00016B/60